OVER THE EDGE

BEAR & MANDY LOGAN
BOOK 4

L.T. RYAN

with

K.M. ROUGHT

LIQUID MIND MEDIA

For information contact:
Contact@ltryan.com
https://LTRyan.com
https://www.facebook.com/JackNobleBooks

THE BEAR & MANDY LOGAN SERIES

Close to Home

Under the Surface

The Last Stop

Over the Edge

Between the Lies (Coming Soon)

Love Bear? Mandy? Noble? Hatch? Get your very own L.T. Ryan merchandise today! Click the link below to find coffee mugs, t-shirts, and even signed copies of your favorite thrillers! https://ltryan.ink/EvG_

1

A BRANCH SNAPPED TO BEAR'S RIGHT. HE HELD OUT A HAND AND crouched low to the ground. Mandy knew to do the same. She was almost as silent as him now. A smile ghosted his face as pride swelled in his chest, but he tamped it down. Time to focus.

Bear stretched his leg forward, planting his foot and then shifting his weight. He crept along a line of bushes until he could peek around the last one and get eyes on their target. This time, he allowed the smile to transform his face. Without looking back, he motioned Mandy forward. Gentle footfalls sounded behind him, and he felt her slipping past him, leaning forward and searching for their prey.

He knew the second she spotted the squirrel. An annoyed huff of air caused the animal to raise its head. "Seriously?" Mandy hissed, no longer keeping her voice lowered. That was enough to send it scurrying away.

Bear's laugh rang out like a gunshot. "Western Gray," he told her, getting to his feet. This one had been almost charcoal, with a bright white stripe along its stomach. "They make a helluva racket."

Mandy pushed to her feet, too. "I thought it was a deer."

"Could've been," Bear said.

A rifle hung over his shoulder, more for protection than hunting.

They'd been living off fish for the last couple weeks. Easier to gather than deer or rabbit. Quieter, too. Though not quite as satisfying, in Bear's opinion. He had the patience to sit up in a hunting blind and wait for dinner to come to him, but Mandy didn't. Her ever-present need to fidget broke his concentration. Leaving her back at the cabin was an option, but she tended to wander off when she got bored, usually leading to trouble.

But like most of his excursions these days, this one was a learning experience. Bear resisted the urge to ruffle her hair. "You did good, kid. Stayed quiet."

A blush crept across Mandy's face. "Thanks."

"Close your eyes."

Mandy groaned, but when Bear shot her a look, she obliged.

He closed his too. "What do you hear?"

A few seconds passed, allowing them both to sink into their surroundings. It was humid under the canopy of trees, but they shaded them from the beating sun. Without the distraction of his sight, Bear's ears grew sharper. He picked out each sound around him, cataloging them to see if Mandy would catch them all.

"Lots of birds. Different kinds." Her voice was soft. Deep concentration emanated from her. This was just another game, like the pop quizzes he sprang on her whenever they found themselves back with the general population. "Insects, too. More rustling. Further off. Maybe a squirrel. Could be something bigger. And water." She paused, straining to hear it. The leaves crunched as she turned on the spot. "North?"

"Northwest," Bear corrected. "Good. What else?"

"The wind?" she asked.

That was a good answer, too. But not what he was going after. "What *don't* you hear?"

"People," she said. "Traffic."

"Do you remember where the road is?"

"South." The answer was instantaneous. "About two miles back."

Bear opened his eyes, looking over at Mandy. Her face was tipped toward the sun, her eyes screwed shut too tightly to be meditative. Her hair was getting long now. It almost touched the center of her shoulder blades, even in a ponytail. She looked older in her orange hunting vest. He could feel time slipping away and couldn't resist ruffling her hair. "Very good."

Mandy was caught between a smile and a scowl as she batted his hand away. "Did I miss anything?"

"Woodpecker in the distance."

The scowl deepened. "I said birds."

"Woodpecker's easy," he said. "You could've named that one."

"Yeah, yeah. What now?"

"You tell me." Bear gestured to the path in front of them. "Where does the trail lead?"

Mandy took a step forward and crouched low, hand on the sheath at her hip. Bear had loaned her one of his smaller hunting knives. It was as useful for foraging as it was for protection, and the grin on her face when he'd handed it to her had been priceless.

Squatting there, looking for signs in the underbrush, she looked too much like a detective trying to find evidence of a crime. Not for the first time, Bear wondered what Mandy would do when she grew up. They didn't talk about it much. They were both too concerned with the here and now.

Escaping. Hiding. Surviving.

That wasn't the life he wanted for his daughter. She was too smart for that. Too skilled. Her brain was like a sponge, absorbing his lessons quickly, and she accomplished anything she set her mind to. Except biting her tongue, one characteristic she couldn't quite conquer. Then again, he wasn't sure she had ever tried.

"Well?" he asked. Not impatient, just pressing. Sometimes you didn't have the luxury of time.

"Give me a second."

Bear squatted down next to her. A few hundred yards behind them, he'd spotted some blood on a broken stem and disturbances along the deer trail they'd been following. It was wet, as it always was out here in Oregon, but this area was too overgrown to spot anything in the mud. They had no clear hoofprints to follow—just the signs of an injured animal. If they were lucky, they would find it and put it out of its misery. In return for their kindness, they'd feast tonight.

Mandy had been all too happy at the promise of something other than fish.

"I think I lost it." The disappointment in her voice was loud and clear.

"There." Bear pointed to another broken set of stems. These didn't have any blood on them, but they'd been crushed underfoot. "See it?"

"How do you know?" Mandy asked, genuine interest in her voice. "That it's the same animal, I mean."

"I don't," Bear answered. "But chances are higher that it is. Lead the way."

Mandy set her course, pacing herself so she didn't cause too much noise. She was silent as she spotted the next few drops of blood, but she looked up at Bear with a grin so wide he couldn't help but match it. Nodding his head, he encouraged her forward.

It wasn't until the next spot of blood that Bear realized something was wrong. A footprint sat to the left of the path. Maybe a men's size thirteen. Some of the grass had already sprung back up, indicating it wasn't too fresh. But the outline was still clear.

Bear put a hand on Mandy's shoulder, freezing her to the spot. It only took her a second to spot the footprint once he pointed it out. There were questions in her eyes when she looked up at him. But she only voiced one, keeping the word just above a whisper.

"Hunter?"

"Probably." A cold feeling crawled down his spine and settled in his gut. It was a feeling he'd had a thousand times before, but one he'd never gotten used to.

He'd thought the animal they'd been tracking was a buck that had been injured by a hunter. It had escaped a day or two ago, given that the blood was on the dry side now. It would lie low while it healed, not take as many risks. He figured it would be an easy target. Even considered letting Mandy take it down and earn them their dinner.

The footprint could belong to a hunter tracking its prey. In fact, that was the most logical conclusion, especially out here on state land, away from the campground they'd come from. All the evidence fit, yet Bear couldn't shake the feeling in his spine. It'd been weeks since they'd come to Arlington, settling into the campground not too far from the highway. A good place to lie low.

Mandy tapped Bear's arm, too cautious to ask her question out loud.

"Stay behind me." He moved forward in a low crouch. Now that he'd seen the footprint, the trail looked different to him. Wider. More haphazard. Less like a deer than a human being running for their life.

A flash of blue caught his attention. Mandy bumped into Bear when he came to an abrupt stop, grabbing his waist to steady herself, still teetering back towards the mud. He could hear the grumble on the tip of her tongue, but she swallowed it down.

Bear put one knee to the earth and listened. He didn't dare close his eyes in case someone was close by, but he utilized the lesson he had taught Mandy just moments before. Birds. Insects. Wind. Water. Everything was the same. No traffic. No people. The likelihood that someone was hiding behind a tree trunk was slim.

But never none.

"Stay." The tone of his voice would keep Mandy in her place, even if her entire body wanted to revolt.

Rifle at the ready, Bear stood and stalked forward, his head on a swivel. The insects nearest to him quieted. So did the birds. Lack of noise could be as telling as a snapping branch. That's why he'd wanted Mandy to listen for all the sounds that weren't there. The silence made him more alert. Gave him an awareness of Mandy behind him and the unknown ahead.

When he reached the piece of clothing caught on a thick patch of brambles, Bear swept the area in a ten-foot radius before motioning Mandy forward. She made no noise as she joined him, looking first at the blue-and-white checkered cloth, then the bloody handprint he'd already spotted on the nearby trunk.

"Not a hunter?" she whispered.

"On my heels," he commanded. They would move forward as one. "At the ready."

Mandy slipped the knife from her sheath and held it in a reverse grip, the blade pointing out. He had taught her all the ways to hold a knife, but this one had come most naturally. She was small and fast, so she could sacrifice range for a deeper cut.

Bear pushed forward at a steady pace. It was never smart to stay in one spot for too long. He'd learned that the hard way, and now so had Mandy. If they kept moving, they'd be a harder target. They could also draw another person out faster if someone were hiding near them. They might not expect an aggressive approach. The element of surprise could save lives. And end others.

Another flash of blue, bigger than before, steered Bear to the right and down a small slope. He paused behind a tree about a dozen feet away, listening for any movement around him, human or otherwise. A branch popped in the distance, too far to be relevant. Mandy jumped beside him, which was good. It meant she was listening.

Hearing nothing, Bear rounded the tree, sweeping his gun and his gaze left and right. Behind him, Mandy would be watching their six. Two taps on his shoulder meant she'd spotted something innocuous. Three meant she'd spotted something deadly.

No taps came as Bear approached the piece of clothing. There was no doubt in his mind the scrap they'd found earlier had once been attached to this one. Blue-and-white checked, probably belonging to a button-down. Not exactly hiking attire. It had been torn from the rest of the shirt, just a breast pocket and a couple of buttons, but he couldn't tell what had done it. The strength of human hands or the sharp teeth of an animal?

When Bear lowered his gun to a forty-five-degree angle, Mandy knew she could talk. "What's that?" she asked, pointing to a slip of folded paper peeking out of the top of the pocket. It was caked in mud.

"Check it," he said, keeping his eyes sharp around them.

Mandy found a small stick and used it to open the paper. "A bunch of numbers. A phone number."

A torn shirt and a phone number. This didn't feel like a hunting accident.

"We're going back," he said.

"What? Why?"

"Not our business."

"What if they're hurt? What if they need help?"

"Blood is at least a day or two old. They're either out of the woods, or they're long dead. Nothing we can do."

"What about the phone number?" Mandy asked, reaching out for the paper. "Shouldn't we—"

"Leave it." Bear didn't like the snap in his voice, but he knew what going down this path meant for them. "Let's go."

Mandy had pulled her arm back, but she continued to stare at the bloody phone number. Most kids would've been more afraid than her, but he could tell she was thinking about the last time she saw blood smeared across someone's shirt. It was a couple months and half the country away, but those kinds of memories stain your soul.

"Mandy," Bear said, firm but patient. "Let's go."

This time, Mandy listened. Rising to her feet, she stayed on Bear's heels all the way home.

2

Iris Duvall sat by herself at a table in Bryant Park. Midtown was not her favorite place in the city—that accolade was reserved for a hole-in-the-wall bar in Sunnyside where she could order three drinks for the price of one here in Manhattan—but this park was one of its few highlights. Much smaller than Central Park, it hosted a different kind of people. The sprawling lawn at its center was for locals who wanted to lay back and stare up at a patch of clear sky. Sure, the concrete towers pressing in on you perpetually lingered at the edges of your vision, but if you squinted, you could almost pretend they weren't there.

Bryant Park was more for sitting than walking. People pressed closer here, but each group was in their own little world. Business meetings over a quick to-go lunch. Friends playing board games rented from a nearby kiosk. Photographers documenting the juxtaposition between green trees and gray buildings. Even in a mass of people, she felt alone. For once, it was a good feeling.

Raising the paper coffee cup to her lips, Iris let the hot liquid rush down the back of her throat, settling amongst the remnants of the overpriced sandwich she'd had for lunch. September in the city was usually hot, but today was cooler. She didn't need the coffee to stay warm, but it helped ground her. Kept her alert.

The sky was overcast, so there were fewer people here than usual. The threat of rain lingered, and every half hour or so it would deliver. Just a few fat drops here and there, but enough to send most people scurrying back to their office buildings or hotel rooms. New parkgoers would replace them a few minutes later, the rain already a distant memory, until the whole event played out once more, as if on an endless loop.

Iris was the one constant. She'd been here a couple of hours already, pulling her hood up when she felt the droplets hit her head, then pushing it back when the sun peeked out from behind a silver-lined cloud. She was content to watch the crowds surge and dissipate, like water lapping at the shore. Even during high tide, with the crowds at their most dangerous, she felt the kind of peace settle over her that she'd experienced only a few times before.

Mind elsewhere, Iris didn't see the man approach her from behind. Despite every movie, TV show, and book on the market, she didn't have a sixth sense to know when danger lurked around every corner. Experience and instinct only got you so far. No one had eyes in the back of their head. And if she did, she wouldn't be in this position.

When he'd swerved around a crowd and bumped into her shoulder, her first instinct was to clutch her coffee. The cup was still half full, and the stain would be a bitch to get out of her gray slacks. They were light, the same color as the clouds overhead, and made of a material you weren't supposed to wash in your machine at home. They had been expensive, but damn did they hug her in all the right places.

Iris' next instinct was to flinch as something dropped into her lap. At first, she thought her cup had slipped out of her hand. But a millisecond later, she realized the man had tossed a small black device at her. It was the size of her thumb. As she realized what it was, her heart leapt into her throat. It took every ounce of her willpower not to let her surprise show. She simply curled her hand over the object and took a delicate sip of her coffee.

The man did not turn around as he walked away from her. Dressed in a navy designer tracksuit, he looked like he belonged here. With a cap pulled down low, you could even believe he was trying to save his hair from the impending rain. But she knew better. It was to hide his identity. From behind, Iris couldn't discern much about the man. White. Fit. Maybe in his thirties or forties, though without seeing his face, that was just a guess. Average height, dark brown hair in a style unknown to her thanks to the hat. His sneakers were the only part of him with any personality. They were two different shades of fire-engine red. Even to her untrained eyes, she could tell they were expensive. Jordans, though she wouldn't be able to say anything else about them, even with a gun to her head.

But the shoes did tell her something important: This was just the delivery guy. He probably had no idea what was on the flash drive and didn't care. As long as he got paid, he'd make the drop and move on with his day, none the wiser to the information he'd just hand-delivered to a federal agent.

Caution kept Iris in her chair for another twenty minutes while she finished her coffee. She tipped her head back to face the sun every time it came out, absorbing the warmth. When her coffee was gone, she made a show of trying to get the last drops before standing and tossing it into a nearby garbage can.

As discreet as the drop had been, there was a chance someone had seen her receive the flash drive. An amateur would've made their move by now—probably sliding into the chair across from her, flirty at first, before dropping the act and pointing a gun at her crotch. A professional would stalk her through the streets of New York to find her base of operations. They'd want to gather the whole picture before revealing themselves.

The nature of her job made her paranoid, but those thoughts had kept her alive throughout the years. Iris joined the crowd and allowed it to sweep her forward and out onto West 42nd Street, like a drop of water returning to the wide ocean. She felt less alone out here. The comfort she'd reveled in a few minutes ago was nowhere to be seen. Women sized her up while men ogled her. Kids looked her in the eyes in a way the adults never did. But they would learn soon enough the dangers of engaging with their fellow New Yorkers, even in such a small way.

Iris followed the crowd wherever it took her. When a few people branched off, she'd follow the larger mass, winding her way around buildings and across streets. North, then South. East and West. She'd turned herself around enough times that if someone was following her, she would've noticed them. And if she hadn't? Maybe she deserved to get caught.

With that thought lodged in her throat, Iris dropped the act. She squeezed the flash drive tight in her hand, which was shoved deep into her blazer sleeve. She peeled off from the crowd and headed for Chelsea. West 17th Street. She would've preferred to meet for the drop farther away from her base to lose any tails on the subway, but Bryant Park was the meeting spot. Non-negotiable.

Her building was under construction, though she didn't have to worry about workers coming and going. A friend of a friend knew the foreman for the site. A little cash passed under the table ensured the site was shut down for the week. Enough time for her to set up a station and do what needed to be done away from prying eyes.

Slipping between buildings, Iris entered through a side door where she had installed a keypad with a code only she knew. She'd replace it with the old doorhandle when it came time to vacate. No one would be the wiser. She punched in the numbers and waited for the gears to turn before shouldering her way into the small lobby and up a flight of dark stairs. Another keypad and a different code awaited her, which she punched in without hesitation. She flicked on the light and took in her ramshackle setup with a sense of pride.

The space she occupied was empty except for her belongings. There were two sets of windows, which had already been covered in thick shrink film. She'd bought a roll of black garbage bags and taped them over the top of the plastic to ensure no one saw her moving around up here. Aside from that, the walls were bare and unfinished. The floor was concrete. Her desk and chair were the only objects that gave any personality to the room, and even they were rudimentary.

She hadn't had time to get the best equipment. Everything had been picked up secondhand except for the interior components of the computer. She'd needed something fast and something good.

Much to her chagrin, Iris didn't know much outside of what her superiors had told her. Her most recent stint aside, she was a model agent. Her arrest record was solid. Even if she didn't get along with everyone in the office, she was a consummate professional. Really, they were lucky to have her.

Iris booted up the computer. Her time on desk duty had gone from one week to two, and then from two to four. Now, she was closing in on two months. Richard Peake had told her to be patient, but her patience had run out a long time ago.

What were they hiding?

It had been bad enough that Iris was pulled from the Reagan case. She'd sacrificed so much during the months she'd spent tracking his operations. She'd lost family who were entangled with the man. He had been within her grasp when she was benched. Now someone else would get the credit for taking him down.

If they ever took him down.

Her disgruntlement wasn't just about professional advancement. There was pain, too. Her cousin Lily was dead, at least in part due to Reagan's machinations. And that was only the beginning of everything Reagan had put her through. She wanted revenge.

Someone was steamrolling her, that was for sure. But she didn't want revenge just for the Reagan case. No, she also wanted it for the man she'd met in Indiana. The one who'd fought for an entire town and asked for nothing in return. The one with the whip-smart daughter, carrying too much of the world on her shoulders already. Her superiors hadn't wanted her to know who he was, but that didn't fly with Iris Duvall. If they wouldn't tell her, she'd find out for herself.

Iris plugged the flash drive into the computer and waited for a dialog box to pop up. The blinking cursor indicated it was ready for her encryption code, which had been hand delivered in a similar manner the day before at a different location by a different man in a tracksuit. She wondered if her contact supplied the tracksuits or if the guys had to buy them on their own. Did they have them on hand for when they weren't undercover?

A combination of sixteen letters and numbers unlocked the drive.

Leaning closer to her screen, Iris took in the various folders and documents before her. Iris steeled herself and clicked on the first icon.

"Okay, Riley Logan," she said, staring at a picture of him at eighteen years old. "Let's see what kind of secrets you're hiding."

3

BEAR PULLED HIS VEHICLE INTO A PARKING SPOT ON THE SIDE OF THE GAS station, away from the cameras facing the pumps. The silver Chevy Tahoe was about ten years old, but it got the job done. He missed his F150, but falling into patterns was a good way to get caught.

Twisting in his seat to face Mandy, he watched as her fingers flew over the screen of her phone, oblivious to everything around her.

"You're staring," she said.

Not totally oblivious.

"You coming in?"

"Catching up with Marcus."

"He doin' okay?" Bear asked. Marcus was the one friend Mandy had kept in touch with since their records had been wiped and they'd decided to live normal lives. Or at least tried to. Marcus' town had been at the center of a pharmaceutical scandal, and nearly every other town they'd stayed in for more than two days had been home to some problem or another. Bear couldn't decide if he brought out the worst in these towns, or if he just couldn't look the other way after uncovering any sort of dark truth.

Maybe a little of both.

"He's good." Her eyes never left the screen. It was a non-answer meant to satisfy the question. "Can you get me a Monster? The pink one? Or if they don't have it, the blue one?"

"Absolutely not." Bear scoffed. "That shit is terrible for you."

Mandy finally looked up. "You know it has less caffeine than a cup of coffee, right?"

"And more ingredients you can't pronounce. You know what ingredients are in coffee?" He opened his eyes wide, mocking one of her trademark sassy looks. "*Coffee.* You're not getting a Monster."

Mandy sighed and returned to her phone. "Fine. Can I have a Frappuccino, then? The caramel one."

Bear didn't want to get that for her either, but it was better than a Monster. Maybe that had been her play all along. And he couldn't get a coffee for himself and not get her something, too. They'd gotten up early to go on their little excursion, and while he'd had a cup of joe back at the cabin, the one at the gas station was like jet fuel in comparison. It kickstarted his system like nothing else.

Maybe the Monster was the safer option, after all. Not that he'd tell her that.

"Beep the horn if—"

"—I see anything suspicious. I got it."

Bear ruffled her hair just to annoy her, then climbed out of the Tahoe and pulled open the door to the gas station. A chime greeted him, and so did the kid behind the counter. That was the other thing about being out here that Bear enjoyed—the people were nicer. More respectful. Say what you want about country folks, but they had better manners than city people. At least in his experience.

Picking up a shopping basket, Bear strolled the aisles, looking for the items on his mental checklist. Beer? Check. Lighter fluid? Check. Batteries? Check. He'd have to ask for the key to the ice machine. And he'd probably have to come back in to get the wood, since he wouldn't be able to carry it all at once.

It felt strange to rely on store-bought products. He could cut the wood himself and start a fire on his own, but it was easier to do it this way. Faster. He'd be able to survive with much less than they had, but Mandy was used to modern conveniences. She'd have to learn those lessons the hard way someday, but he couldn't bring himself to teach them to her just yet. They'd had a long, tumultuous few months. Few years, if he was honest.

Plus, he missed beer. Even the shitty kind from a gas station cooler.

Bear approached the counter and set his basket down. He'd seen this kid before—tall and lanky with ginger hair and an unfortunate sprinkling of adult acne—and noticed how he always looked a little nervous when Bear walked in. He was used to the reaction, and most of the time it served him well. But there was no purpose in scaring the guy, so Bear tried a smile instead.

"Find everything okay?" the kid asked. The tag on his shirt said his name was Ryan.

"Yep. I'll need a couple bags of ice, too. And I'll come back for three bundles of wood."

"No problem." The chime of the door interrupted the beep of the price scanner as a man and a woman walked in. Ryan offered them a tentative smile. "Hello!"

Bear turned to take in the newcomers. The man was big, his chest muscles bulging out of his too-tight shirt and a leather jacket that appeared to constrict some of his movement. A gold watch glittered from his wrist, matching the gold chain around his neck. Bear couldn't tell from his vantage point whether they were real, but the impression remained the same.

The woman was tiny in comparison, wearing a pair of cut-offs and a baggy t-shirt. Her hair was long and blonde, and a little stringy at the ends. A pair of sunglasses rested on top of her head, but otherwise, she wore no jewelry of any kind. If they hadn't walked in at the same time, Bear never would've guessed they were together.

The man ignored Ryan's greeting while the woman clung to his arm. She talked to him in a low whisper that Bear couldn't make out, but her face gave away her discomfort. Was it the company she kept, or the place they'd decided to visit? Whatever she said, the man didn't seem to care, and he tried unsuccessfully to shake her off.

Bear turned back to the register and handed the kid a pre-paid debit card, but a crash had him spinning around again. From the looks of it, the guy had shoved the woman into one of the displays, dislodging a shelf and scattering containers of nuts everywhere.

"I said," the man roared, stepping closer to her, "get back to the car. Now."

"Hey," Bear called, keeping his voice even. "There a problem?"

The woman looked at Bear in surprise and fear before scampering back through the door. The chime was too cheerful amid the tension inside the store. Ryan cleared his throat as if to say something, but no words came out. Probably for the best.

The man stepped up to Bear. "You say something to me, pal?"

"Is there," Bear repeated, loud and slow, "a problem?"

"Keep your nose out of other people's business," he said.

Bear wrinkled his nose against the stench of the man's cologne. "Don't make your business everyone else's problem."

Gears turned behind the man's eyes, and Bear could see the moment this stranger decided to try his hand at intimidation. It would've worked on the kid behind the counter, but Bear was another breed. And this guy was an amateur.

The man stepped forward and shoved at Bear's chest. But Bear had already planted his feet in anticipation of the move. He stayed still as the other guy stumbled backwards. A moment of shock gave way to sharp anger, and the guy reared his fist back to punch Bear in the face. But when Bear didn't even flinch, the guy had second thoughts. Instead, he brought his hand down on a magazine rack, scattering the contents across the floor, before turning on his heel and stalking out of the store.

"Sorry about that." Bear knelt to pick up the magazines. "Hopefully, none of these are damaged."

Ryan scrambled around the counter and gathered up a handful. "It's okay. We have a monthly allowance of damaged items for this reason. Gas stations don't always bring in the best characters."

"You know that guy?" Bear asked, looking out through the front windows and watched the man climb into an army-green Dodge Challenger.

Ryan hesitated, busying himself with the magazine rack. He didn't meet Bear's eyes. "No, I don't know him." It was a lie, but one Bear didn't feel like calling out. They moved on to the overturned almond shelf. "I'm only part time. I usually only work the morning shift. Not experienced enough for the nightshift yet."

"Hopefully he doesn't come back." Bear picked up a couple containers of nuts and put them back on the shelf. "If he does, call the cops."

"Won't do much good," the kid said. "The cops are worthless around here."

"You just don't want to get into a tangle with a guy like that."

Bear knew the type. Guys like him thought they were invincible because they had muscles or money or both. But for all his bulk, the guy had no form. He was a street brawler. Bear had no doubt his fist could pack a punch, though it'd lack the skill Bear had in his own. He was more used to intimidating people than fighting them.

Guys like him were so quick to anger, to act in violence, were threatening. Abusive. That woman was in a dangerous position. If Bear had his way, if this were a lawless country, he wouldn't have let the guy walk away. It was better to take him off the streets before he did something that couldn't be undone. That was not an attitude he wanted to pass on to Mandy, but it was the stark reality of their world. People like him usually showed their true colors well before ever acting on impulse.

And yet, nothing could be done until they pulled the trigger.

"Sir?" Ryan asked. Bear realized the kid had been talking to him. "Are you okay?"

"Yeah." Bear walked back over to the register now that the store was in order again. Ryan pulled a key out from behind the counter. "I'll have this back in a few."

"Take your time," he said. "And sir?"

Bear didn't even turn to look at him. He knew what was coming next. "Yeah?"

"Thank you."

"Don't mention it." He hoped the kid took that literally. Better not to make an impression, but the situation had forced his hand.

Bear piled his supplies into the back of the Tahoe, returning twice more to add ice to their cooler and to stack the wood against one side so it wouldn't roll around. Somewhere between the second and the third trip, the Challenger peeled out of the parking lot and Bear caught a glimpse of the couple inside. There was no doubt the man had seen Bear and the make and model of his vehicle, though from the angle he probably hadn't caught a glimpse of the license plate. Bear had the urge to turn the SUV in and get something else, just to be safe.

Climbing into the front seat, Bear was surprised to see Mandy's nose wasn't buried in her phone. Instead, she looked up at him with wide eyes, her mouth in the shape of a deep frown.

"Did you see that woman come out of the store?" she asked, taking the coffee that Bear handed to her, but not opening it.

Bear knew exactly who she was talking about. "What about her?"

"She's in danger," Mandy said. "And we need to help her."

4

BEAR STUCK THE KEY IN THE IGNITION AND TURNED IT, WAITING FOR THE Tahoe to rumble to life. "We can't get involved in the lives of everyone we meet. It always causes such a shitstorm and we need to be laying low right now."

"But Bear—"

"But nothing."

Mandy huffed. "What if she's in trouble?"

"Then she needs to go to the police."

"You know that can cause more harm than good." Mandy fit her unopened coffee into a cupholder and turned to face him. Her eyes were full of worry. "Please. Something's wrong and I can't let it go."

"How do you know?" he asked.

"She came out of the store crying. What happened in there?"

Bear thought back to the incident involving the man. Maybe the woman had been hurt worse than he thought. "The guy she was with shoved her. Knocked over a shelf. Told her to go back to the car."

"Did you do anything?"

Bear lifted a shoulder and dropped it in a half-hearted shrug. "Asked him if he had a problem. He got all up in my face about it."

"Did he try anything?"

"Shoved me." A grin split Bear's face. "Bounced right off. Was pretty funny, actually."

Mandy scowled, but he could see a smile twitching to life just beneath the surface. "Then what?"

"Then he left." Bear shook his head. "Sometimes guys like that are more bark than bite."

The ghost of Mandy's smile faded. "Is that the impression you got?"

Bear shook his head. "No, it's not." After a moment of silence, he asked, "What did you see?"

Mandy tucked a piece of hair behind her ear. "For a minute, she stood there, sort of just looking into the distance. Almost like she was trying to figure out if it was worth it to just start walking in any direction."

"Can't say I blame her if that's who she's going home to every night."

Mandy nodded. "Then she took a phone out of her back pocket and money fell out. I thought she'd notice it, but she didn't. Just stared at her phone, not even using it. Like she was debating on calling someone. Maybe the cops. Maybe a friend. I don't know."

"If you tell me you got out of the car—"

"She was scared," Mandy snapped. "And alone. And if she was gonna run away, I wanted her to at least have some money in her pocket."

Bear closed his eyes and took three deep breaths before looking at her again.

"I walked up to her and picked up the money. I don't know if she even saw me approach her. She was so out of it. Jumped a little when I said something. Then she just stared down at the money like she couldn't even comprehend what it was. I asked her if she was okay. And then we—" Mandy broke off for a moment, and Bear saw her cheeks blush pink. "We had a moment."

He made sure to keep his voice even. "You had a moment?"

"Yes, a *moment*." The huff that escaped her mouth was more forceful than the last one. "I don't know how else to describe it. We looked at each other, and I could tell she was scared. She'd been crying. She was so lost, and I didn't know what to do. So I asked her again if she was okay. That's when she snapped out of it. Said her boyfriend was being a jerk."

"Understatement," Bear muttered. He blew into the hole in the lid of his coffee. It was still too hot to drink.

Mandy continued as though she hadn't heard him. "But I could tell it was more than that."

"Sometimes it's easier for people to open up to strangers, but sometimes it isn't."

"I swore she was going to tell me something after that, but that's when her boyfriend came out of the store. He looked so mad."

"Yeah, he was." Bear chuckled. He couldn't help himself.

"He was furious. He yelled at her to get into the car. Then he spotted me."

All the humor left Bear's body. "Did he hurt you?"

"No. *No.*" Mandy looked frustrated, like Bear wasn't listening even though he was tuned in. "Something switched in her. She got this cold, mean look on her face. Like she was looking down her nose at me. She shoved my hand away—I was still holding the money out to her—and laughed. Said really loudly that she wasn't going to buy me beer. Then they just walked away."

Bear waited for more, but when it didn't come, he placed his own coffee in a cupholder and put his hands back on the wheel. "Even if I wanted to get involved—which I don't—we don't have any proof. The guy was an asshole, but we don't know if there's more to the story. She said he was being a jerk, but that doesn't mean anything."

"You know he's worse than that. You know it." Mandy looked pissed now. "You can tell. Just like I can."

Bear sighed. "We don't know anything about her."

"Her shirt was from a local bar. It was called The Magic Tap. I'm pretty sure she works there."

"Just because she was wearing their shirt doesn't mean she works there."

Mandy threw him a look. "Trust me, that's the only reason she'd wear it."

"Look, if someone wants my help, they need to knock on my door and ask for it themselves."

Mandy waited until Bear met her eyes, then pulled out a folded bill from where she'd tucked it under her leg. Unraveling it, he saw that it was only a dollar. Even if the woman had been trying to get away, it wouldn't have gotten her very far. Not even a snack from a vending machine these days.

Then something else caught Bear's attention. Written in black sharpie across the front were the words *HELP ME.*

5

THE HOURS SPENT AT HER COMPUTER HAD TAKEN A TOLL ON IRIS' BODY. Her feet tingled, and her shoulders were tight from hunching over her keyboard. Not to mention her back throbbing in sync with her heartbeat.

She pushed away from her desk, stood, and paced the room, pulling her shoulders back and wiggling her toes. The last thing she wanted to do was take her eyes off the computer screen for more than a few seconds, but her body needed a break, and her mind needed a minute to fit some puzzle pieces together.

Maneuvering herself into mountain pose, Iris slowed her breath, inhaling deeply and pushing the air out of her lungs in a powerful exhale. Her heartrate hadn't been elevated, but she could feel it slow as she moved into a more meditative state. She moved through a vinyasa, bending forward at the waist, and then kicking one leg back into a deep lunge, then exchanging it for the other. It felt good on her hips after all that sitting. Pressing down into a plank, she kicked her other leg back and worked through the cobra pose before shifting into downward dog, which finished stretching out her back. Moving back up into mountain pose, Iris felt looser, clearer.

Maybe it was just an excuse to lie down for a minute, but Iris leaned back into corpse pose with her hands splayed out to her side and her eyes closed. She'd swept the floor and cleaned out as much of the debris as she could when she'd first moved in, so there was no worry she'd get her pants dirty. Besides, that was the least of her concerns now.

An image of Bear popped into her head from her time in Indiana. She'd been surprised by his quiet nature. Most guys that big were used to sticking out in a crowd, not bothering to moderate their voices or actions. Bear had been different. When he did talk, it was with a measured tone. He had a sharp, unexpected intelligence behind his eyes as well. And then there was the way he'd interacted with his daughter. A smile crept over Iris' face as she remembered the teen. Mandy was a handful, but she was a good kid. And even though Bear was overprotective, he treated her like an adult. Validated her feelings and helped her feel powerful. In a world where women and girls had to practice constant vigilance, that strength and confidence would serve Mandy well. With a jolt of surprise, Iris realized she missed her.

Bear's skills in the field hadn't been surprising. Most guys his size knew how to throw a punch, but not many could move like him. Despite his bulk, Bear was quiet and quick. Tactical. Purposeful. She'd half-expected him to start brawling whenever there was trouble, but instead, she'd been met with someone whose form was—as much as it pained her to admit—better than her own.

It made sense now that she had read through some of his backstory. He'd enlisted in the Marines at the age of eighteen. Nearly a quarter of those who wanted to become a Marine never made it past basic training. Not only did Bear succeed, he became a top recruit. It had driven him into the CIA and eventually to a program called the SIS, led by a man named Frank Skinner. She hadn't been able to find much on Skinner, other than the fact that he was dead. After that, Bear had become an independent contractor.

Details about that time in Bear's life were sparse. It had occurred to her that maybe he hadn't always worked for the right person. The sense she'd gotten from him was that he wanted to do the right thing. But life didn't always allow that. Guilt had clung to Bear's shoulders like a shroud. She couldn't begin to guess what had happened to weigh him down. Lord knew she could understand, given the job she'd taken on. Her experience lent a sense of compassion for Bear. She wanted to offer him the benefit of the doubt after fighting side by side with him, but she also knew that kind of naiveté could get her in trouble. Even killed.

At some point during his journey, Mandy had entered the picture. The girl had been so young when Jack Noble, Bear's longtime friend and partner in crime, had first found her on that street corner. Iris didn't think either of the men could've guessed that she'd grow up to be so powerful. The smile that had crept over her face now cracked open into a wide grin. A laugh escaped her mouth. Mandy was a spitfire who had seen too much of the world already, but all things considered, she handled it well. And a lot of that had to do with Bear's guidance.

The smile dropped as Iris remembered what had happened in Indiana. Mandy had killed someone. In self-defense, sure, but she was too young to have had that experience. Too fragile still, despite her inner strength. In that moment, Iris could understand Bear's thoughts and actions. His incessant need to keep her safe and protected for as long as possible. Sooner or later the world would chew Mandy up and spit her out, like it did with everyone else. As long as he could delay that fate, there might be a few more bright days on the horizon.

Thinking of that day reminded Iris of her cousin. Lily had been a good person, despite the fact that she'd always wound up with bad people. Maybe that was why—they saw her light and wanted to take it for themselves. In an odd way, it made Lily feel good to help them. Life had been particularly cruel to Lily. She'd deserved to die at an old age surrounded by her children and grandchildren, not in some cornfield at the hands of a lowlife scumbag.

Taking two deep breaths in and pushing out once, Iris refocused. She had no proof that Riley Logan and Mr. Reagan were connected, but something in her gut told her the whole situation was off. Her superiors had taken her off the Reagan case in the same breath they'd mentioned Bear. Why was Bear so important? How would the FBI taking him out of the picture serve their best interests? There were still too many questions and not enough answers.

Maybe it had to do with Jack Noble. He was as enigmatic as Bear, but her previous research had shown that he'd been involved in some major scandals. The FBI's operatives had been informed to call in backup before even approaching the man, a request that had come from the very top of the food chain. She'd heard the name before, whispered like he was the boogeyman, but considering she'd never crossed paths with him, she hadn't committed his story to memory. Finding out more about him would take money and time, both of which she was running out of.

Besides, Peake hadn't mentioned Noble. He'd focused on Bear. The answers had to be with Bear.

Iris sat up and went back over to her desk. Sinking down into her chair, she turned back to the drive. The details were piecemeal at best. Scraps of information that had been collected and sorted into a haphazard system. Much of it was scanned material, as though the man had left no digital footprint. But the picture it painted was clear.

Riley Logan was dangerous.

Over the years, he had killed hundreds of people. Some hits were sanctioned, others were not. Details of his time as an independent contractor were murky at best, but she had gathered enough of an overview to know that the man she'd met in Indiana was not what he seemed. There was enough here to raise some serious questions with the FBI and the CIA, not to mention various other organizations around the world. More than that, there was enough here to bring Bear in and keep him locked up for a long time. The question wasn't whether he should be brought in—it was why she'd been told to steer clear.

If a perfect person existed to get close to him in order to take him down, she was a top candidate. Gritting her teeth, Iris clicked through folders and documents without really seeing them. He'd been within her grasp, and she'd let him go with a smile on her face. It was clear he knew how to stay off the radar, and now that he was out of reach, there was a chance they'd never see him again. And if she couldn't get to him, she couldn't get to Reagan.

Iris backed out of one folder and clicked into another, then froze when she saw a video file in front of her. Holding her breath, she hit play and watched as a group of people stormed into a boardroom. A man with a deep, resonant voice spoke, and even though the camera never showed his face, Iris recognized its familiarity.

Leaning forward, she studied the video, pausing and rewinding as needed. The speech he gave was informative, speaking about HealTek poisoning local water supplies as they attempted to create chemical warfare in secret. With a jolt, she realized she'd seen this before. It had gone viral on social media, and the news had spread across the country, both on television and in print.

She'd had no idea Bear had been involved.

Even more suspicious was that she and her team had suspected Reagan of funding HealTek's research, though they hadn't found any proof. It was exactly the sort of operation he'd want to get involved with. Considering how long they'd gotten away with poisoning local residents, it was no surprise that the government—and therefore Reagan—had been involved. Whether the townspeople knew remained to be seen.

How interesting that Bear had been there as well.

It was clear Bear wasn't working with Reagan—not if he'd been party to taking down two of his operations—but that didn't mean he was just a simple bystander either. Did he know who Reagan was? Had he worked for Reagan in the past? He'd feigned innocence the last time they spoke, but now that Iris knew what he was capable of, she wasn't about to take him at his word.

Though she didn't know where Bear was now, she knew where he'd been. Pulling up a map to pinpoint the exact location of the town, she was happy to see it was only a couple of hours away by car. A dark grin spread across her face.

"One way or another," she whispered to the empty room, "I'll find you."

6

Bear pulled into the dirt parking lot of The Magic Tap, a small local brewery. Its rustic appearance was meant to invoke the idea of a shack in the middle of the woods, but Bear could tell the banister had been recently replaced and the sign, though crooked, was bright and clean. He hadn't bothered going to the website yet, preferring to get his own eyes on it first, but he'd bet money someone who'd lived his best years in the seventies had opened it and still maintained it to this day.

A handful of cars sat in the parking lot already, which was more than he had expected. The place had only opened about twenty minutes ago, but it looked like all the regulars were already inside. It would be a good sign if his only reason for being here was to grab a drink. But thanks to Mandy, he had other plans.

He'd dropped her off at their cabin against her will. She'd wanted to come with him to scope out the bar, but that would've drawn a lot of eyes given she was only fifteen. Besides, they'd just bought all that ice, and he'd needed to stock it in their freezer at their home-for-now. Mandy had relented, but only if Bear promised to go inside the bar and figure out what was going on. She'd made him promise to find out if the woman was okay.

He'd seen a lot of people—not just women—stay in bad relationships because they had nowhere else to go, and the woman from the gas station fit the bill. Had she been waiting for Bear to follow them out of the store, or had she seen Mandy watching from the Tahoe's passenger seat? If he'd confronted the man, what did she expect him to do? Bear had no room in his life—or his cabin—to take in strays.

That hadn't stopped him from following her trail to the bar's doorstep, though.

The sound of gravel crunching under tires caught Bear's attention, and he turned just in time to see the brute of a man whip into the parking lot and pull into a spot near the side door. Now that Bear had a better vantage point, he could tell the Challenger was one of the newer models, with a pair of racing stripes down its middle. The car was pristine on the outside. Bear wondered if the only reason he'd beaten the man to the bar was because the guy had just gotten it washed and waxed.

Ducking down to make himself less conspicuous, Bear watched as the man got out of his vehicle, walked around the back, and opened the passenger side door. The front seat contained the woman from the gas station, her long blonde hair now pulled back into a sleek ponytail. The gesture would've been chivalrous if the man hadn't proceeded to grab the woman's elbow and yank her out of the car, making her stumble and grab onto to him to keep her balance.

Bear sat up in his seat. He should've been trying to stay out of view, but he couldn't help it. He hadn't liked the guy before, but now his internal alarms were blaring. The woman wasn't trying to get away, though it was clear she didn't appreciate being manhandled. She walked toward the side door of her own volition, twisting her arm as though trying to get out of the man's grip. The look on the guy's face was caught somewhere between frustration and anger. Regardless of which one won out, the woman could be about to have a very bad day.

Bear hadn't bothered looking at the details of the woman's shirt too closely before, but now that he was familiar with the Magic Tap's logo, he could see it plain as day in the center of her chest. Mandy had been right—there was no way you wore a Magic Tap shirt to the bar unless you worked there.

The look of strain on her face had Bear reaching for the door handle, only to pause when the side entrance to the bar opened and a man stepped out. He was a big dude, probably taller than Bear, and likely had a good eighty pounds on him, too. The mop of curly red hair on top might've looked ridiculous if the guy hadn't been so menacing. It would be a safe bet to guess he was the bouncer.

That alone wouldn't have been enough to stop Bear from getting out of the car and asking what was going on, to see if the woman needed to get away right then and there. He'd done stupider shit in his life and lived to tell the tale. Over the years, he'd gotten downright brazen just for the hell of it.

But as the big ginger held the door open for the newcomers, his jacket fell open just enough for Bear to see the shoulder holster hanging by his side. When he'd first spotted the guy, he thought it had been strange he was wearing a jacket in this heat, as thin as it was. Now he knew why.

Bear cursed and sat back, letting his hand drop from the door. He'd been willing to bet he could get the upper hand on the guy from the gas station, even if the man did have a weapon. But with the bouncer in the mix, it wasn't worth throwing himself in the middle. Especially because he didn't know the full extent of it. If the woman needed help, he had to make sure he would improve her situation, not make it worse.

The three figures disappeared into the brewery, and Bear waited five minutes before climbing out of the Tahoe and filing through the front door. Since you had to have a license to conceal carry a handgun in the state of Oregon, he left his own weapon in the glove compartment of his vehicle, making him feel undressed in the worst way possible. Especially when he found himself face to face with the big ginger bouncer.

The guy already had his hand out. "ID?"

Bear thought about being difficult, but it wouldn't serve him in the moment. He didn't want to make an impression, not if he had to come back to keep an eye on things. The idea of causing a little trouble just for the hell of it threatened to bring a smile to Bear's face, and he had to tamp down on the urge.

"Kinda early for a bouncer, isn't it?" Bear asked, handing over his ID.

It was a real New York State license with a real address he hadn't visited in almost a year. But the name was fake.

The man took the ID and looked it over in detail. His voice was casual when he spoke. "Owner likes to have security on hand." The man looked up at Bear, comparing his face to what was on the license. "Not gonna turn down easy money."

"Hear you there," Bear said, taking his ID back and slipping it into his wallet.

The bouncer had seemed at ease, but Bear wondered if it was a practiced lie. Most of the patrons of the bar were sixty and above—regulars who wanted to get away from their family or had no family to get away from. The guy guarding the door could toss them out two at a time, if necessary. And then there was the handgun, which had stayed hidden beneath that windbreaker.

Seemed like a lot of security for a little brewery in a town of about six hundred.

But now wasn't the time to ask questions. It was a time to observe. Stepping past the bouncer, Bear sidled up to the end of the bar closest to the door and sat down. Most of the other patrons were on the other side, near the kitchen and flatscreen TV. Fine by him.

The woman behind the bar was blonde, but not the same one Bear had seen at the gas station. Her hair was cropped just above her shoulders, and she was unnaturally tan. There was a small diamond stud in her nose. Her makeup was heavy, but not unflattering. He'd guess her age to be around twenty-five. The tag on her shirt said her name was Monica.

"Welcome to The Magic Tap," she said, throwing a napkin down in front of him. The ease with which she talked to him indicated she wasn't new to the job. "What can I get for you?"

"Any recommendations?"

The woman pointed to a sign on the wall above them with a list of their beer. "We have all the staples on tap, but we also have our own line. Can't go wrong with the Magic Brew. It's got a classic taste with a hint of honey. Nothing too crazy."

Bear raised an eyebrow. "Do I look like a guy who isn't into anything too crazy?"

A laugh trickled out of her mouth. "You look like a guy who likes what he likes. But if you're looking for something a bit more adventurous, we've got a chocolate chili beer."

Bear involuntarily winced. "I'll try the Magic Brew, thanks."

"Thought so." Monica retreated a step or two and reached under the bar, pulling out an ice-cold bottle with the Magic Tap logo front and center. He'd seen it at the gas station, but it had looked too highfalutin for his taste. "Let me know what you think of it."

Bear lifted the beer to his lips and took a healthy slug. It was crisp and smooth. As it moved down his throat, he got the sweet taste of honey, just enough that he knew it was there. Classic. He smacked his lips. "Wow."

"Pretty good, right?"

"Who makes this?"

"The owner, Edison Tapp. He's a genius with that sort of thing."

"His last name's actually Tap?"

"Two p's," she said, drumming her fingers on the bar. Monica moderated her voice to sound deeper and gruffer. "Would've been a dancer, but I've got shit knees."

Bear couldn't help himself. He laughed loud enough to turn a head or two. "Sounds like a fun guy."

"Can be." Monica shrugged. "Strict but fair. I've had worse jobs."

Bear took another sip of his drink. "Think I saw this at the gas station down the road. You can get it in stores?"

"Funny you should ask that." Monica's grin was wide and excited. "His son finally convinced him to send out samples to a few places. We've carried these locally for years, but Ethan got Ed to ship out a couple bottles to a few people in Portland. They loved them, and now we've got a new revenue stream."

That explained why the place looked brand new. He'd probably taken that money and put it right back into the brewery. Smarter than pocketing it, at least. Bear couldn't help but share in the excitement.

He'd only been here a few minutes, but he was already invested in Ed's story.

Another question settled on the tip of his tongue as the woman from the gas station stepped through the doors to the kitchen, wrapping an apron around her waist and pinning a nametag to her shirt. She looked flustered, though unharmed. The moment she approached a customer on the other end of the bar, a wide smile was in place, her terrible morning a distant memory.

Monica saw how Bear's attention had shifted and looked over her shoulder, then down at her watch. "Lunch time. Kelly will take care of you. Need anything else before I go?"

Bear took a casual sip of his drink and rearranged his face into a blank expression that he hoped didn't betray the gears turning in his head. He held up his bottle, still half full. "What's your next recommendation after this one?"

"You like orange?"

"Who doesn't?"

She smiled. "Orange Cascade. Has a bit of a caramel flavor in there, too, but it's more citrus than sweet."

"Thanks." Bear pulled out a five-dollar bill and handed it to her. "In case I'm gone before you get back from lunch."

Monica pocketed the cash with a smile, then turned on her heel and headed through the kitchen door, giving Kelly a gentle pat on the shoulder as she passed. The other woman smiled in her direction, and as her eyes traveled the rest of the bar, she spotted Bear and froze. It was just for a second or two, but long enough to overflow someone's beer. Shaking the liquid off her hand, Kelly placed it in front of the customer and took their cash, depositing it in the register and then turning her back on Bear, busying herself with menial tasks.

It didn't bother him. He had time to kill and enough people to watch as he enjoyed the rest of his beer. Two more patrons filtered through the door, though Bear noticed the bouncer just wave them in. They must've been regulars. Bear hadn't wanted to stick out, but perhaps that wasn't a possibility in a town this small. The bouncer had probably known he was an outsider from the second he laid eyes on him.

Eventually, Bear's bottle ran dry, and he made a point of pushing it away from him and waited for Kelly to meet his eye. He could tell when she noticed he was staring. Her shoulders tensed and she kept her back to him for another couple of minutes. But she needed to do her job. It was only a matter of time.

Eventually, she made her way down to his end. Refusing to meet his eyes, she pointed to the bottle. "Another?"

"Monica mentioned trying the Citrus Cascade. Got any of those?"

Kelly startled, chancing a glance at him. "You know Monica?"

"Just met her. Asked for a few recommendations." Bear watched Kelly's eyes, rimmed in black eyeliner, though not as heavy as Monica's. The area below her eyes was puffy and dark, but it looked more from lack of sleep rather than a bruise. "You a fan of Citrus Cascade?"

Kelly bent down to grab the beer for him, replacing the old bottle with the new. "Not a fan of citrus." Her tone wasn't conversational like Monica's had been.

Bear's gaze found her nametag, but it said Karla instead of Kelly. He picked up a bottle and tipped it toward her. "Which is it?"

The woman furrowed her brows. "Which is what?"

"Karla," he said, looking at her nametag. "Or Kelly?"

She looked down, her shoulders sagging when she spotted the mistake. "Grabbed the wrong one."

Bear leaned forward, careful not to invade her space, but wanting to keep the conversation between them. "Are you okay?"

Halfway through removing the nametag, Kelly stiffened. Her eyes found his. "I'm fine."

"My daughter Mandy found your note. She talked to you this morning out in front of the gas station."

Warring emotions waged a battle across her face, finally won over by dread. But was she more afraid of Bear or the man in the back room? Would she refuse Bear's help for fear of discovery, or would she take advantage of this one-on-one conversation?

Kelly's gaze shifted to her right, just over Bear's shoulder. A shadow fell over him, and without turning around, he knew the hulking mass of the bouncer was standing behind him. Bear turned to face him. "There a problem?"

The man's eyes never left Kelly's face. "You tell me."

Kelly met the bouncer's eyes, more guarded than she had been a minute ago. "It's fine, Robbie." She glanced at Bear, and then away again. "I need to grab the right nametag. I'll be right back."

Robbie the bouncer looked down on Bear. "Don't bother the waitresses."

Bear held up his hands. "Just making conversation."

Robbie held Bear's gaze for a minute, then walked away, settling back on his stool next to the front door. Even though Bear had his back turned to him, he could feel the other man's gaze bore into him. Even if Kelly wanted to talk to Bear, it'd be impossible now.

A few minutes later, Kelly returned and busied herself at the other end of the bar, ignoring Bear even after he finished his second drink. Leaving a twenty on the countertop, he had to resist writing his number down. It wouldn't do her any good to get caught with another man's number, and he didn't relish handing that number out to strangers.

Tipping his head to Robbie, Bear pushed through the doors of the bar and back out into the sunshine, wondering how the hell he was going to tell Mandy he'd come back empty handed.

MANDY WAS BORED OUT OF HER MIND.

No, she was beyond bored.

Was there a word for that?

She'd look it up on her phone except they didn't have any service out here.

With a huff, Mandy tossed her phone on the bed and launched herself to her feet. She'd already paced the tiny cabin a hundred times since Bear left, but what was a hundred more? Or a thousand? Maybe she'd wear a track right through the floor and dig her way to China. It'd be better than just sitting here doing nothing.

Everything they'd gotten at the gas station had been put away since Bear had dumped the supplies and left her to go track down that woman. She hadn't been too happy to be left behind—like always—but he'd made a good point that she couldn't exactly stroll through the front doors of a bar and order a drink like he could. So, she'd resigned herself to putting away their purchases and waiting for his return.

Mandy had even cleaned up the cabin, scrubbing what few dirty dishes Bear had left in the sink, making the beds, sweeping. Doing chores? Yeah, she was that bored. Bear would be happy about her pitching in, but she hoped he wouldn't let it go to his head. It wouldn't be a regular occurrence. A shudder ran through her at the thought.

The clock on the wall said Bear had only been gone half an hour, and it made her feel worse that even thirty minutes was excruciating. Might as well have been a whole day. Sometimes she could trick her brain into speeding up time instead of slowing it down, but apparently today was not one of those days. She blamed it on the cabin, too small even for the two of them. A couch, a small round table, and a minuscule kitchen took up every last inch of space in this room. One door led to the twin bed where she'd been sleeping, since Bear had insisted on taking the couch. The next door led to the bathroom, which had a shower stall barely big enough for Bear to navigate. And the last door led outside.

She'd considered going out there to work on cleaning up the flower beds, but that was even worse than chores. Sure, it'd be less suffocating than staying in the tiny cabin, but at least in here, she didn't have to keep her head on a swivel. No one was after them, as far as she knew, but they'd run into more trouble accidentally than not. Better safe than sorry.

As her anxiety rose, Mandy felt the usual urge to make sure everything was in its place. The coffee cup handles had to face out for easy access. She'd checked the outside door to make sure it was locked six or seven times. Turned the gas stove on and then off again. Made sure her book was precisely where she'd left it last—perfectly in line with the corner of her nightstand. She wanted to fight the compulsions, but giving in to them provided her with overwhelming relief.

Without her phone, there were only two forms of entertainment here—cards and her book. She was sick of solitaire, and as much as she was enjoying *The Forbidden Library*, it was too hard to read right now. The main character, Alice, could enter books and explore other worlds, and instead of letting Mandy escape, it just reminded her how trapped she was. Plus, she only had a few chapters left, and it was the last book in her pile. Bear said they wouldn't be able to pick up more for at least another couple of days.

Worse, Mandy couldn't stop thinking about the torn piece of clothing they'd found in the forest that morning. More specifically, she couldn't stop thinking about that phone number on the slip of paper. She hadn't meant to memorize it. Really, she'd only looked at it for a few seconds, but the numbers had seared into her brain. Even as she paced around the cabin, she caught herself whispering it without realizing what she was doing.

That phone number was driving her crazy. The torn, lined paper had come from a notebook, like something she'd used in school. There was nothing fancy or different about it. And the numbers had been written plainly. Not rushed or messy. There was really nothing to learn from the slip, other than the fact that it had been found at the scene of a possible crime.

And who did the shirt belong to? What had happened to them? Had they made it out of the forest alive, or had their dead body been lying somewhere nearby? Bear had said he'd go check it out later, but they'd gotten distracted by the crying woman at the gas station.

Before Mandy realized what she was doing, she unlatched the lock to the door outside. She watched as her hand reached out and turned the doorknob, like she wasn't in control of her own body. Stepping out into the sun, she shut the door behind her, careful to lock it and slip the key into her pocket where it wouldn't get lost. Then she turned to her little motorized scooter leaning up against the cabin.

It was bubblegum pink, which wouldn't have been her first choice. At least her helmet was black. Bear had bought it a couple weeks ago, bringing it back from some garage sale he'd passed on the way home from one of his longer trips. For once, Mandy hadn't wanted to go with him on a supply run. They'd been cooped up in the cabin for too long already, and being even more cooped up in the car with him didn't sound too appealing. Besides, she couldn't read in the car without feeling sick, so she'd elected to stay home with her book.

A few hours later, Bear returned with the scooter. Mandy had been too excited to care about the color. This meant freedom! Kind of. Bear only let her ride around the campground. There were enough paths to keep her entertained for a couple of weeks while she memorized them, but she'd explored them enough that now they held no more mystery.

Today, she had another destination in mind.

Strapping on her helmet, Mandy gave into her impulse. As she stepped onto the scooter, she switched it on and squeezed the handle. She headed down the bumpy gravel driveway away from their cabin, then out onto the paved roads of the campground. They were old, and she had to dodge plenty of potholes, but it was much smoother than the loose stones. She'd wiped out a few times, coming in too fast from the other road. A nasty cut on her elbow was still covered up with a Band-Aid. After complaining that they didn't have any cool Band-Aids with fun designs on them, Bear had drawn smiley faces on their pack of plain ones. It wasn't quite the same, but it still made Mandy grin.

Her palms were sweating, and she kept having to wipe them on her shorts, one after another. Bear would be pissed if he found out she left, which was all the more reason to get this over with as soon as possible. If she could make it to her destination and back in about half an hour, she had a chance.

If only the stupid scooter would go faster.

It was a little over five minutes to the camp entrance because Bear had insisted on renting the cabin in the deepest part of the campground. She hadn't complained when they'd first arrived because she liked being surrounded by all the trees with no neighbors to bother them, but now she was cursing under her breath as she crested the hill next to the battered and faded Bull Pine Campground sign.

Without slowing down, Mandy maneuvered her scooter across the street and along the shoulder so she faced traffic. That way, she could see what was headed in her direction. It was ten minutes of highway to get to the rundown shopping center, which meant a total of fifteen minutes to get back to the cabin after she did what she needed to do. That left little to no wiggle room for cooling down and catching her breath. And that was only if Bear took his sweet time coming back from the bar.

Movement and a mission helped Mandy focus. The adrenaline didn't hurt either, and she found herself enjoying the ride to the shopping center. Although she had complained when Bear said they'd be going to Oregon instead of California, she couldn't deny that it was beautiful out here. The forest felt thick and mysterious, calling her name like a mystery to be solved. But Bear had told her how easy it was to get lost out here, and she wasn't about to make him call in a search party to find her. So she stuck to the highway.

A little winded when she arrived at the shopping center, Mandy forced herself to take a few deep breaths, in through her nose and out through her mouth. It was less from exertion and more from anxiety. Without slowing down, she hopped the curb and made straight for the building on the left. There were several shops connected here, including a clothing outlet store, a shoe store, and a restaurant, but they all looked run-down. If it weren't for the half a dozen or so cars in the parking lot, she might've thought it was abandoned.

But being a relic of its time was a good thing in this case because she knew from their singular trip out here a couple of weeks ago that there was a payphone around the corner. Mandy knew what it was in theory —she'd watched movies and had the internet, after all—but she'd never used one before.

Not like it was hard. Put in a couple of quarters, push the buttons to dial a phone number, and wait until the other person answered. Parking next to the dilapidated phone booth, Mandy pulled out her cell, knowing that it had finally gotten service when she'd reached the shopping center. There were no texts or missed calls from Bear, but there were a dozen messages from Marcus. She got a little thrill seeing his name on her phone, but she convinced herself it was because there was a chance he'd uncovered something about the phone number—not because she was happy to hear from him.

Back in New York, Marcus was leading a normal life. He went to school, had dinner with his mom, and researched all the weird things Mandy texted him whenever her phone got service. Part of her envied how mundane his days were, but the other part knew she'd be even more bored out of her mind than she was here. If she were Marcus, she'd be happy to have someone like Mandy in her life. He got to practice his hacking skills and learn a whole bunch of random things from her weird questions. Plus, she was pretty awesome.

Opening the messages revealed that Marcus did not, in fact, find anything else out about the number. The area code had told him it was a local number, but that didn't lead to anything useful. Mandy blew a piece of hair out of her face and tucked her phone away. She'd reply to him later when she was on less of a timetable.

For now, her mission was the priority.

Leaning her scooter against the outside of the payphone, she pulled a pair of quarters out of her pocket. She'd found one on the sidewalk last time she was here, and the other one had been in the gas station parking lot when they'd first arrived in Arlington. It's not like fifty cents was a lot of money, but she was happy she'd found the change and hung onto it.

Slipping the quarters into the slot, Mandy didn't hesitate to dial the number. For a split second, nothing happened. Were you supposed to dial and then put the quarters in? Maybe she should've read the instructions first.

But then the phone rang once, and someone picked up the other line. A woman with a smooth, confident voice. She didn't sound old or young, and she didn't sound bored, exactly. More like this was just another day at an uneventful job.

"Operations."

Mandy waited. There was no noise in the background. She couldn't even hear the woman breathing. Maybe she was wearing a headset with a noise-cancelling microphone. Or she was all alone in her office or wherever she was answering from.

"Operations," the woman repeated.

Mandy didn't know what to say. *Operations?* That sounded official, and the thought made the hair on the back of her neck stand on end. She'd had a few guesses as to who might pick up the other line, but none of them had come close to this. If anything, she'd figured it would've been someone's mom. Or their girlfriend or boyfriend. Maybe a hotel, though that one was less likely, considering Marcus hadn't been able to find the number online anywhere.

When the woman still got no answer, she asked, "What's your code?"

Now it was really time to panic. This wasn't someone's loved one. This was an operation. That required a code. Mandy opened her mouth to reply with something—anything—but the only thing that came out was a strangled sort of squeak.

After a moment, the line went dead, and Mandy realized she'd been able to hear one thing—the slight buzz of static. She pulled the phone away from her face as if to check if they were still connected, only to realize she was using a payphone, not a cell. Biting down a curse, Mandy put the phone to her ear again and closed her eyes, hoping to pick out even the most minuscule sound.

When the static returned, Mandy jumped at the sound of the woman's voice in her ear. "A car has been dispatched to your location."

8

BEAR PULLED INTO THE BULL PINE CAMPGROUND'S ENTRANCE. HE'D ONLY been gone an hour, but it felt like he'd wasted most of his day. The trek out into the woods this morning had been nice, especially because Mandy had seemed to soak up his lessons, but it had ended in mystery and confusion. Then there was the gas station incident. And the strange atmosphere in the bar. It was only midafternoon, but what had he accomplished today?

Returning to the campground wasn't quite like returning home, but a similar sense of peace washed over him. It was a sprawling area with a good mix of wooded trails, paved paths, and plenty of camp-sites for all sorts of adventurers. He would've enjoyed staying in a tent under the stars, but a cabin provided extra safety. Besides, he was getting too old to sleep on the ground for too long. He was still spry for his age, but he was slower than he used to be, back in his prime.

He turned on the path that led back to the cabin. The trees here were thin, and he could see through to some of the campsites occupied by those who just didn't want to go home yet. These were the final days of summer as school would be starting in the next couple of weeks. Bear still hadn't decided what to do with Mandy. She wouldn't appreciate being sent off somewhere, but she needed to be around kids her own age.

As the trees grew thicker, Bear got lost in his thoughts. He'd traveled these roads enough to know where he was going without needing to think about it. The last couple of weeks had been good. He'd enjoyed the isolation Oregon had to offer. Reconnecting with nature always reinvigorated him. And he felt closer to Mandy. After her trauma in Indiana, Bear had worried she'd retreat into herself. He'd noticed her OCD getting worse, and sometimes she had full-blown anxiety attacks. But when he asked her how she was, how she was handling everything, she was honest with him. He wouldn't take that for granted.

Bear directed the Tahoe into the single parking space in front of the cabin and shifted it into park. Looking at the cabin usually settled him, but there was a detail his subconscious had noticed that the rest of his brain had not. He grabbed his pistol from the glovebox and climbed out of the vehicle, shutting the door without making a sound.

Straining his ears, all he heard was birdsong and a distant rustle of leaves as the wind blew through them. Bear hesitated long enough to take a deep breath and center himself. Would he walk in on his worst nightmare, or would Mandy be sprawled across the couch, her nose deep in her book? She'd laugh at him for being so paranoid, and he would join in with her because he'd rather be paranoid than make a mistake that got Mandy hurt. Or worse.

The door was closed. Bear tested the handle and found it locked. A good sign. Pulling out his key, he fit it into the keyhole and twisted, keeping his gun aimed at a forty-five-degree angle. Shouldering the door open, he stepped inside and did a quick sweep with his eyes, his gun following along with the trajectory. He stepped into the bedroom and the bathroom. He checked anywhere a person could be hiding and found nothing. But that gave him no sense of relief.

Mandy wasn't here.

Keeping his gun at the ready, he slowly swept the room, looking for anything out of place. To his surprise, he found the cabin in a better state than when he'd left. Mandy had washed some dishes and put everything from the gas station in its proper place. Her book was lined up on the nightstand, just how she liked it. She'd either been extremely bored or anxious while he was gone. Maybe both.

A locked door and a clean cabin should've put Bear at ease, but he'd told Mandy to stay put while he checked on the woman from the gas station. Something still scratched at the back of his head, and the fact that he couldn't place it drove him crazy. There was a detail missing, and if he could flesh it out, maybe he could figure out where Mandy had gone.

With no sign of a struggle inside the cabin, Bear stepped back through the door and circled the little house. No tire marks from a car or a bike. No scuffles written out in the dirt. No dropped items that might've been a clue as to what happened to her. Mandy had just disappeared into thin air.

Before Bear could let panic settle in, he took two calming breaths and returned to the Tahoe. Staring at the front of the cabin, it took him another minute before he realized what was off. Mandy's scooter was missing. The little pink vehicle should've been resting up against the front of the house and under the overhang so it wouldn't get wet when it rained. It had become a part of the scenery to the point that Bear had subconsciously noticed it was missing.

Mandy had left of her own volition. She might be riding around the park to let off some steam, but she would've left a note in case Bear got back, knowing how much he'd worry. If she hadn't left a note, that meant she either snuck out or was chased out. Considering there was no sign of trouble, Bear was leaning toward the former.

Still worried, now with a little bite of anger to complement it, Bear got back in the Tahoe and reversed out of the driveway. If she was bored, she'd likely gone out for a joyride. But where? Lack of a note made him think it was somewhere off limits. Had she gone in search of the bar herself? Maybe, but her chances of being caught were high, and he didn't think she'd risk that. Then maybe the shopping center? She'd be able to get there on her scooter without much trouble, even if it meant breaking the rules by riding along the shoulder of the highway.

Bear's worst nightmare shifted from finding his daughter dead inside the cabin to finding her dead on the side of the road. A car could've hit her at sixty miles an hour. The injuries would be catastrophic, even if the crash wasn't fatal. The thought made Bear press down harder on the gas pedal.

As he crested the hill next to the sign at the entrance to the campground, he didn't bother slowing down. There were no oncoming cars. He mashed the pedal down harder and peeled out. It would only take him a few minutes to get to the shopping center. If he found her, he'd hug her and then chew her out for disobeying him. If he didn't? Well, he'd think about that when the time came.

But Bear never made it that far. Finally looking to his right as he pulled out onto the highway, he saw a flash of color and heard a thump against the side of his door. A curse escaped his mouth as he slammed on the brakes, then threw the car into park right where it was. He'd been so wrapped up in making sure there were no cars coming that he hadn't been looking for pedestrians. Granted, not a lot of people walked along the highway out here, but it wasn't unheard of. He'd seen a few making the trek into town over the last couple of weeks.

Jumping out of the Tahoe, he circled around the back, hoping the person hadn't been seriously injured. It took a moment for his brain to catch up with his eyes. Pink scooter. Black helmet. A small girl sitting up and rubbing her shoulder. Quiet and colorful curses that would've brought a smile to his lips if he hadn't been losing his mind.

"Mandy?" The name was more breath than voice. He didn't have enough air in his lungs to speak.

Mandy looked up at him, her eyes wider than he'd ever seen them. "You ran me over!"

Bear knelt next to her and began checking for injuries. Her helmet was still intact. She held her arm and rubbed it. When he twisted it in one direction, then another, she winced. But when he felt along her bone, nothing was broken. Maybe a fracture or just deep bruising. He chose a couple of colorful curses himself, and then continued his examination. Her other arm seemed fine. So did her legs. Even the scooter was still intact, though the Tahoe had a little scratch along the passenger side door now.

"Are you okay?" he asked. "Can you stand?"

"I think so." Mandy's voice was too quiet.

Bear helped her to her feet and watched to see if she swayed on the spot. When she stood steady, he opened the door and helped her inside, throwing the pink scooter into the back seat. Then he jogged around the back of the vehicle and jumped in, reversing into the campground enough that the cars along the highway didn't have to drive around him anymore. He'd left the front end of the Tahoe out in the middle of the road while he checked on Mandy. It was a miracle someone hadn't accidentally hit them and made the situation ten times worse.

Now parked along the entrance road, Bear turned in his seat to Mandy. He was still more concerned than angry, though he could feel his adrenaline fading. "Are you sure you're okay? Do you think your arm is broken?"

"No, just bruised. I kind of just bounced off the car. I saw you coming and braked, so I didn't hit that hard. Just didn't have time to swerve."

"Good." A deep breath calmed him down another level. He didn't want to yell at her right now, but— *"What were you thinking?"*

"I'm sorry—"

"You mean you're sorry you got caught?"

"No. I mean, yes. Obviously. But—"

"I know you think my rules are stupid, but they're in place to keep you safe. It only takes one wrong move. One bad day. When I came home and you weren't there, a million scenarios ran through my head. I've seen too much. Lost too many people—"

Mandy's face distorted, but instead of arguing, she burst into tears.

Bear's mouth snapped shut on the rest of his sentence. He'd seen Mandy cry before, but rarely like this. Fat tears rolled down her face, and she was breathing hard like she was having a panic attack. Burying her face in her hands, her whole body shook as she sobbed.

Not knowing what else to do, Bear pulled Mandy close to him, careful not to jostle her bad arm, and let her cry. For once, she let him hold her, and after a few seconds, she snaked her arms around his waist and squeezed. Tears sprang to Bear's eyes, and all his anger and disappointment slipped away. Right now, all that mattered was that Mandy was okay.

A few minutes passed like this. Her breathing slowed and her sobs dissipated. He let go when she sat up, a hiccup escaping as she sniffled. She swiped at the tears on her cheeks, but they kept falling.

"I'm sorry," Bear whispered. He didn't know what else to say.

Mandy looked at him, her eyes red and puffy. "Dad?"

Bear's stomach churned at the pain in her voice. "Yeah?"

"I think I really messed up."

9

BEAR'S HEART SQUEEZED IN HIS CHEST, AND HE TOOK THE TIME TO WIPE his own tears before he could find the words he wanted to say to Mandy. Ruffling her hair usually got a reaction out of her, but this time, she just closed her eyes like it was painful.

"You didn't mess up—"

"Yes, I did." Mandy's eyes snapped open, and even though she was still crying, she pinned Bear with a look. "I called that number."

"What number?"

"The one we found in the woods."

It took Bear a second to trace his thoughts back to that morning. The slip of paper in the pocket of the tattered shirt. He'd told Mandy to leave it alone. It had still been there when they'd headed home. Trying to keep his voice neutral, he asked his next question. "Did you go back to find it?"

"No." Mandy's eyes pleaded with him to believe her. "I memorized it. On accident."

"On accident?"

"Yeah." She had to clear her voice of emotion before she could get out her next sentence. "I didn't mean to, I swear. It just got stuck in my head, and I couldn't stop thinking about it. Repeated it over and over again."

"That's why you left?" He wasn't going to blame her for getting the number stuck in her head. It would be too hypocritical—that situation in the woods had been eating at him, too.

"I knew the shopping center had a payphone. I had a couple quarters. I just wanted to see who would pick up. Maybe find out who that person was. You know, like, If they were missing."

"Did anyone answer?"

"Yeah."

The fear in Mandy's voice confused Bear, and it caused goosebumps to erupt down his arms. "Who?"

"I'm not sure. Some woman. Sounded older. American. There was no background noise." She rattled off the information, knowing Bear would want every detail. "When she answered, all she said was, 'Operations.'"

Bear stilled. "Did she say anything else after that?"

"She said 'Operations' again, then she asked for my code. I didn't know what to say. Then the line sort of went dead, and then she came back on and said a car had been dispatched to my location." The words were rushing out of Mandy now, like a waterfall over a cliff's edge. "I'm so sorry. I didn't know that was going to happen. What if they know it was me? What if they find us? I didn't mean to cause any trouble, Bear, I swear. Please—"

Bear gently shushed her, wrapping an arm around her shoulders, careful not to jostle her injured arm. "You didn't do anything wrong."

"But—"

"You didn't do anything wrong," he repeated, more firmly this time. "You didn't know. It's okay. And now we know something else is going on around here." Despite his constant desire to stay out of other people's problems, he found that comforting. Better to know what was heading his way. "You said you went to the payphone at the shopping center?"

When Mandy nodded, Bear put the Tahoe in drive and pulled out onto the highway—making sure to look both ways this time.

"What are you doing?" she asked.

"We're gonna see if anyone shows up."

"What if they see us?"

"You said you didn't talk at all on the phone, right?"

"Right."

"Well," Bear said, getting up to speed, "then they won't know you were on the other line. There are no cameras over there, so there's no chance they know it was you. It's gonna be okay."

"You're just saying that because you ran me over."

Bear had to tamp down a chuckle. "I didn't run you over. Only bumped you with the car."

Mandy's laugh was watery, but it was good to hear. "You promise it'll be okay?"

Bear hated making promises he couldn't keep, but right now, Mandy needed the comfort those words would provide. "I promise. All we're doing is observing. No one can tie us to that number or the shirt we found in the woods."

Mandy was silent, but Bear took that as a sign that she believed him. The shopping center was only a couple minutes away by car, so it hadn't been long since Mandy had made the phone call. Depending on where the dispatched car was coming from, someone could show up in a matter of minutes or hours. If this were an extraction, there'd be a car waiting nearby for a phone call from the operative.

Bear slowed down as he approached the entrance to the shopping center, but only to see if there was a car already pulled up to the payphone. Most of the cars were on the other side of the parking lot. Mandy looked over at him to see if he realized he'd missed their turn but said nothing.

Taking the next turn, Bear drove into a residential area. This was one of the first places he'd explored as he drove around to become more familiar with Arlington. It was also where he'd spotted the garage sale where he bought Mandy's scooter. It wasn't a large area, but he knew you could see the other side of the shopping center and the payphone from one of the streets back here.

When he reached a stop sign, Bear turned left and drove straight until he was lined up with the end of the mall building and the area they were scouting. Pulling off the side of the street, he parked outside someone's house. Didn't look like anyone was home. Even better.

"Now we wait?" Mandy asked.

"Now we wait," Bear said.

Parking on the side of the highway would've been too obvious to whoever pulled into the shopping center entrance, and parking too close to the payphone would tip them off as well. From this vantage point, it would be more difficult to follow whoever arrived, but he hadn't decided whether that was an option yet. That was dependent on who showed up. With Mandy in the car, he might not want to risk it.

The first fifteen minutes were silent. Bear and Mandy kept their eyes on the payphone, only occasionally looking around at their surroundings to make sure no one approached them. The next fifteen minutes were filled with whispered speculation. With more than a half hour behind them, Bear wondered if they'd already missed someone arriving. Maybe they'd left as soon as they realized no one was waiting at the payphone.

Another fifteen minutes, and Mandy's whispers grew into grumbles. Bear could sit still for hours if needed, but Mandy was used to constant motion. She'd been sprinting through life from the moment he and Jack had found her, and there was no indication she'd stop any time soon. Her impatience was infective, and Bear started shifting around in his seat.

After an hour, Bear considered calling it quits. They'd probably missed whoever showed up. They hadn't had eyes on the payphone for about fifteen minutes between Mandy leaving and Bear showing up in the Tahoe. Plenty of time for a car to arrive, then leave when they realized it was a false alarm. He couldn't decide if he was disappointed or relieved. It was one less thread to unravel, sure, but he couldn't help wondering if the person who'd shown up had caught Mandy leaving the shopping center. He hadn't asked her, but he felt certain she'd been too frazzled to check if she'd been followed.

Bear reached to put the vehicle in gear when a flash of white caught his attention out of the corner of his eye. A panel van had turned the corner and was headed toward the payphone. Next to him, he felt Mandy lean forward to peer around his bulk. With bated breath, they both watched as the vehicle turned and came to a standstill. A splash of orange covered the van's side doors. It took a moment for Bear to realize what it said.

Then he started laughing.

"What?" Mandy asked, leaning forward to see better. "What is it? Why are you laughing?"

"It's the phone company," Bear said between chuckles.

"Are you sure?" A laugh escaped her mouth, too. "Really?"

"Says ConnectCom Services right on the side of the van." Bear pointed to the contraption sitting on top of the van's roof. "That's a boom lift. They stand in the bucket at the end, and it lifts them up so they can work on the phone lines."

Mandy's laughter came out in wheezes now. "All that for a phone company?"

"Guess so." Bear turned to her. "Better that than the alternative."

They hadn't discussed it, but Mandy had been in Bear's life long enough to draw her own conclusions. She'd probably thought the same thing he had—that it was some sort of agency.

"Explains the phone number," Mandy said, having caught her breath. "But not the blood or the shirt."

Someone had been hurt out in the woods, that was for sure. He'd had the number to the phone company in his breast pocket, but there could be a reasonable explanation for that. The blood? Not so much.

Bear opened his mouth to bounce some theories off Mandy when the sudden chirp of a police siren made them both freeze. Looking in his rearview mirror, Bear saw red and blue lights dancing across the top of a cruiser parked behind them.

10

It hadn't taken long for Iris to arrive in the upstate New York town that Bear and Mandy had once called home. It was a few hours' drive from the city, during which she'd mulled over what she'd do when she got there. With time of the essence, launching a full investigation into Bear wasn't worth it. Instead, she'd bypass witnesses altogether and go straight to the source.

Sheriff Josephine McKinnon's picture was plastered all over the internet, having been at the center of the operation that finally exposed HealTek's pharmaceutical scam. With fiery red hair and a splash of freckles across her face, she looked fierce and formidable. Iris had done her due diligence and investigated the woman. Though she hadn't been looking to unearth any dirt on her, Iris was disappointed she hadn't found any. It would've made getting answers out of the sheriff that much easier.

McKinnon was one of the good ones.

Pulling into a spot in the center of town, Iris put her car in park and turned off the engine. A few cars down on the opposite side sat the Sheriff's cruiser, parked in front of a local coffee shop.

Through the wide windows of the coffee shop, Iris could see McKinnon standing in line, chatting with a customer behind her. All smiles, the woman talked with her hands, gesturing this way and that, as though regaling the person with some heroic story. Or maybe she was just giving them directions. The conversation broke off as McKinnon stepped up to the counter and ordered her morning beverage. Iris' mouth watered at the thought of getting some coffee for herself, but she swallowed down the temptation. The fewer people who saw and remembered her, the better. No point in going into a shop full of witnesses when she could talk to McKinnon one-on-one with no chance of anyone overhearing them once she was outside.

As money exchanged hands, Iris stepped out of her car and crossed the street. Both foot traffic and street traffic were light at this point in the day. That had its pros and cons. Nothing to slow her down, but nothing to cover her tracks, either. She'd stick out like a sore thumb, especially to someone like McKinnon, who probably knew every single person in this town by name.

Iris slowed down to time her arrival outside the coffee shop just as McKinnon stepped through the door. Either the woman was distracted or at ease because she didn't even cast a glance Iris' way as she strolled down the sidewalk toward her cruiser. There was a bounce in her step, and Iris couldn't help but wonder what was going through the sheriff's mind. Just another beautiful day on the force? Was there someone waiting for her at home? Or did she just really love coffee?

Iris waited until she was a couple of paces behind the woman before speaking. "Sheriff McKinnon?"

McKinnon stopped and turned toward Iris. The woman was stockier than she'd expected, and even though she was shorter than Iris, she looked like she'd be tough to take down in a fight. Not that Iris was going to let it get that far. Beating information out of a sheriff was no way to stay off the radar.

Though McKinnon didn't betray any anxiety on her face, her body had gone rigid. She didn't know Iris, and therefore, she didn't know what to expect from her. "Yes?"

"My name is Iris Duvall, and I'm—"

McKinnon surprised her by turning around and continuing to her car. "If you want a comment, you have to go through the hotline. No exceptions."

Iris pinched her eyebrows together in confusion. "I'm sorry?"

"The hotline," McKinnon said with more force, and Iris had to scramble to catch up to hear the rest of her words. "If you want a comment, you have to call it. We've been pretty clear about it. All journalists—"

"I'm not a journalist."

McKinnon stopped a foot before her car and Iris mirrored her, leaving little space between them. McKinnon turned and looked Iris up and down, finally assessing her. "No, you're not, are you?"

Was she that obvious? "My name is Iris Duvall." She'd gone over how she'd introduce herself a hundred times, and she'd decided to be as direct as possible without giving too much away. "I'm a friend of Bear and Mandy's."

McKinnon couldn't hide her reaction. A flash of surprise was followed by one of trepidation. Was she afraid of Bear, or of what Iris might discern from their conversation? The only evidence that Bear had been involved in the HealTek disaster was the viral video, otherwise he'd only been referred to as an inside source. That look on McKinnon's face told Iris all she needed to know—McKinnon and Bear had worked together to crack the case.

"Bear doesn't have friends," McKinnon said.

"You're friends with him, aren't you?"

McKinnon smirked. "Friends? No. Acquaintances? Barely. But I owe him one. More than one, if I'm honest. I'm sorry, but I can't help you."

Iris stepped forward as McKinnon turned to leave. "Please." She wracked her brain for what to say next. Desperation wasn't a good look, but this was the closest she'd come to Bear since she'd seen him last. "I think they're in trouble."

"What makes you say that?"

"I first met him a couple months ago. We ended up in the same small town in Indiana."

"Let me guess." McKinnon's smirk grew into a smile. "Bear got involved in something he didn't want to stick his nose in. Ended up saving the day. Didn't ask for anything in return."

"That about sums it up." Iris couldn't help matching McKinnon's grin. He'd hate that description, but it didn't make it any less true. "Turned out the town was the center of a drug distribution chain. There was this guy—he was blackmailing half the townspeople. Bear helped take him down."

"Sounds like Bear." McKinnon looked more relaxed now. "And Mandy? How's she doing?"

"Good." Iris' face twisted. She didn't want to go into detail about everything Mandy had been through. That wasn't her story to tell. "I think. Look, I haven't actually talked to them in a while. That's why I came here."

McKinnon took a sip of her coffee, but Iris could tell she was using the pause in conversation to gauge the situation. "You said they're in trouble?"

Iris took a big breath and blew it out, warring with herself. When she pulled out her identification, it was with the awareness that she was showing her hand. "I work for the FBI." She let that sink in before tucking her badge away. "I was undercover on a case that led me to that town in Indiana. Bear helped me out, and we went our separate ways. But when I got back home, my boss relegated me to desk duty. Gave me some bullshit excuse about why. Doesn't take a genius to figure out it was about the case I was on. But I also think it's about Bear."

"They know who he really is," McKinnon said, not missing a beat. "And you don't. That bothers you."

"Yes."

"I can't help you."

"Please—"

McKinnon held up a hand to stop her. "It's not that I don't want to. Like I said, I owe Bear plenty. But I can't help you. I know nothing about him. Don't know where he's been or where he's going. And something tells me he's the kind of person who won't be found if he doesn't want to be found."

The next question came out before she could stop herself. "Do you trust him?" she asked. "Do you think he's"—she floundered for the right phrase—"a good person?"

McKinnon played with the lid of her coffee as she considered the question, popping it off and on again. The seconds stretched on, but finally, she met Iris' gaze again. "Yes."

"That took a while."

McKinnon shrugged, that same smirk from earlier playing around her lips. "Bear's complicated. I only knew him for a little while, but you tend to get an idea of a person when you're fighting side by side with him."

"I know what you mean."

McKinnon nodded in solidarity. "He loves Mandy more than anything. Would go to the ends of the earth for her. Does that make him a good person? In her eyes, sure. In someone else's? Maybe not."

"But you said—"

"It's a matter of perspective," McKinnon continued. "In my eyes, Bear's a good person. He helped us when he didn't need to. Solved a cold case and took down a corrupt corporation. For all his grumbling, he cares about people. About righting the wrongs in the world. I got the impression that it comes from a place of guilt, maybe. He didn't tell me much about himself, but I came to understand he did some things in his past he's not proud of. Now that he's got Mandy, he wants to keep his nose down, keep her safe. Prepare her for the world she'll eventually step into. The one she's already in. It's not easy when you can see the darker side of humanity better than most. But for all he knows about that, he's still driven to help people, even if it means sticking his neck out when his first instinct is to turn the other way."

Iris had gotten the same sense from Bear, but she wasn't sure she trusted her instincts. The evidence laid out in front of her spoke of a man who was highly trained and highly dangerous. Just because he was a good dad didn't mean they were fighting for the same thing. "You really trust him?"

This time, McKinnon didn't hesitate. "I really do."

"Then help me find him. Help me warn him." Iris rushed on before McKinnon could run the same lines on her as before. "If you don't know where he is, you might know someone who does. He lived here for a while, right? He must've had friends."

"Like I said, Bear doesn't have friends." McKinnon's face twisted in thought. "There were a few people he'd talk to on occasion. And Mandy was at least a little less prickly."

"I just want to help," Iris said, and she was struck by how true that was.

"You got a car?"

"Parked across the street."

"I'll show you where the Moores live. Mandy was friendly with Marcus. Best I can do."

"Thank you," Iris said, infusing as much gratitude as she could into the words.

"Sure." McKinnon didn't look convinced as she said it. "Bear deserves to have someone watch his back. I just hope he doesn't hate me for it."

Iris didn't know how to respond. McKinnon had said it herself—she wasn't friends with Bear. Hardly knew the guy. Yet she was going out of her way to help him.

Once again, Iris was struck by the idea that the evidence didn't match the testimonials. On paper, Bear would kill someone as soon as he looked at them. But in reality, he helped more than he hurt. At least, he did now. Why was there such a disparity between the two? Could a person really change that much?

Consumed by the thoughts, Iris followed McKinnon as she drove to the other end of town. Pulling to a stop outside a modest house, the Sheriff pointed to the mailbox, and Iris saw where the name MOORE had been written out in white decals across the black surface. If Iris had any doubts about McKinnon staying to introduce her to the family, they were confirmed as the McKinnon pulled away from the curb, washing her hands of the situation.

Iris was on her own.

Pulling into the driveway, she didn't hesitate as she climbed out of her car and walked up to the front door. With three sharp knocks, she waited until a woman in her forties opened the door. A suspicious look settled on her face as she took Iris in.

"If you're a—"

"I'm not a journalist." Iris had been here for less than an hour, and she could already paint a picture of what life had been like over the last year. The story of HealTek had made national news, and everyone wanted a slice of the story. "My name is Iris Duvall. I'm with the FBI."

The suspicion on the woman's face turned to fear. "What do you want?"

"I'd like to talk to you about Bear and Mandy Logan. I just have a few questions—"

"How do I know you're not a journalist?"

Iris fished her ID out of her pocket, along with her card. She flashed the former and handed over the latter. "Please, it'll just take a few moments."

"I don't know anything about them, I'm sorry."

Iris had to slap her palm against the door to keep the woman from shutting it in her face. She felt guilty as she saw terror erupt in the woman's eyes. "Please. I'm afraid they might be in trouble."

"I don't know them," the woman repeated, though she didn't try closing the door this time. "We weren't friendly."

"But your son," Iris said, diving back into her memory to recall his name. "Marcus?"

"They went to school together. That's all."

Iris tamped down on a curse. "Would he have any idea where they are now?"

"No."

"Any information at all that could help me find them?"

"No."

"Okay." It was hard work to keep her voice even, but she did. Pressing the issue, forcing an answer out of the woman, wouldn't do her any good. Maybe Marcus had known Mandy, but the chance that he knew where they were now was a stretch. Mandy had been with Bear long enough to understand how to keep valuable information under wraps.

Iris had noticed that within the first few minutes of talking to her. What was Iris doing here, looking for scraps they would've been too smart to leave behind? This trip felt more and more like a waste of time. "Thank you for your time. If you think of anything, please don't hesitate—"

The woman didn't let Iris finish before slamming the door in her face.

Iris clenched her hands into fists and returned to her car and back to square one.

11

"Bear?" Mandy's voice was full of questions.

"Play it cool." Bear watched in the rearview mirror as the cop ran his plates. "They don't have anything on us."

"Never stopped them before," Mandy mumbled.

She wasn't wrong. They'd met good cops and bad cops. At the end of the day, police officers were just people. They could fall on either side of the line. A prickle of apprehension crawled up Bear's spine. They hadn't done anything to give the cop a reason to flash his lights or his siren. So, what was this about?

A minute later, the cop opened his door and strolled toward the Tahoe with a practiced ease. Bear stared straight ahead while Mandy plastered a bored look on her face. When the cop tapped on the window with a single knuckle, Bear made a show of reaching over and pressing the button to lower it.

"There a problem, Officer?"

"License and registration."

"Can I ask what this is about?"

"License and registration, son," the officer said. "I won't ask again."

Bear looked up into the man's face. It was hard to tell from his current vantage point, but he seemed on the shorter side, and he was stocky. A mustache sat on his upper lip, thick and wiry. Pockmarks marred his face on either side of a wide and greasy nose. His hair was thin and swept to one side. There was nothing particularly interesting about the man, and Bear had seen dozens of guys like him over the years.

Bear had issues with men like him, throwing their weight around just for the hell of it. They liked feeling big by making other people feel small. His natural reaction was to bristle at the condescension, but he bit back the barb on the tip of his tongue. With Mandy in the car, it wasn't worth causing trouble.

Yet.

"Of course." Bear leaned over to open the glove compartment and pulled out his registration with deliberate slowness. Then he reached into his wallet and pulled out his ID card. With a smile on his face, Bear handed them both over. "Here you go, Officer."

The man took his time going over Bear's details. He seemed more interested in the ID than the registration. When he looked up, it was like he was trying to match the name and the face. "Carl Larson?"

"That's me," Bear said.

The fake ID had been a necessity for this exact reason. Bear didn't feel the need to constantly check over his shoulder these days, but he wasn't naïve enough to think that couldn't change at the drop of a hat. Better safe than sorry, and this way, his name wouldn't flag in a system if someone was looking for him. Plus, he wasn't going to trust a cop like this with his real name.

"New York. You're a long way from home. What's your business out here, son?"

It took everything in Bear not to bristle at the use of the word *son*. The man looked like he was only about a decade older than him. It was a tactic to make Bear feel small, but instead, it just made him angry.

Taking a deep breath to steady his voice, Bear flashed the man a smile. "Camping. Always wanted to come out here when I was a kid. I figured, now that I've got one of my own, might as well make it happen."

The officer made a show of looking all around him. "Doesn't look like a campground to me."

"Went for a drive with my daughter." Bear gestured to Mandy, who gave the officer a little wave. "Pulled over to have a little father-daughter chat about how important it is not to sneak out of the house when I'm gone. Don't talk to strangers. All that good stuff."

Mandy huffed and crossed her arms over her chest. It was a real reaction to Bear's excuse—the best lie contained a partial truth—and it was believable enough that the officer didn't press the issue.

But that didn't mean he was ready to let them off the hook.

"I need you to step out of the vehicle."

Bear tensed. There was no reason the officer would want him out of the car. Bear might have been able to drive away while sitting behind the wheel, but he'd pose much more of a threat once he was standing across from the guy. Then again, the cop wouldn't know that.

"Look, Officer"—Bear searched the front of his uniform for his name—"Padulano, what's this about? Have we broken any laws?"

Bear knew they hadn't, and Officer Padulano knew it too, but that didn't stop him from repeating his command. "Step out of the vehicle. Now." The man's hand moved to rest on his weapon. "I won't ask a third time."

Bear held up his hands in a placating gesture, slowly moving one to the door handle. Padulano backed up, one hand still on his gun while the other clutched Bear's information. Pushing the door out slowly, Bear let it bounce open before twisting in his seat and letting both feet hit the ground.

"Dad?" Mandy's voice was small. Worried.

"It's okay," Bear assured her. "I'll be right back. Just hang tight."

"Okay."

He hated the fear in her voice, and it was the only thing keeping him from giving Officer Padulano a piece of his mind. If something happened to Bear, what would Mandy do? Where would she go? He had a backup plan, of course, but that was only if the worst were to happen. It wasn't the life he wanted for her.

Pressing forward, Bear climbed out of the Tahoe and moved to the side. As he suspected, he towered over Padulano. Even the officer seemed taken aback by Bear's height and build. In a fair fight, there was no question as to who would win. Which meant Padulano would never fight fair.

"Turn around," he instructed. "Hands against the vehicle. Spread your legs."

"You're going to frisk me?" Bear was incredulous, and he felt another barb on the tip of his tongue. "What did I do wrong?"

Padulano unsnapped his holster. "Do it."

Bear kept a growl from escaping his throat, just barely. Better to get this over with. Not wanting to make any sudden movements, he lifted his arms and turned around, pressing his body against the vehicle and spreading his legs. This wasn't the first time he'd been patted down, wouldn't be his last, but it was aggravating all the same.

Padulano was quick and efficient, feeling along Bear's arms, legs, and midsection. It was a good thing Bear had replaced the gun he'd pulled out of the glove compartment earlier. And that Padulano hadn't seen it when he'd retrieved his registration.

"All right, you're clear."

Bear turned to face him, crossing his arms over his chest. His patience was wearing thin. "Could've told you that myself."

"You'll understand that I couldn't take your word for it. Especially not after assaulting Chip Greyson."

Bear's eyebrows shot up. "Who?" Realization dawned on him a second later. "That chump from the gas station." He couldn't stop the laughter that bubbled up from his chest. So that's what this was about.

"You think this is funny?" Padulano looked like he wanted to get in Bear's face but thought better of it. "Assault is no laughing matter, son."

"If you actually thought I'd assaulted him, there'd be handcuffs on my wrists already."

"I could take you down to the station," Padulano said. "Then we'll see who'll have the last laugh."

"I'll give you a hint," Bear said. "It's not gonna be you. But hey, let's see who's right. I'll go downtown, and you can pull up the security cams from the gas station. Talk to the kid who worked there." He shook his head, a sour smirk still on his face. "Your boy's lucky I don't press charges."

Padulano looked like he wanted nothing more than to pull his weapon on Bear, but Bear wasn't giving him any reason to do so. It didn't look like the man was wearing a body cam, but there was a high chance he had a dash cam. He needed probable cause to make a move, and Bear was fresh out.

"This is your one and only warning." Padulano stepped forward. It seemed like he finally grew a pair. "Stay away from Mr. Greyson. If I hear about another encounter or see that you've been to his place of work, I will bring you in and you'll sit your ass in a jail cell until I've decided you've learned your lesson."

Bear resisted throwing up his arms in case Padulano took that as an aggressive maneuver. "I don't even know where he works."

"Like hell," Padulano said. "Stay away from Greyson. Stay away from The Magic Tap. I suggest you wrap up your time here in Arlington and be on your way."

Bear had to keep the amusement off his face. Not only did he find out the name of the man from the gas station, but he also confirmed he worked at the same bar as the woman. The question was whether Greyson had seen him or if Kelly had told him he'd paid her a visit. Bear couldn't imagine the woman putting herself in that position. Maybe it'd been the bouncer.

"Yes, Officer. Whatever you say. Are we done here?"

"You got an attitude on you, Larson. I don't like that. We'll be watching."

"Ominous," Bear said, not bothering to hide his bored tone. He pointed to the ID and registration in the man's hand. "Those are mine."

Padulano looked like he wanted nothing more than to toss them on the ground at Bear's feet, but he thought better of it. Chances were he could get away with murder, but the fact that Bear hadn't been intimidated at all had thrown him off-kilter. It appeared Padulano wasn't used to anyone sticking up for themselves. The man was all talk.

Bear climbed into the Tahoe, slammed the door, and rolled up the window. Padulano retreated to his own vehicle, climbing inside and bringing a phone to his ear. If he were calling the station, he would've used the radio on his shoulder. Was he calling Greyson, or someone else?

"What now?" Mandy asked.

"I don't know about you, but I'm starving."

Mandy snorted. "Got anywhere in mind?"

"Actually," Bear said, starting up the Tahoe and pulling away from the curb, "I do."

12

THE REASON BEAR HAD WANTED TO GO OUT FOR LUNCH BECAME APPARENT as soon as they pulled into the parking lot of the Meadowlark Diner.

It was directly across the street from The Magic Tap.

Mandy turned to Bear and gave him a look that said *you're not slick.* All he gave her in return was a shit-eating grin. As annoyed as she was, she couldn't stop the corners of her mouth from twitching up in response.

"Really?" she said, voice full of mirth.

"What?"

Mandy rolled her eyes. "You're gonna get in trouble."

"They said I couldn't go to the bar. Didn't say anything about eating lunch across the street. Should've been more specific."

Mandy climbed out of the Tahoe and looked up at the Meadowlark. It was the kind of diner they'd been in a hundred times—a relic of a time before she was born that smelled of bacon grease and coffee. The sign was hand-painted, with black letters surrounded by a yellow outline and a little bird sitting where the dot to the 'i' in 'diner' should've been. Even peering through the dirty windows, Mandy could tell whoever owned this place had a color scheme in mind and stuck to it.

"Seems they have a theme," Bear said, echoing her thoughts.

"Hooray," Mandy drawled. She wouldn't let Bear know, but she kind of liked it. Made everything simple and easy. Need to decide on a color for your dinnerware? Yellow or black, take your pick.

A chime sounded when Bear pulled open the door, and a waitress behind the counter looked up at them with a smile already plastered on her face. Mandy could tell it was fake, but she couldn't blame her. Imagining a life where she had to be nice to everyone day in and day out sounded exhausting. What would happen if the waitress just snapped one day? Would anyone blame her?

"Sit wherever you like," the woman said. She had a husky voice, like she'd been smoking her entire life. Mandy would've guessed she was in her sixties, but she knew cigarettes could age a person. Maybe she was closer to thirty. That'd be a tragedy. "Be with you in a minute."

"Sounds good," Bear said. Then he turned to her. "Your pick."

There was really only one option—the booth at the other end of the room. Not only would it provide the best view of everyone in the diner, but it was farthest from the door in case trouble walked in. Plus, no one was sitting that far from the counter, so Bear and Mandy would be able to talk in peace. Assuming their waitress wasn't too nosy.

Inside, the yellow-and-black theme seemed more potent, and she wondered how hard it was to spot a bumblebee amidst the décor. The tables and chairs were yellow with black accents. The décor on the walls consisted of little yellow-and-black birds. That must've been what a meadowlark looked like.

Learn something new every day.

Mandy let Bear slide into the seat that faced the room while she kept her back to it. It sent prickles of discomfort down her spine, but she pushed the feelings away. At least this way, she wouldn't have to keep an eye on the room. The view outside the windows was better, even as dirty as they were.

As soon as they sat down, Mandy prepared for the phrase Bear lobbed at her more and more often these days—*pop quiz*. But it never came. She frowned. Was he preoccupied with what had just happened between him and the cop, or had he finally trusted that her observations were not only more accurate, but second nature?

She studied Bear's face. He would've looked relaxed enough to anyone else, but she saw the way his eyes were unfocused, as though he were trying to solve a complicated math problem. There was no reason he should be concerned about what had just happened. It's not like it was the first time the cops had tried to push Bear around. A smirk crept over Mandy's face just thinking about the way Officer Padulano had tried to intimidate him and failed.

"Welcome to Meadowlark Diner," the waitress said, walking up to their table and setting a menu down in front of each of them. "Have you been here before?"

Mandy studied the woman's face, now that she had a chance to look closer. Aida, according to her nametag, definitely wasn't thirty, but she didn't look sixty either. Heavy makeup covered her face, and Mandy could see where the woman hadn't blended it along her jaw. The foundation was at least three shades darker than what she needed. But the waitress smelled like fresh muffins and her smile was kind.

"No, ma'am." Bear added some southern hospitality into his voice. "Been here a few weeks now but didn't know this place existed. Came at the recommendation of someone I met in town. What was that man's name?" He paused for a few seconds, acting like he was deep in thought, before snapping his fingers with a smile. "Chip Greyson, that's who it was. Do you know him?"

Aida's body went rigid, and she looked around, as though making sure no one had heard Bear utter the name. "Chip is a regular here."

They both waited for her to say more, but when she didn't, Bear looked down at the menu, as though the atmosphere of their conversation hadn't shifted dramatically in the last few seconds. "Any recommendations?"

"Our meatball sub is a local favorite." Aida's tone was not unkind, but her words had become monotone, as though she were trying to get through this interaction as quickly as possible. "It comes with bottomless fries. Our BLT is also a classic. Thick-cut bacon. And you can't go wrong with our classic turkey club."

"What do you think, kiddo?" Bear asked, the twang still in his voice.

"I'll take the BLT," Mandy said, affecting her own words. She wasn't as good at accents as Bear, but they'd been practicing. The detail could throw an opponent off their tracks, should it come to that. Or sweeten a deal with a potential ally.

"And I'll take the meatball." Bear passed the menus back to Aida. "May we also get a couple glasses of water, and a couple glasses of lemonade?"

"Do you have raspberry lemonade?" Mandy asked.

"Sorry, just regular," Aida said, already backing away from the table.

"Thank you, ma'am," she said, ever the dutiful daughter. Mandy waited until Aida was back behind the counter before she leaned toward Bear conspiratorially and said, "That was weird."

"Not surprised," Bear said, his voice back to normal. "Not like Greyson was winning any friendship awards."

"It was more than that," Mandy insisted. "She looked scared."

"But why?" It was less a question for Mandy and more just Bear thinking out loud. "Is he an unruly customer? Shit tipper? Or is he holding something over her head?"

Mandy looked out the window to the bar across the street. She could imagine what the inside looked like after Bear had filled her in, but the details were blurry, like they'd been drawn from a hazy memory. If she were older, she could've gone in there herself. Maybe Chip Greyson never would've known Bear had been inside, which meant they wouldn't currently be on Officer Padulano's radar.

Aida returned with their drinks, setting them down without a smile. "Food will be out shortly."

"Thank you, ma'am," Bear said, his smile disarming and pleasant.

Mandy offered the woman her own smile, and Aida returned it gingerly. Mandy watched Bear's face as the waitress retreated from their table, the way he slipped off his mask and tucked it in his pocket for later.

Not for the first time, Mandy's chest swelled with something akin to pride. For him or herself, she couldn't tell. Bear wore a thousand faces depending on who he was with, but Mandy liked to believe she got the real deal. Sure, she was still just a kid, and he kept things from her to keep her safe, but he trusted her more than almost anyone in the world.

That meant something to her, and she wanted to prove to him she deserved it. What would it take for him to let her strike out on her own, to be an extension of himself?

Mandy wasn't in the habit of thinking about her future. With Bear, there usually wasn't much time for those kinds of thoughts. But she was almost sixteen, which meant she'd be able to drive soon. And two years after that, she'd be eighteen. A legal adult, in the eyes of the government. It wasn't lost on her that she could get away with a lot more now, since she was a minor, but the idea of wielding some small amount of her own power in just over two years was enough to make her sit up straighter in the booth.

She'd been reading a lot lately. Stories about girls who were thrust into leadership roles as they navigated strange worlds. Bear's training meant she could often see where the story was going faster than the main character—it was easy for her to distinguish friends from foes— but that didn't make the journey any less enjoyable. She wanted nothing more than to climb into the pages of her books and save the world, just like Bear had, once upon a time.

Sure, being a kid had its advantages, but she couldn't help feeling like it had even more drawbacks. Especially for someone like her. It's not like her life had been easy, yet she wasn't ready to go off on her own just yet. Bear had been clear about how dangerous the world was, and she'd seen enough to know he wasn't exaggerating. But she'd be lying to herself if she didn't admit she wanted to explore as much of it as she could.

The books she'd been reading had taken her around the world, and sometimes out into the vast universe. What would it be like to go to Italy and navigate the streets on a moped? To travel to India with a scarf around her head, slipping into the crowd and away from her pursuers? Could she survive in the jungles of South America, with nothing but a hunting knife and her wits?

If Bear could do it, she could, too.

A series of buzzes in her pocket made her pull out her phone. She had at least a dozen text messages from Marcus. Had he found more information about the number they'd found in the woods? Now that she was thinking about it, she found it strange that they hadn't been able to find any information earlier, considering it belonged to a local telephone company.

"Phones away at the table," Bear said. He waited until she complied before pointing to her arm. "How are you feeling?"

"Probably have a bruise," Mandy said, downplaying how sore she was. "But I don't think it's fractured or anything."

"I'll check it out when we're back home. Just in case."

Mandy opened her mouth to tell Bear to stop smothering her, but Aida arrived at the same moment with their food. It smelled amazing, and even Mandy was impressed by how much bacon they'd stacked on her sandwich. Bear's meatball sub looked like it would give even him a run for his money. Maybe if she asked nicely, he'd share his fries with her. All she got was some chips, which were already soggy because of the juice from her pickle.

"Can I get you anything else?" Aida looked like she hoped the answer was no.

"I just want to apologize," Bear said, laying it on thick, "if I made you feel uncomfortable before. Mentioning Chip Greyson, I mean. I got the sense you don't like him much, and I didn't mean to put you on the spot."

"It's okay," Aida said, her voice shaking slightly. She looked at Mandy, and that's when it became clear they had her. Mandy might have not been able to go out on her own missions, but people trusted him a lot more with her by his side than on his own. "I'm not one to spread rumors or stick my nose in other people's business."

"Has he caused you trouble before?" Bear asked.

"No, no. Nothing of the sort." Aida twisted her hands before her. She glanced at Mandy again. "Just be careful. He's rough around the edges. I wouldn't recommend getting close to him."

"Ma'am—"

"Enjoy your meal." Aida plastered a smile back on her face and left before Bear could say anything else.

"What now?" Mandy asked, picking up her sandwich and preparing to take a huge bite.

"Lunch." Bear dove into his sub. "And then while I go for a drive, you're going to deep clean the cabin."

"Aw, c'mon, Bear. I already learned my lesson. You ran me over, remember?"

"It was just a little bump. And something tells me cleaning the cabin will do more for reminding you to listen to me in the future."

Mandy took a bite of her sandwich to stop herself from talking back. Getting one more shot in wasn't worth whatever punishment he'd come up with next. Maybe he was right about cleaning the cabin.

But she'd never admit that to him.

13

BEAR KNEW IT WAS CRUEL TO MAKE MANDY DEEP CLEAN THE CABIN. SHE'D tried to occupy her mind to keep from doing something rash, but Bear wanted to believe she'd done everything in her power to keep from breaking his rules.

The urge to laugh bubbled in his chest. Bear allowed the sound to escape his lips and break the relative silence inside the Tahoe. The engine rumbled, only drowned out by cars passing him on the highway. He could've turned on the radio, but for once, he wanted to be lost in his thoughts.

The kid had done good at lunch today. It had become a force of habit to quiz her on her surroundings, but she'd become proficient in a short amount of time. It was time to move on to other skills. Her accents needed work, but to the uninitiated, they sounded good enough. He was proud of the way she'd picked up on his cues without needing him to point her in the right direction. And at the end of the day, Mandy's presence had put the waitress at the Meadowlark Diner at ease enough to give him a small piece of the puzzle.

Chip Greyson was not a beloved community member.

Not shocking information, but the waitress had looked terrified at the mere mention of his name, even peering around to see if anyone had overheard. Which told Bear that Chip had friends everywhere. Bear could tell he was a real piece of work from the moment he'd walked into the gas station but having a cop on his side had upped the ante. And it seemed Padulano wasn't the only one.

What was this guy into?

Bear didn't know where to start, so he put his mind to solving a different problem. The torn shirt and phone number had been bothering him since they'd first found it. They'd been miles from the closest campground trail, and if the torn shirt hadn't been suspicious enough, the bloody tree confirmed something else was afoot. While he would've preferred to stay out of it entirely, a dead body in the woods would bring the cops knocking on his front door. If he could get ahead of that, maybe he and Mandy wouldn't have to pack up and leave so soon.

He'd come to enjoy Arlington, despite everything that had happened in the last twenty-four hours.

That thought brought him back to his present predicament. Mandy had told him she'd sent the number to Marcus so he could research it, but to no avail. He'd proven himself adept at solving these sorts of problems in the past, so Bear took his word for it.

But that presented another issue—the van that had shown up after Mandy placed the call looked legitimate. It had a logo slapped on the side and a boom on the tail-end. The phone number splashed across the doors had been different from the one they'd found in the woods. The one on the slip of paper was likely for the workers, not the clients.

Bear had called the number, but it was perpetually busy. The company name, ConnectCom Services, led to a simple website with minimal information, as though they weren't concerned with bringing in more clients. Maybe word of mouth gave them more than enough work. Or maybe it was a cover, for what Bear didn't have any idea.

The website hadn't provided an address, but Bear had memorized the ID number on the driver's side door and the license plates. The truck had been registered, and Bear had found ConnectCom's offices after all. If this was a legitimate company, they certainly weren't doing themselves any favors. Maybe if they had a suggestion box at the front desk, he'd give them a couple of tips to improve their presence online. He snorted at the thought. Mandy would be so proud.

ConnectCom was halfway between Arlington and Portland, taking Bear about an hour to get there. That lined up with their wait time at the shopping center, so at least Bear knew he was headed in the right direction.

The office didn't look like much. It was a small brick building with a couple of tinted windows and a tiny sign that would've been hard to read from the road. The parking lot was empty except for a black Audi A4 from a couple of years ago. The word *uninviting* popped into his head, and he found he couldn't have come up with a better one to describe the premises.

Bear parked the car and sat there, debating his next move. There was a chance that whoever owned this company was just a terrible business owner, but there had to be more to it. And there was only one way of figuring out exactly what.

The problem was the cameras on the outside of the building. They looked standard, nothing too fancy or technical, but Bear wasn't sure why a phone company would need them. For unruly customers? Sure, the public got up in arms about increased phone bills all the time, but why the extra security? Bear decided not to risk it. Staying off the radar was his number one goal, and a cheap camera jammer would ensure that happened.

There was no chime as Bear opened the door, but the woman at the front desk looked up at him as though a gunshot had gone off in the office. Looking around, Bear spotted all the trappings of a typical workplace. A pair of uncomfortable looking chairs and a small table constituted the waiting area, though there were no outdated magazines to read. A small bookshelf filled with titles in a rainbow of colors sat to one side, topped with a small potted plant. The desk in the center was cheap pine, and though there was a computer and various desk supplies, like a cup of pencils and a stapler, it all looked incredibly staged. Like they had never been used.

The woman behind the desk appeared friendly enough. The red of her lipstick matched the color of her cardigan, draped over the shoulders of a navy dress and covered with her dark brown hair. Nothing about her stood out or drew attention, though she was attractive. He'd guess she was in her late twenties, and though that wasn't an unusual age for a secretary, something about the sharpness of her dark gaze and the tautness of her muscles told him she'd be better suited for a different vocation.

"Good afternoon, sir." The woman's smile didn't reach her eyes. "We're undergoing a little construction in the back, so I'm afraid we won't be able to help you today. If you place a call—"

"Line's been busy for hours," Bear said, keeping the accent he'd affected at lunch but putting a little less charm into his words. "Couldn't get through."

"Yes, unfortunately, we're quite busy now. A terrible time for our plumbing to go out."

"Will you be open tomorrow?"

"I'm not sure. It'd be best if you kept trying to call."

"I just need you to look up the number of one of your vans." Bear gestured to the computer in front of the woman. "I want to file a complaint."

"I'm sorry, sir, but our Wi-Fi is out, too." Her smile turned into a sympathetic frown. "It's just one of those days, I guess."

"Guess so." Bear studied the woman closer. The way she kept her hands out of sight, under the desk. How she never took her eyes off his face, as though memorizing it for later. "You have a pen and paper?"

They both knew she did. It was sitting on the corner of her desk, untouched. It looked like it pained her to reach over and drag it in front of her. "Of course. Would you like to leave a message?"

"A complaint." Bear crossed his arms over his chest. He didn't want to be memorable, but he had a part to play. "About one of your drivers. Almost ran over my kid. Lucky she didn't break anything, otherwise you'd be getting a copy of her hospital bills."

The woman's face bunched in concern, and though it was believable, there was something distant about her words, as though she were reading from a script. "I'm so sorry. Is she okay? I could send her a little gift basket as an apology. What kind of candy does she like?"

"Candy?" Bear's huff of frustration was real. "She doesn't want candy."

The woman leaned forward, as though she were sharing a conspiratorial secret. "I think all kids want candy."

"I want to meet the driver." Bear put a little extra growl in his voice. "I demand an apology from him. And I want him to be reprimanded."

Whether it was simply to deescalate the situation or because Bear wouldn't accept an alternative solution, the woman sat up a little straighter in her chair, pen poised above the notepad. "Of course. Can I have the van's license plate and ID number? Plus, your name and a phone number where we can follow up?"

Bear rattled off everything she asked for, giving her a fake phone number that would forward to his real phone without them knowing. This one had a voicemail set up for Carl Larson. He doubted they'd call him, but he went through the motions, just to see what she would do. "And your name is?" he asked.

"Anne." The woman smiled, pushing the pad of paper off to the side. It didn't even have the company's logo on top. "I hope you have a wonderful day, sir. We'll be in touch."

"I sure hope so." Bear kept the edge in his voice sharp. "I'd hate to have to go to the papers with this. Don't think you'd be in business much longer after that."

Anne's face dropped into a deep frown, and this one seemed more authentic than the others. "Of course. The moment our internet is back up, I'll contact the driver and the owner of the company. We'll get this sorted for you as soon as possible."

"And the name of the owner?"

"Oliver Warner, sir." The name came out smooth. If it was a lie, it was a practiced one. "Is there anything else I can do for you today?"

"Apparently not," Bear said. He looked around the office one more time, but it was so perfect it bordered on sanitary. There were no clues here for him. "But I expect a call within twenty-four hours, otherwise I'm filing a police report and going to the news station."

"That won't be necessary," Anne said, though she sounded as though she were speaking through gritted teeth. "We'll be in touch. Have a good day, sir."

Bear didn't bother saying goodbye. He spun on his heel and barged through the door, paranoia creeping up his back to settle onto his shoulders like a two-hundred-pound weight. There were enough hidden cameras inside and outside the premises that ConnectCom could've doubled as a security company. Thanks to the jammer in his pocket, nothing would tip them off to who he really was, but once they checked their feed, they'd know he was more than he appeared.

14

BEAR DRUMMED HIS FINGERS ON THE STEERING WHEEL IN A STACCATO rhythm belonging to no song in particular. He'd kept the radio off, even though the buzzing of his own thoughts had started to drive him crazy.

After leaving ConnectCom's shady office building, Bear took off back to Arlington, unsure of his next step.

He'd hit a dead end with Chip Greyson, short of showing up at the bar and causing trouble. Normally, he'd be more than happy to oblige, but he had to think about how his actions could affect Kelly. Chip had known Bear had been to the bar, but had Kelly suffered the repercussions of his actions?

There was a chance that if he got Kelly alone for a one-on-one conversation, she might be willing to say more than she had with witnesses around, but he couldn't be sure. Short of stalking the woman, there was no way of figuring out where she lived. Besides, if Chip was as well-connected as he seemed, then there was a chance he'd find out anyway. Bear wasn't about to risk the woman's safety like that.

Merging onto the highway, Bear's thoughts returned to Connect-Com's offices. It didn't take a genius to figure out it was a front for something—but what? Bear had his guesses, but he wasn't ready to lay his money on any particular one just yet. Anne had been professional and cool under pressure, and the company itself was legitimate enough in the eyes of the law. That meant they had money to spend on making it all look real. Maybe whoever was behind the company was less important than why they were there to begin with.

Bear had used one hand to look up Oliver Warner on his phone while the other kept the Tahoe heading in the right direction, but there were no promising results. The most relevant link returned him to ConnectCom's shoddy website, and most of the others were for obituaries or Facebook pages in foreign languages. Warner's lack of social media presence didn't surprise Bear, but finding no information on the man sent up red flags.

Did the guy even exist?

To someone walking in right off the street, they'd probably see a business they wouldn't want to work with. Poor customer service, long wait times, and little information. Anne had probably become adept at driving customers away, so they could continue to operate whatever scheme they were hiding behind ConnectCom's façade. If Bear had been anyone else, he would've written them off completely. But he hadn't made it this far without listening to his gut.

In that moment, an epiphany struck him so hard, he almost slammed on the brakes. Tossing his phone onto the seat next to him, and gripping the wheel with both hands, Bear let autopilot take over as he worked through his moment of realization.

ConnectCom was, in fact, a cover. Isn't that what Mandy had heard on the phone, when the woman picked up? They'd laughed off the idea once the truck had shown up, but what if their first assumption had been right all along?

Bear's mind snapped back into the present as he came up on an exit, and he jerked the wheel over in time to get off. Someone blared their horn behind him, and he threw up a hand in an attempt at a half-hearted apology. He was still a good half hour from the campground, but now he had a gameplan.

It took him twenty minutes to find another payphone, but luckily the exit had taken him down a stretch of highway past seven or eight gas stations. Most of them didn't have one, and just when he was about to give up and circle back for a second look, he spotted one on the corner of a small convenience mart. It was just rundown enough to have poor security, too. A perfect location to call the truck again.

Dialing the number, Bear waited to hear what Mandy had described to him earlier. Sure enough, a middle-aged woman with no discernable accent picked up the phone. The first word out of her mouth was, "Operations." She sounded less bored and more detached. The second time she said the word, there was a bit more curiosity in her tone. Without any background noise, Bear couldn't begin to discern any clues as to who this woman was and where she was located. At the very least, he knew it didn't sound like the woman from the office, Anne.

He debated saying something, or pretending he was in pain, but it was better to play this exactly how Mandy had, by staying silent. It was the best way to ensure they reacted as they had before—by sending out a truck to assess the situation. And this time, he'd be prepared.

There was a chance the driver had previously spotted the Tahoe when he and Mandy had waited for him to show up the first time, so Bear parked as far from the payphone as possible, hoping he'd be harder to spot with the pumps between them. Then it was just a matter of waiting.

Half an hour later, right on time, the truck pulled into the gas station and right up to the payphone. It only took one glance at the number on the door to conclude that it was the same vehicle as before. From what Bear could tell, it was the same driver, too. Same build, same sandy hair. But he was still too far away to see any of his facial features clearly. Bear might have been able to spot him in a lineup, but only just.

It's not like Bear had bought Anne's bullshit, but this also confirmed that the driver had been reachable via phone. The woman at the office had gotten rid of Bear as efficiently as possible, promising him everything he wanted without allowing him to stick around to witness whatever was going on behind closed doors.

The driver scanned the area, then walked up to the payphone, lifting it to his ear, and dialing a number. Bear could only guess that he was calling the same number he'd just dialed, though this guy clearly had his own code. Was the number on the door? The likelihood of that was low, though perhaps it was worth a try at some point.

If Bear had his usual equipment, he could've bugged the payphone in less than ten minutes. It would've been worth the risk of being spotted, but he lived a stripped-down life these days. His best assets were his brain and his gun, in that order. And a couple of tiny tricks up his sleeve. Anything else would weigh him down.

After about two minutes, the man hung up, scanned the area again, and then entered the convenience store. If there were cameras inside, Bear would probably be able to gain access to them one way or another, though that wasn't the priority right now. Sixty seconds later, the guy exited without having made any purchases, jumped into his truck, and pulled out of the parking lot.

Any worries Bear had that the technician would recognize his vehicle were swept away in the gust of wind that followed as the truck headed back toward the highway. The driver hadn't even looked in Bear's direction, which meant he could follow without worrying about giving himself away.

Pulling around, Bear waited until he saw the man merge onto the highway before following behind. There were at least a couple miles between this exit and the next, so he'd be able to catch up in no time without showing his hand too early.

Sure enough, Bear kept a steady pace just over the speed limit, coming up behind the van in only a couple of minutes. He stayed a few cars behind, and one lane over, so as not to be too obvious about following. The technician rode in the middle lane at the pace of the surrounding traffic, staying steady and giving Bear no causes for concern.

The van took the exit he had just returned from—the one that led back to ConnectCom's headquarters. Bear slowed down, hoping another vehicle would pass him and get off the exit between them, but he had no such luck. He took the off-ramp at a snail's pace, and by the time he reached the end, the stoplight had turned green, and the van had pulled out onto the road.

From his vantage point, Bear couldn't tell if the driver had noticed him in his sideview mirrors, but now that they were off the highway, it would be trickier to track the vehicle in front of him at a safe distance without losing sight of it.

What caught Bear's attention was that the van had turned right instead of left, back toward the offices. Tapping the gas, Bear pulled onto the road behind the other vehicle, careful to maintain his distance. The other driver stayed within the speed limit, not indicating at all whether he was nervous about the Tahoe that had been following him for miles.

Bear kept a mental map of the area in his head, logging the van's route for future reference. It was a vital skill, one that had become second nature to him and had saved his life. Once Mandy got her driver's license—God help them all—it would be one of the first lessons he taught her. Even though he wasn't ready for his daughter to be old enough to drive, he knew it was better to embrace the moment rather than fight it. At least that was his attitude now. Who knew how he'd feel once the day was staring him in the face?

A few turns later, the van pulled into an empty lot with a warehouse in its center. Bear was smart enough to keep driving so as not to bring any more attention to himself. Was this the van's final destination, or had the driver finally noticed Bear and decided to see if he'd walk into a trap? Maybe this was where the drivers stored their vehicles once they were off the clock. Or maybe this was ConnectCom's real headquarters.

Bear drove by slow enough to get a solid mental picture of the place. He didn't spot any security cameras, but at this distance and low speed, he couldn't be sure of his assessment. The one way to know for certain would be to get up close and personal.

The area surrounding the warehouse was predominantly scrub brush, with overgrown meadows and rundown doublewides. It didn't look like the best part of town, but there was enough space between residences that Bear didn't think anyone would pay him much mind, as long as he stayed out of eyesight. Not easy for a guy his size, but he'd spent his entire life getting away with more than most people half his height and weight. This would be no different.

Pulling into a vacant lot about a half mile down the road, Bear prepared himself for whatever answers he'd uncover inside that warehouse.

15

AFTER HITTING A DEAD END IN NEW YORK, IRIS HAD FLOWN OUT TO North Carolina. It was the only other location she knew for certain that Bear had lived. She also knew his family had owned a house in the area at one time. Another news report had cited an anonymous Good Samaritan who had helped take down another drug ring. This one had been using various residences to hide the product, then forcing local businesses to launder the profits for them.

The new information had sent a jolt of electricity down Iris' spine. She could believe that Bear had stumbled onto one, maybe even two. But three drug operations? That wasn't coincidence. It was a pattern.

But Bear had almost single-handedly taken down each one. Any far-fetched theories about Bear being or working for Mr. Reagan had to be tossed out the window. But Iris couldn't wrap her head around the facts that remained. Was Bear working for a rival? Had he picked up another independent contractor gig? Would he do that, even with Mandy in tow? If he had no other choice, maybe. But Bear was a ghost. She'd tapped into every last one of her sources to get the bare minimum on him. Whoever was blackmailing him, if that was the case, would be powerful.

Iris shook her head to clear it. Before heading to North Carolina, she'd scrubbed her little base of operations in New York and returned the building to normal. There was no doubt in her mind now that she was on the right track. She just had to find one person who knew something about Bear and would be willing to talk to her. But that was starting to feel like a needle in a haystack.

Iris parked her car in a shopping store parking lot in Hatteras and chose to walk to her first destination. It was a little cooler here on the coast, every gust of wind bringing with it the smell of the ocean. If she'd had more time, this would've been an idyllic area to take a vacation. When was the last time she'd had a day off? Long enough, she couldn't remember.

But dreaming about the impossible wouldn't get her where she needed to go. She'd learned about the Logan's summer house from public records on the flash drive. They hadn't owned it in some time, but it stood to reason that Bear would stay in a location he was familiar with. And maybe it was nostalgic. Taking his kid to the place where he grew up and all that.

Not for the first time, Iris wondered about the source of her information. The channels she'd tapped into to find this information hadn't all been legit, but they had been reliable. Without that flash drive, she wouldn't have been able to follow Bear's trail to North Carolina.

Looking at the information, she could spot Bear's fingerprints all over the town that had been saved from criminal activity but finding that clip would've been impossible on her own. Maybe her source was better than she was. Or maybe they'd had their own eye on Bear for some time.

Now was not the time to question where the information came from. All she needed to know was that it was real. Standing outside Bear's childhood vacation home, Iris was convinced that it was. There was no outward indication that it had ever been owned by the Logans, but records had shown the deed exchanging hands. It had belonged to a family until earlier this year, around the time Bear had swung through town. Then it was snatched up by a management company who rented it out to vacation-goers. Even now, it was filled with a family taking advantage of the last dregs of summer before school started up again.

For a moment, she thought about knocking on the door and asking if they'd ever heard of Riley or Mandy Logan, but it would be a long-shot, and the fewer people she talked to, the better. The Agency had no idea she was here, and she wanted to keep it that way. Raising eyebrows and making people nervous was a fast-track to getting caught.

Iris meandered through the area of town, circling around to get a better view of her surroundings before allowing herself to stroll past Logan's old house. Now she headed back toward town, unsure of what she'd expected to get out of this trip. There was a reporter she could talk to, but that was a risk. Who knew if he would write about a federal agent asking questions about the incident? And, like it was back in New York, she wasn't sure any of the locals would be willing to speak with her, either.

An elderly couple sat on their front porch, enjoying the breeze and the fresh summer air. She smiled at them as she approached the house, and the man raised his arm in greeting. A skein of blue yarn sat in a basket on the ground at the woman's feet, unraveling bit by bit as her needles *clicked* and *clacked*. From her vantage point on the sidewalk, Iris wasn't sure what the woman was knitting, but it was long enough to be a scarf or a blanket.

"Good afternoon," Iris called, stopping outside their gate. "It's a beautiful day today."

"Usually is out here," the man called. "And if it's raining, all you have to do is wait five minutes for it to clear."

"Unless it's a hurricane," the woman said, smiling at Iris. "Then it might be a good idea to get inside."

"I bet." Iris wasn't sure how to respond to that. The couple seemed nice enough, but she wasn't one for small talk. "Hope you guys don't get hit too bad this year."

"Right in the middle of the season now," the man said, looking up at the sky as though he could read the future in the fluffy clouds. "Hurricane Arthur hit us pretty good. We're about due."

The old woman tsked. "Don't say that."

"It's true. Wasn't nearly as bad as Floyd, though. That was back in '99."

Iris froze. They'd been here a long time. "This might be a longshot," she started, her mouth suddenly dry. "But I'm trying to find a friend of mine. His family used to vacation here when he was a kid. And he visited earlier this year. Riley Logan? He's got a daughter named Mandy."

The couple exchanged a glance, worry creasing their faces. A silent conversation passed between them, and when they turned back to Iris, the man looked more guarded. The woman wouldn't meet her eyes.

She asked, "Why are you looking for Riley?"

Relief flooded Iris' body. Someone was smiling down on her today. "He's a friend of mine." Remembering what Sheriff McKinnon had said, Iris amended her statement. "Sort of. We met a couple months ago in Indiana. My cousin was involved in something. She died, and Riley helped me find who was responsible." That was close enough to the truth. "I think he might be in trouble, and I just want to find him. To make sure he and Mandy are okay."

"Sweet girl," the woman said, focused on her knitting.

"Riley lived next door to us for a while," the man said, pointing to the lot to his left. "Helped us out with some work around the house. 'Course all that went to waste when we lost it in the fire."

Iris' gaze traveled to the house, noting for the first time how it looked newer than the rest on the block. "Did he help you build a new one?"

"In a way," the man said. "He helped us all. We owe him a debt. The whole town does."

"Do you know how I could get in touch with him? A phone number, or an address?"

The man shook his head, looking sad. "I tried. The number I had for him was disconnected. Wish I could thank him for everything he's done, even though it wouldn't come close to being enough."

"You should talk to Rosie," the woman said, finally meeting Iris' gaze. "She owns an ice cream shop downtown. She might know how to get in touch with him. They were close for a while. And if you do, tell him the Murrays are grateful for everything he's given us."

"I'll do that." Iris had a thousand more questions, but her main objective was finding Bear. "Thank you for your time. I hope you have a good rest of your day."

"You too," the man said, giving her a friendly smile.

Iris wasted no time heading back into town. On her way through, she'd noticed Rosemary's Ice Cream Palace situated on the main strip. It had to be the little shop the couple had meant when they told her to talk to Rosie.

A chime sounded when she walked through the door, and the woman behind the counter flashed her a hurried smile as she completed someone's order. She was tall and lean, with short blonde hair half pulled back and a pair of dark-rimmed glasses perched on her nose. Her smile was infectious, and she seemed to know each customer personally. They'd have a little chat, then she'd hand them their ice cream, and each one inevitably dropped a couple dollars into the tip jar.

Much like the Murrays' house, the ice cream shop appeared to have been recently renovated. All the seating looked brand new, with fresh vinyl and shiny chrome. The appliances in the back looked impressive, even if Iris didn't know what half of them were for. She'd gotten the sense that while Bear hadn't helped the Murrays rebuild their home, perhaps he'd sent them some money to help. Had he done the same for Rosie?

The shop was busy, which had its pros and cons. There was enough of a murmur that she and Rosie might be able to have a private conversation if they went into the back, but she wasn't sure she'd be able to convince the woman to leave her station with customers lining up for their afternoon snack. At the mention of Bear's name, the Murrays had become suspicious, even if they ultimately gave up some information, the same way McKinnon had. Would Rosie react the same way, or would she kick her out of the shop with nothing but an ice cream cone to show for it?

Someone else walked through the door after Iris; she let the man and his kid ahead of her on the pretense of still trying to decide what she wanted. By the time Iris got to the counter, she was the only one waiting, exactly what she'd been hoping for. If she could do anything to increase her chances of getting this woman to talk to her, she'd do it.

"Hello," Rosie said, her twang subtle and welcoming. "What can I get for you?"

Iris leaned a little closer, careful to keep her voice down. "I'd love to order something for the road, but first I have a question for you." Iris didn't miss the way Rosie's eyes narrowed in suspicion. "The Murrays sent me here to talk to you. They thought maybe you could help me."

Surprise made Rosie's eyes widen this time. "Help you with what?"

"I'm a friend of Bear's. An acquaintance," she amended. "I'm trying to find him. Or at least get in touch with him. It's important. I'm afraid he and Mandy are in trouble."

Rosie looked around the ice cream shop at all her customers. There were at least a dozen people chatting and laughing, licking ice cream from their fingers or slurping up milkshakes through oversized straws. Was she worried that they would overhear, or was she looking for witnesses in case Iris wasn't who she seemed?

When Rosie reached under the counter, Iris tensed, and her hand twitched toward the firearm she had strapped to her side under a jacket that was too warm for this weather. She'd debated whether she needed it, but as she drew closer to Bear, the dark tendrils of paranoia seemed to inch ever closer. Better safe than sorry.

But Rosie hadn't gone for a weapon. Instead, she brought up a sign that read *Be Back in Ten Minutes* and motioned for Iris to follow her into the back. Relief flooded her system, working to counteract the adrenaline that had pumped through her veins seconds before. Rosie didn't look dangerous, and the chances of her attacking Iris in front of a shop full of people were low. But Iris was trained to stay vigilant, regardless of the circumstances.

Iris slipped through the opening in the counter and stepped into the back room, which held more machines, a large walk-in freezer, and overstock for the many syrups and toppings found out front.

Rosie closed the door behind them, and though Iris felt trapped, the woman didn't look like she was trying to intimidate her. In fact, she looked crazed with worry. But that suspicious look never left her face. "Who are you?"

"My name is Iris Duvall. I met Bear a few months ago in Indiana. He helped me in the same way he helped you and the Murrays and everyone else in this town." Not the exact same way, Iris thought, but close enough. The details weren't important. "We went our separate ways, but in the last few weeks, I've started to worry that he's in trouble. Do you know where he could be? Do you have a phone number for him?"

Rosie shook her head. "It's been disconnected. And he didn't tell me where he was going. Didn't tell anyone."

"Have you spoken to him since then?"

She shook her head again. "There was too much between us." The woman had to clear her throat of emotion before she could go on. "Too much baggage. It wouldn't have worked."

Iris blinked back her surprise. A romantic involvement? With the way Bear was constantly on the move, she was surprised that was even a possibility for him. Then again, those kinds of relationships weren't always planned. She spoke her next words carefully. "Were you close?"

"For a time." Rosie's smile was sad. "We both grew up around here. He and my brother were friends. When we reconnected, I thought it was fate, you know? Like the universe telling me something. But then everything went down, and"—she looked down at her feet—"I made some mistakes. He forgave me, but it wasn't enough for him to stay." Finally, she looked up at Iris again. "I owe him everything. My shop would be gone if it weren't for him."

Not for the first time, Iris was torn between what she knew about Bear and what other people said about him. Which was the truth? More than likely, it was some blend of both, but it bothered her to not have the full picture. She had avoided thinking about it as much as possible, but at some point, she'd have to decide what she'd do when she came face to face with him—help him or put him in cuffs?

Iris hadn't realized she'd been quiet for some time until she caught Rosie searching her face. Standing up straight, she forced herself to think about the here and now. "Are you sure you have no way of getting in touch with him?"

"I'm sorry. He doesn't leave a lot of breadcrumbs behind."

That was for sure. "What about Mandy? Did she have any friends while she was here."

"One," Rosie said, with a nod of her head. "Jenny."

Iris' heart jumped. "Do you know where she lives?"

"Yes, but it won't do you any good. I don't think they talk anymore. There was an incident. A long story. It wasn't entirely Mandy's fault, but Jenny's parents still blamed her."

Iris couldn't help but feel dejected. "Was there anyone else? Anyone that can help me reach them?"

"Not from around here," Rosie said. "But Mandy used to talk to this other kid quite a lot. I think he was from somewhere up north. They would text constantly."

"Marcus?" Iris said, reaching for hope even though she knew she shouldn't.

"I think so. Mandy didn't seem to make friends easily. A lot of the kids around here picked on her. But she and Marcus were close. Closer than even her and Jenny, I think." Rosie frowned. "But I don't have his number or anything. I can't even remember where he was from."

"That's okay." Iris' head was spinning. Mrs. Moore had been quick to get rid of her—not because she had nothing to say, as Iris first thought, but because she didn't want Iris to know that Marcus and Mandy still talked. Or maybe she had no idea. "One last thing."

Rosie was fixated on Iris. "What?"

"Can I get a double scoop of butter pecan in a waffle cone?"

16

BEAR KEPT THE TAHOE STOCKED, JUST IN CASE. MOST OF HIS TOOLS WERE multi-purpose, so he wouldn't be loaded down with too much junk. But on days like today, he was grateful for the myriad of items he kept on hand.

Despite the heat of the day, Bear threw on a light windbreaker—easy to ditch, if necessary. Someone might spot a man in a green jacket, but he could toss it anywhere between here and the cabin.

A plain cap pulled low would hide most of his face, and his beard would do the rest. Jamming the cameras could alert the people inside to his presence, so he'd save that as a last resort. As long as he knew where the cameras were, Bear could avoid showing any of his defining features. And, as much as it pained him to admit it, he could shave his beard and look like an entirely new person. He'd had to do it a few times in the past, an uncomfortable experience every time. Mandy wouldn't be too happy, either.

Bear also grabbed a pair of binoculars and a slim book on bird-watching in Oregon. The former would double as surveillance equipment, but the latter would explain why a man like him was out here by himself, scoping the area. He'd memorized a few of the more famous native species, like the Western Meadowlark, just in case he was stopped. If he was convincing enough, the ruse could work.

Unless the cops searched him for weapons. The jacket concealed his pistol in a shoulder holster, and the pockets of his jeans were deep enough to hide his hunting knife. But he knew better than most that if the police suspected you of a crime, they could find a reason to frisk you. Hell, it'd happened to him earlier that day. Only this time, they'd find something.

"Better not to get caught," Bear mumbled to himself, locking up the car and trekking across the road. There was a house down the opposite way from the warehouse, but the trees made it difficult to see much, which worked in his favor, too. If he worked fast enough, no one would get suspicious of the abandoned vehicle, and he'd be gone before any alarms were raised.

Then again, that all depended on what he found in the warehouse.

On the other side of the road, Bear made his way through an overgrown field. Patches of pavement told him this had been a parking lot at some point, probably decades ago given the number of weeds that had sprung up. The grass was about as tall as his hip, allowing him to duck low enough to hide whenever a car went by. Luckily, he only had to do that once. The light traffic had to be at least part of the reason why ConnectCom—or whoever was masquerading as the phone company—chose this area.

Bear resisted letting his mind spiral out of control looking for possible answers. He'd find them soon enough. And when he did, he'd decide whether it was worth sticking around in Arlington, or if it was time to move on to the next place. Maybe they'd disappear into a city next, change it up a little. Mandy would like that.

On the other side of the meadow, Bear hit a line of trees. They were sparse this close to the road, but further in, they were darker and denser. He headed in that direction. Once he couldn't see the road anymore, he walked the half mile back toward the warehouse.

It was cooler under the shade of the trees, and Bear was glad he'd thrown on the jacket. The birdsong was loud enough to drown out any other noise, and he had to work to tune it out in case he wasn't alone in the forest. The chance of ConnectCom having someone stationed in the trees was slim, but not zero.

But he hadn't needed to worry. When he felt certain he'd crossed the distance to the warehouse, Bear turned back toward the road. He'd come out a little earlier than he'd meant to, but it gave him time to scope the area behind the warehouse. And there wasn't a single person in sight.

Getting close enough for a direct view, Bear crouched down and leaned against the trunk of a large maple to steady himself. Pulling out the binoculars, he held them to his eyes and surveyed the warehouse, confirming his initial suspicions that just because there were no sentries didn't mean no one was watching.

The warehouse looked abandoned, but solid. It was three stories tall, and though he had no idea what it had once housed, it looked large enough to have belonged to some sort of processing plant. It had clearly been derelict for a couple of decades, but there were a few signs that it had been touched up recently.

All the windows on the first floor had been boarded up, and none of them looked like they had been out in the weather for any length of time. Given how much it rained out here, Bear figured it'd been in the last couple of months.

The second floor's windows were mostly intact, though a few had been broken. It had probably happened years ago, and there weren't enough of them that whoever was inside felt the need to board them up, too. He'd bet money ConnectCom's operators worked out of the first floor and didn't even bother going upstairs except for the occasional perimeter check.

Bear grinned behind the binoculars. That would be his way in.

There were no escape ladders on this side of the building. A drainpipe ran the height of the structure. It wouldn't be a fun climb. If the bolts held firm, he could make it up to the second floor and crawl through one of the windows. He'd have to break his way through. Climbing up to the third floor where the windows were open was more risk than he was willing to take.

His main obstacle would be the camera set over the back door.

They'd mounted it in the very center of the building, giving a wide view of the back parking lot where two white vans had parked as well as the tree line. Watching it for a few minutes, Bear confirmed it wasn't on a swivel, which was a point in his favor. He'd have to circle back around and approach from the side, but he was certain he'd be able to climb up without the camera spotting him. The problem would be if anyone spotted him from the road. Or if another van arrived and pulled around back as he was making his way into the warehouse.

The longer he was out here, the higher the chances that he'd be caught or the Tahoe spotted, so without wasting any more time, Bear retreated into the trees and retraced his steps for a few hundred yards before creeping forward and bringing the binoculars to his eyes once more. With no visible cameras on the side of the building, it was time to make his move.

Straining his ears for the sound of an approaching car or nearby voices, Bear determined there was no time like the present. He dashed forward at full speed, not slowing down until he hit the side of the building with a grunt. His shoulder stung from the impact, but it would be worth it if he got in and out without getting caught.

The drainpipe was old, and the bolts holding it in place were rusted but still fastened to the building's brick façade. He couldn't see how it was holding up past the second floor, but with any luck, that wouldn't matter. Bear wedged the fingers on both hands around the pipe, testing its strength with a solid tug. When the pipe stayed in place, he prepared for his ascent.

It was a slow, grueling climb. Gripping the drainpipe took a toll on his hands and arms, and it wasn't long before they started to cramp. His method was straightforward as he shimmied his way up—his upper body held most of his weight, while his feet scaled the building and provided some balance. Without footholds, it was slow going. If one of his feet slipped, he'd likely fall to the ground, possibly taking the pipe with him. Then it'd be game over.

He was halfway to the second floor when he heard a car coming down the road. Looking down, he growled in annoyance. Too far from the ground to turn back, and too far from his destination to crawl through the window before the vehicle passed. Unable to plaster himself against the building without losing his grip, Bear froze, praying his strength held out and that the driver wouldn't spot him.

The seconds ticked by as the car approached. It sounded like it was slowing down. His heart ratcheted into his throat, and his fingers twitched like they had a mind of their own. His right foot slid a few inches down the face of the building, but he readjusted just as the minivan sped by, the driver none the wiser.

Before Bear could breathe a sigh of relief, however, he felt a fat drop of water hit his head. Then a second. And a third. Rain would make the pipe too slippery to grip. If he were smart, he'd turn back now and try again another day. But he was already here, a thousand questions begging to be answered. If he could get through the window above him before it started to rain in earnest, he'd deal with the descent when the time came. No point in worrying about it now.

With renewed vigor, Bear put hand over hand along the pipe, inching his way up. As he came even with the window, he felt the drain shift, and looked up to see a loose bolt along one side. It wasn't enough to send him tumbling to the ground, but if he wasn't gentle, he could pull the whole thing loose.

At least one part of this plan seemed to be going in his favor. The sill in front of the window was wide enough that Bear could step onto it and relieve the strain on his arms and legs. Though Bear shook with the effort, he wasted no time putting his elbow through the windowpane. Hoping the steady drizzle was loud enough to mask the sound, Bear used his jacket to clear the area enough to climb inside.

Now the real work began.

17

THERE WERE ENOUGH WINDOWS ON THIS FLOOR THAT BEAR DIDN'T NEED to let his eyes adjust to the room. Not that there was much to see, anyway. This room ran half the length of the building and half the width. The floor was full of dust and debris. No abandoned equipment or furniture. There were a few empty beer cans and plenty of graffiti, but they were old and faded.

Dust tickled Bear's nose as he stepped forward, testing the floor. One good thing about a building like this was it had been built to withstand the weight of heavy equipment. Unless he tripped and fell, the people below him would have no idea he was up here.

Still, Bear kept his footsteps light. It was harder to keep himself from sneezing. Between the visible dust particles in the air and the pungent smell of mold coming at him from all sides, his nose tingled and burned. Pinching it until the feeling passed, Bear pulled out his gun and set off toward the door closest to him.

Leaning against the door, Bear listened for voices on the other side. He heard none. He used a single finger to press down on the handle, waiting for it to unlatch and then letting it swing open on its own. The hinges didn't squeak, and Bear slipped through without a sound. He found much of the same on this side of the building, though there was significantly more water damage, and the smell of mold was much stronger.

Stepping back through into the first room, Bear noted that the drizzle had turned into a steady downpour. He'd either made it inside at just the right time or had chosen the worst possible moment to scale the building. Getting back down would be a pain in the ass, but he could use the rain to his advantage and slide down the pipe like a fireman's pole. It'd be much less work. And a lot more dangerous.

Repeating his process from the last one, Bear stepped through the next door once he was sure the coast was clear—and found exactly what he was looking for. There was a short hallway and another door that led to the other side of the building, plus a door labeled with a sign for the staircase. Paranoia forced him to clear the rest of the floor before heading downstairs. He didn't find anything of significance, and it made him feel better about not clearing the third floor before going down to the first. If the second level was this bad, there was no chance the people in the vans would be on the third.

Like most of the rest of the building, the stairs were concrete. It was much easier to avoid making an echo than it was to avoid a creaking staircase you were unfamiliar with. Small victories bolstered his confidence.

Bear made it to the ground floor and flattened himself against the wall as he worked his way over to the door. The walls weren't sound-proof, and he could hear voices on the other side, even if he couldn't make out what they were saying. Steeling himself, he took only two seconds to peek through the small window in the center of the door before leaning back and analyzing what he'd seen.

His view had been limited, but he'd been able to make out a group of desks in the center of the floor, maybe forty feet from the door. Unlike upstairs, the ground level was completely open, allowing him to see everyone in the room without being able to get any closer.

The desks looked like a typical command center, with a couple of computers and various other pieces of equipment. If he had to guess from a glance, there were also likely cameras, some printers, audio equipment, and various weapons. Maybe four or five people stood talking or hunched over the computers, and while he didn't know who they were or what they were doing there, he'd seen plenty of setups like this before. Whether it was a private security firm or government agency was anyone's guess.

Bear ducked below the window and crossed to the other side, closer to the doorhandle. Squatting low and bracing his back against the door, he reached up and once again used a single finger to depress the handle as gradually as he could. As long as he made no sudden movements—and as long as the hinges were as quiet as the ones upstairs—he'd be able to open the door without anyone noticing.

The *click* of the latch opening sounded like a gunshot in the hallway. Bear froze, waiting for someone to notice what he'd done. But given the distance of the command center and the noise of the men and women on the other side, he doubted anyone had heard it. Still, it took him a few seconds to realize he was holding his breath. He let it out as quietly as possible.

Opening the door a millimeter at a time, Bear only risked an inch or two before he shuffled closer to listen to whomever was on the other side. No one was trying to keep their voices down, but with half a dozen conversations going on at once, all he could catch was a word here or there.

Footage. Weapons. Phone lines. No movement. Source. Headquarters.

Bear listened for a few more minutes, but he couldn't figure out their objective. Were they aware he was in town, or were their conversations unrelated? No one was supposed to know who or where he was these days, but information could have leaked through the cracks. After making enemies everywhere he went over the last couple of decades, he had to be careful.

Without more information, the risks he'd been taking would be for nothing, so Bear pushed the door open wider, inch by inch until he was able to fit his head through. The chance of gaining valuable information was worth getting caught, though he was confident he'd be able to get away without being spotted.

Pivoting on his heels, Bear gripped the doorframe and peered through the crack, noting an old conveyer belt and a pile of debris in the corner. He swept his gaze along the wall; he didn't spot anything—or anyone—in the immediate vicinity. A good sign. He eased his head through the opening and took in the room, filling in the gaps from his first glimpse at the command center.

He'd been right about the number of people sitting and standing around the computers, though now he could see there were three men and two women. The people at the computers were likely the techs—analyzing video and audio or searching through databases. Sure enough, one woman wore large headphones over her ears, and her eyes were closed as she attempted to distinguish the voices on the other end. The man to her right had his eyes glued to his screen, his nose inches away. He never seemed to blink.

The others stood over the techs' shoulders or pointed at maps or scrolled through their phones. What the hell was going on in here?

One voice rang out above the general chatter, and Bear drew back behind the door. "Look alive. We've got company."

For a moment, Bear thought they were talking about him. He prepared to sprint upstairs and throw himself out the window. He could still hear the rain coming down as hard as it was before, and he cursed himself for being arrogant enough to think he'd be able to get in and out without being detected. He'd be lucky to not break his neck on the way down.

"Never mind, they're just turning around."

There was a collective sigh from the group, and Bear got the sense that this happened several times a day. Risking another glance through the door's opening, Bear searched until he found the source of the voice. It belonged to a tall Black woman with her hair braided tightly against her scalp. Even from this distance, Bear could tell she meant business, and he had no doubt that she was the leader.

It was too bad they weren't wearing shirts or jackets emblazoned with the name of their company or agency.

"*Shit.*"

Bear jumped at the curse, ducking back behind the door, his heart pounding. The woman with the braids spoke. She sounded a few feet closer now.

"What is it?"

"Water's leaking from upstairs. Landed in my coffee. Disgusting."

"Byers?"

"Yeah?" This voice sounded younger, timid.

"See if you can find the hole. Patch it."

"Yes, ma'am."

That voice was already close. Too close. Bear didn't think before launching himself to his feet and scrambling up the stairs, not bothering to close the door behind himself. If he was lucky, Byers might think they'd left it cracked by accident or that the wind had somehow forced it open. If he wasn't lucky, Byers would raise the alarm and the whole squadron would be after him.

Bear passed through the door into the hallway upstairs just as Byers came through the one at the bottom. He paused before ascending the stairs, maybe to think about the door or to draw his weapon. Bear didn't risk looking through the little window to find out. He slipped into the room that would provide his exit and walked over to the opening on the opposite wall.

The rain came down in sheets, buffeted by a strong wind that hadn't been there before. Even if he managed to hang onto the drainpipe, the wind would knock him clean off. And that was only if he could get a solid grip on it to begin with. With Byers right behind him, Bear knew he didn't have enough time.

He crossed back over to the door and slipped into the corner just as Byers entered the hallway. The man sighed like he'd done this a dozen times before, and pushed his way through the door Bear was hiding behind. It smacked Bear in the arm, but the rookie didn't notice. What he did zero in on, however, was the broken window Bear had come through.

Before Byers could inspect it closer, Bear surged forward from his hiding place, wrapping one arm around the kid's neck as he slapped his other hand over his mouth. Byers was no match for Bear's size or strength, but that didn't mean he would give up without a fight. The kid bucked, trying to shake Bear off, scrambling at Bear's arm with one hand while he went for his firearm with the other.

Bear removed his hand from the kid's mouth and grabbed his wrist, bending it at an awkward angle just as he pulled his weapon free. Byers couldn't get enough air to scream out even though his mouth was now uncovered. His weapon fell out of his hand and clattered to the floor, skittering away where it was no good to either one of them.

Seconds later, Byers went limp in Bear's arm, the oxygen having been successfully cut off from his brain. He wouldn't stay out for long, but his confusion as he came to would buy Bear a few extra seconds.

The urge to go through the man's pockets to find out who he worked for was strong, but a shout from the bottom of the stairs sent Bear careening for the broken window. Someone must've heard the gun hit the floor, and when Byers didn't answer, another agent would come looking for him. And they'd be more on guard than Byers had been.

Bear climbed out the window and wrapped his hands around the drainpipe. Rain stung his face and chilling rivulets of water slid under the collar of his jacket and down the back of his shirt. Spending just enough time to make sure he had a good grip, Bear shifted his weight until he could press his feet around the pipe to give him some extra traction. After that, he let gravity do most of the work.

The pipe scraped the palms of his hands. He was making good time until he hit the halfway point. A strong gust of wind and the popping of the loose joint above unbalanced him enough that his foot slipped out. He scrambled at the metal in the hopes of regaining his grip, but it was no use. The ground was already rising to meet him.

Bear landed with a thud, and the air rushed out of his lungs. He'd landed on his forearm and hip, stopping him from hitting his head. His ankle had met the ground at a bad angle. Though he was sure nothing had snapped, a sharp pain told him he'd probably sprained it.

There was no time to worry about that now. Bear pushed himself to his feet and followed the path he'd taken earlier back to the woods. He only stopped once to look back over his shoulder and up at the window he'd climbed out of. A figure stood there, watching him retreat, but Bear took some comfort in the fact that he couldn't make out whether it was Byers, the Black woman with the braids, or someone else. If he couldn't see them through the rain, chances were they couldn't see him either.

Not that Bear was going to take any chances. Ignoring the pain in his ankle, Bear sprinted through the woods and out into the field, stumbling as he hit the road. Regaining his balance, he launched himself back into the Tahoe and peeled out of the empty lot he'd parked in, heading in the opposite direction from the warehouse.

Once Bear was back on the highway, he pulled off his wet windbreaker and tossed it on the seat next to him. Ten minutes later, he was pulling out of a gas station where he'd thrown it in a dumpster along with his cap. He'd need to get a new set to keep in the car, but that was a problem for a different day.

Though he'd been cursing the rain earlier, he was grateful for it now. There was next to no chance they'd been able to catch up quickly enough to follow him back to Arlington, but even if they had, the rain would make their job more difficult. Still, every time he spotted a van in his rearview, he made a detour off the nearest exit and circled around until he was sure it wasn't one of ConnectCom's. It doubled the amount of time it took him to get home, but it would be worth it in the end.

The rain had let up somewhat by the time Bear pulled into the driveway, and he wasted no time shoving his way through the door. His mind was still frantic, and he couldn't decide if he wanted to get out of his wet clothes or pack up Mandy and get the hell out of dodge.

"Bear?" Mandy had been lying on the couch, holding her book over her face, when Bear had returned home. Now she was standing in the middle of the living room, the novel forgotten on the floor. They stared at each other for a moment, taking in the other person's visage. Bear sopping wet and breathing heavily, Mandy laced with concern.

"What's wrong?"

A loud banging on the door cut off any answer he could've given her.

18

BEAR AND MANDY STARED AT EACH OTHER FOR THE LENGTH OF A SINGLE heartbeat before they were both in motion. They'd been over their contingency plans enough that Mandy knew what to do.

As soon as they'd arrived at the cabin, they'd gone over dozens of possible scenarios. This one called for Mandy to go into her room, take up her knife, and use her judgement to either stay hidden or help Bear should he be attacked.

Bear pulled his gun from his holster and pressed himself flat against the cabin wall. He lifted the corner of the curtain covering the window with the tip of his finger. Outside, he caught the flash of a familiar face, but it took a second for his memory to catch up with him. He'd been expecting someone from the warehouse, not the bartender from The Magic Tap.

Bear shifted his gaze to the beat-up old Civic parked behind his Tahoe. He couldn't see any other figures on the other side of the door. The bartender appeared to be alone, but appearances could be deceiving.

Another knock came. Bear wasn't sure if the woman had softened her knock or if Bear was just now hearing it correctly, without the hint of aggression. Taking in a sharp breath, he pulled open the front door, keeping his gun down but ready, and locked eyes with her.

"I'm so sorry to show up unannounced like this." Her words came out like an avalanche. "I'm not sure if you remember me. My name is Kelly. From the bar?"

Bear stepped close to her, and he could see her eyes go wide for a split second before she realized he was only checking if she was alone. Though it was still difficult to see in the rain, Bear didn't hear or see anyone else, and her car had no passengers. Unless Chip Greyson was hiding around back.

"Come in," Bear said, not bothering to modulate his voice to make it sound less gruff.

When he stepped to the side, Kelly shuffled through the door, carrying nothing but a small purse. Not too small to hold a weapon, but he doubted she'd come all the way to his cabin just to try something like that.

Bear checked the surroundings again, then shut the door, locking it and turning to face the woman in front of him. It only took a quick glance at her face to notice the panic. He realized too late that he had shut her in and was now standing between her and the only exit. When her gaze slipped to the gun in his hand, she backed up a step, attempting to put the couch between them.

"I-I shouldn't be here," she said. "I'm so sorry. I'll come back later."

"How do you know where I live?" He didn't bother hiding the gun. Maybe it would convince her to tell the truth.

"I was on my way home, and I had recognized your car pulling in." Kelly kept eye contact with Bear, though it seemed like she was struggling not to keep glancing at his gun. "I didn't mean to ambush you. I-I'm so sorry." When Bear didn't say anything, a tear slipped down her cheek. "Please. I have a daughter."

Mandy slipped out of her room, tucking her little knife into her pocket before the woman could see it. "Bear, you're freaking her out."

Whether it was Kelly's pleading or Mandy's voice that finally shook him out of his current state, he wasn't sure. Either way, he tucked his gun into his shoulder holster. He wasn't quite ready to take it off, but Kelly seemed to relax now that she wasn't alone with Bear.

"Hi," Mandy said, sticking her hand out for the woman. "We were never properly introduced. I'm Mandy."

Kelly shook her hand for a brief second before dropping it. Her gaze flickered to Bear, then back to Mandy. "I'm Kelly."

"My dad told me." Mandy steered Kelly to the couch. "Can I get you anything to drink? We only have water and orange juice. Well, and beer, I guess."

"A beer would be great," Kelly said. Her voice was steadier now, but her back was still ramrod straight. She glanced at Bear. "As long as you don't mind?"

"Make it two, kid," he said, working to keep his tone light.

"Coming right up." Mandy pulled two bottles out of the fridge and cracked them open on the edge of the counter like a pro. Bear winced at the display of expertise, but Kelly just laughed.

"Thank you." Kelly took the beer from Mandy and chugged at least a third of it.

"You're welcome." Mandy handed Bear his bottle with a glare, then sat down next to Kelly, putting herself between him and the woman. "Is everything okay? Are you in trouble? Do you need help?"

"Not me." Kelly fiddled with the label on the beer. "My boyfriend."

Bear barked out a laugh. Still too amped to sit, he started pacing the length of the room. "You expect me to help that asshole?"

"Not him," Kelly said. "Not Chip."

"You two aren't together?" Mandy asked.

Kelly wouldn't make eye contact with either one of them. "We are. But—"

"He's an asshole?" Mandy asked.

Kelly's lip twitched into an almost-smile. "You could say that. Look, it's complicated."

Mandy waved her off. "Who are you talking about, then?"

"Ethan." Kelly's voice was softer, tinged with worry and hope. "Ethan Tapp."

"Edison's son?" Bear recognized the last name. "The owner of the brewery?"

Kelly nodded; her brows creased. "Do you know him?" Her eyes went wide. "Do you know where he is?"

Bear shook his head, sorry that he got her hopes up. "Monica was telling me about him when I was at the bar. Said he finally convinced his father to send beer samples out to Portland. Wanted to get them into more local shops and convenience stores." Bear took a swig of his own beer—some cheap brand that didn't taste great but got the job done—and finally let himself settle enough to lean against the wall. If Kelly was here asking about Ethan, who she was clearly in a relationship with, then she wasn't working with Chip. She was risking everything just by showing up at his door. "Why do you think he's in trouble?"

"Because he's not answering any of my phone calls or text messages." She looked between Mandy and Bear. "That's not like him."

"Is his father worried about him?" Bear asked.

Kelly shook her head. "He thinks Ethan's on a work trip."

"What makes you think he's not?"

"He told me he was leaving for Florida, but he never texted me when he got on the plane or when he arrived there. And then he sent me pictures from the beach. But they're wrong."

"Wrong?" Bear asked.

"Can I see the pictures?" Mandy asked.

Kelly dug her phone out of her purse as Bear went to stand behind them on the other side of the couch. Pulling up the pictures, she scrolled through seven or eight of them. They were all either of the beach or the ocean. One was a seagull eating a French fry.

"They look fine to me," Bear said, not that he didn't believe her. He just didn't want to stick his nose where it didn't belong. He had enough problems on his plate.

"Ethan always sends me goofy pictures of himself when he's away." Kelly scrolled up to the last time he went on a trip. They were all selfies of him making funny faces or posing in front of random signs. "I know it sounds stupid, but this isn't him. I know it isn't him."

"We believe you," Mandy said.

Bear shot her a look. "Maybe he didn't feel like taking pictures of himself that day. Or ..." Bear paused, feeling a brief tinge of guilt. "He's hiding something—or someone."

Kelly glared at him, and Bear was taken aback by the fierceness in her eyes. "Ethan wouldn't do that. I know him. He wouldn't."

Before Bear could respond, Mandy spoke. "Bear." Her voice was deep and serious. She still had Kelly's phone in her hands. "Look at this."

Bear bent over to look at a picture of Ethan standing in front of a sign that used to say DANGER, but now was missing the first letter. He had his face all scrunched up like he was pissed off, and his hands were balled into fists like a bare-knuckle boxer from one of those old cartoons. But that wasn't what had caught Mandy's attention, and it wasn't what caught Bear's. That was reserved for his blue-and-white checkered shirt.

Bear sighed. "Could be a coincidence." The hair was standing up on the back of his neck now. "Most guys have one of those in their closet."

"One of what?" Kelly leaned forward to try to look at the picture.

"You don't," Mandy said, staring him down.

"I'm not most guys."

"One of what?" Kelly took her phone back, her eyes searching for whatever it was they were talking about.

"Bear—" Mandy started.

Bear held up a hand, then walked over to the counter and put down his half-empty beer. When he returned, Kelly was staring up at him with true fear in her eyes. As much as the picture didn't prove anything, Bear had to admit it was strange—finding the shirt, the blood, the number that led to a surveillance team just outside Arlington.

"Was Ethan involved in anything?" he asked.

Kelly gawked at him. "Anything like what?"

"Anything illegal? Dangerous?"

Kelly swallowed a lump in her throat, and for a split second, Bear saw doubt in her eyes before it was replaced by resolve. "No."

"Are you sure?"

"Yes, I'm sure. He's a good person. A good man."

Bear decided not to point out the fact that you could be a good person and still be involved in illegal or dangerous activities. "If there's anything, you have to tell me."

"What's going on?" Kelly stood. Her knuckles turned white from the grip she had on her beer bottle. Bear was afraid she'd shatter the glass right in her hand. "What do you know?"

"Maybe nothing," Bear reassured her.

"Bear," Mandy warned. She was standing now, too. "It's worth looking into."

Kelly slammed her beer bottle down on the coffee table. She didn't look afraid anymore. She looked pissed. "What's worth looking into?"

Bear sighed. There was no avoiding it now. "Sit down. Let me start from the beginning."

19

MANDY WOKE UP AS SOON AS SHE HEARD BEAR MAKING COFFEE IN THE kitchen. With her blanket half on the floor, she felt the morning chill caress her skin, but she was too tired to pull it back on top of her. Besides, the cool air would help her wake up faster. Bear would be shocked to see her up by the time he knocked on her door, and she wanted to see the look on his face.

Out of all the lessons Bear had been teaching her, rising early was the one she struggled with most. Give her a knife or a gun, or ask her what color socks any given person was wearing, and she'd ace those tests. But being up before the sun? That was just cruel and unusual punishment.

This morning was different. A thrill snaked through her as she remembered everything that had happened last night. It wasn't like she'd been happy to see Kelly in distress, but after weeks of boredom, it was an exciting change of pace. As much as Bear wanted to stay out of other people's business, she'd seen the glint in his eye, too. There was nothing quite like solving a problem that had felt impossible just hours earlier.

When Kelly had walked through that door asking for help, it took everything in Mandy not to pump her fist in the air. From the moment she'd met the woman, she'd known something was seriously wrong. As much as Bear had tried to deny it at first, he couldn't now. Not when Kelly was knocking on their door. Literally.

A grin spread across Mandy's face as she squinted into the early morning sky through the window at the foot of her bed. Her instincts had been right, and now Bear knew it, too. If she could help Kelly find out what happened to her boyfriend—the good one—then maybe she could prove to Bear that he should trust her with more responsibilities. Sure, she'd messed up by going to the payphone and calling that number, but she'd also gotten them one step closer to the truth.

A knock at her door had Mandy sitting up in her bed, trying to look like she hadn't woken up just a couple of minutes ago. A few seconds passed before Bear peeked inside, freezing when he caught sight of her not only awake, but looking ready to start her day.

The surprise in his eyes lasted only a fraction of a second, but that was enough for her.

"How'd you sleep?"

"Pretty good. What about you?"

"Not bad." Bear shrugged as he said it, and Mandy didn't miss the stiffness in his shoulders.

He had insisted on staying on the couch, giving her the bedroom, even though she could fall asleep anywhere. But it wasn't worth arguing over. Bear would rather be the first person an intruder encountered. It was safer for both of them that way.

"How's your ankle?" she asked him.

"Fine. Good night's sleep took care of it. How's your arm?"

"Hurts a little, but not bad." She hopped out of bed and put on a pair of socks. "What's for breakfast?"

"Bacon. Eggs. Coffee."

"Sounds good to me."

Mandy wondered how many other kids her age lived life like a forty-something-year-old man, reading the newspaper while holding a steaming cup o' joe to her mouth. Waking up early enough to see the sunrise, then going for a five-mile hike in the woods. Complaining about kids not respecting other people's property. What would she be like at Bear's age? And where would he be? Would he even be in her life anymore? Would he even be alive?

It wasn't the first time she wondered how long she had with him. It's not like he was that old, but his lifestyle wasn't for the faint of heart. They had discussed it, of course. Bear didn't like leaving anything to chance, and as difficult as that topic was, Mandy felt better knowing they had a plan. They both knew that it wasn't a matter of *if* Bear's past caught up with him, but when.

The thought made Mandy sad, so she pushed it away, burying it deep down with all the other painful memories she carried in the recesses of her mind. The urge to fiddle with the knobs of the stove was so strong, she found herself doing it before she could stop herself. Normally, she didn't like doing that sort of thing in front of Bear, but she felt much better after tapping each one, making sure they were off. She did it a second time, just to be sure. Then a third.

"Everything okay?" Bear asked.

"Yep," Mandy answered too quickly. She spun from the stove and sat down at the table. "But I'm starving."

"Good, because I had to use up the rest of the eggs before they went bad."

Mandy waited for Bear to set her plate down in front of her, a pile of scrambled eggs and at least ten pieces of bacon making her mouth water. His portion was double hers. Between the two of them, they could eat their weight in breakfast foods. If only they had pancakes, too.

The silence stretched on, only broken by the sounds of chewing before Bear stopped to take a sip of coffee and then level her with a look.

Mandy rolled her eyes. It was like he expected her to read his mind. "What?"

"You nervous?"

"About a worldwide shortage of bacon?" She stole a piece off his plate. "Eating this much every morning can't be good for you."

"I'm fit as a fiddle," Bear said, puffing out his chest. "All the doctors say so."

She snorted. "When's the last time you actually went to a doctor?"

"Good point." He turned serious. "We should probably make an appointment. It's been a while for you, too."

Mandy groaned. "Never mind. Forget I said anything."

"Too late, can't take it back." Bear stabbed a forkful of eggs and shoved it in his mouth. "I meant about watching Kelly's kid today. It's a lot of responsibility, Mandy, being in charge of another person like that. It's okay if you're not ready."

Mandy huffed. "I told you, I can handle it."

Last night, after Bear had explained what they'd found in the woods, Kelly had insisted on going to see the tattered shirt herself. She would've left right then and there if Bear hadn't reminded her that it was still pouring outside and that it would be dark soon. Mandy had chimed in, despite the glare on Bear's face, and said he'd been planning to go back out there anyway, suggesting that they all go together. Now that they were getting closer to some answers, Mandy was itching to uncover them.

Kelly had perked up at the thought, then deflated in the next breath, telling them that she didn't have anyone to look after her daughter, Flora. She'd started crying, begging Bear to let her come along. That she'd know Ethan's clothes anywhere, that if she could only see the shirt in person, she'd be able to tell whether it was his.

While Kelly's face was buried in her hands, Mandy and Bear had exchanged a look. Kelly was desperate to do something, to be proactive in uncovering answers. It was obvious to Mandy that Bear didn't think the woman should be out in the woods with him in case he came across Ethan's body, but he couldn't deny that Kelly would be invaluable in identifying the man if they came across him.

That's when Mandy had blurted out that she'd babysit Flora, despite having no previous experience taking care of a kid. Even though she'd sacrificed her chances of going back out in the woods, it was better than missing the opportunity to find out more than if Kelly stayed behind. Though Bear didn't like the idea, Mandy knew it would offer him the opportunity to get to know the woman better and collect other relevant information. It didn't take a world-class detective to know she was hiding something.

Kelly had looked doubtful at first, but Bear had backed up Mandy's suggestion, saying that they'd only be a couple miles away, and that Mandy was extremely responsible. If there was an emergency, they had several escape plans depending on the situation. And with any luck, Bear and Kelly would only be gone for a couple of hours.

In the end, Kelly had agreed, relief and anxiety warring across her face. Mandy hadn't known what that anxiety was for—the potential for finding Ethan's body or letting a stranger look after her kid—but she doubted it was the same as the look of trepidation passing between Mandy and Bear. They both knew there were other threats out there than Flora accidentally tripping and hitting her head or choking on a piece of food.

After Kelly left, Bear had filled Mandy in on everything that had transpired during his research trip. She'd been mad that he hadn't told her where he was going or what his plan was, but the anger was soon swept away by relief that he had come back in one piece. And then it was replaced by fear that they had gotten involved in something much larger than they had initially realized.

But that was part of the reason why Bear had agreed to bring Kelly along. If the clothing in the woods indeed belonged to Ethan Tapp, then he was tied to whatever was going on with ConnectCom. They both agreed it was better to figure out what was going on than run the risk of having to constantly look over their shoulders for the foreseeable future.

Been there, done that, and Mandy was not a fan.

The truth was, Mandy was a little excited to babysit Flora. She wanted to prove she was responsible, that she could follow the rules. If everything went off without a hitch, maybe Bear would let her do something a little bigger next time. And if she kept it up, he'd trust her more than he ever had before. It was all she wanted.

A knock on the door had Bear getting up from the table with a stifled grunt and crossing the room. Kelly stood on the other side, dressed in workout gear and hiking boots. A little girl about three years old sat on her hip, looking up at Bear with wide eyes. Without any fear, she reached up and tugged on his beard.

"Santa?" she said, her voice high and lilting.

Bear chuckled. "Out of the mouth of babes. Guess I'm getting old."

"I'm so sorry." Kelly peeled her daughter's hand away from the beard, her face torn between embarrassment and laughter. "She thinks every man with a beard is Santa. I swear you don't have that many gray hairs."

"I'm choosing to take that as a compliment," Bear said. "Come on in. Need any help?"

"I got it." Kelly stepped inside and set her bag down in front of Mandy. "Flora, this is Mandy. She's going to play with you while Mommy and her friend go for a walk, okay?"

Flora wiggled until Kelly set her down on the floor. The little girl took off running around the cabin, checking out everything within her reach. Kelly unzipped the bag and started pulling out the essentials—stuffed animals, books, and plenty of snacks.

"She's pretty independent. Probably won't even miss me," Kelly said, sounding both relieved and sad. "She's curious, which gets her into trouble, so just keep an eye on her. She'll get tired in a couple hours. Reading usually puts her down faster. If she gets upset, try giving her Mr. Elephant." Kelly held up a stuffed hippo, and Mandy quirked an eyebrow at her. "I tried to explain it to her, but she thinks all gray animals are elephants."

"And all gray men are Santa, apparently," Bear added.

Kelly stared at Flora, who had pulled a towel down from the handle of the oven and was pretending to catch imaginary butterflies with it. "Maybe I should get her eyes checked." Kelly turned back to Mandy. "Are you sure about this? It's not that I don't trust you," she rushed on. "I just know kids can be a lot sometimes."

"It'll be totally okay," Mandy said, sounding more relaxed than she felt. "Go do what you have to do. It'll be fine. We'll be best friends by the time you get back."

Kelly looked relieved, then turned to Bear. "Are you ready?"

"Are you?" he asked, the question heavy with meaning.

"No." Kelly grimaced, but she looked resolute. "But I need to do this."

"All right," Bear said, swinging his backpack over his shoulder. "Let's move." He looked at Mandy, a thousand emotions crossing his face at once. There was a lot Bear and Mandy left unsaid because sometimes words just weren't enough, and she was glad this was one of those times. "See you, kiddo. Be smart."

"Always." Mandy watched as the pair of them stepped outside. Then she turned back to Flora, wondering if the kid would prove to be her biggest challenge yet.

20

NEITHER BEAR NOR KELLY FELT THE NEED TO EXCHANGE WORDS AS THEY began their trek deep into the woods. Half of Bear's mind was back with Mandy, hoping the kid would be okay. It's not that he didn't trust her—quite the opposite. He'd seen Mandy with other kids before, had noticed how she stepped up to the plate when necessary. Having to focus on taking care of Flora would keep her out of trouble.

But he still worried.

If something happened with Flora, Mandy'd have to run up the road for better cell service in order to call the police or an ambulance. If someone came knocking on the door, she'd have to defend the both of them. She was more than capable of taking care of herself, but Bear couldn't shut off that part of his brain that wanted to lock her away so nothing ever happened to her.

Mandy was fifteen, though. She'd have to learn sooner or later. Bear was torn, wanting to show her the worst of the world to make sure she was prepared. But he wanted to shelter her from anything or anyone who could possibly break her heart. Knowing neither of those options were realistic or practical, it was hard not to think in extremes when his life experiences had been full of them.

Bear broke the silence. "Flora seems like a handful."

"Yeah," Kelly agreed.

"Reminds me of Mandy when she was little." Flora had bouncy brown curls and bright eyes and tiny dimples on either side of her cheeks. But it was the curious look in her eye that really did it. Mandy had been the same way when she was younger. "Cutest kid I'd ever seen. Can't imagine how anyone could toss her aside like they did."

Kelly was behind Bear as they walked the trail deeper into the woods, but he could imagine the expression on her face from the tone of her voice when she asked, "Toss her aside?"

"I adopted her a while back. My partner found her standing on a street corner, all alone. Father dead. Mother didn't want her. It's a long story." He wanted to ensure the woman wouldn't ask any questions Bear didn't want to answer. "But it has a happy ending."

"She's lucky to have you."

Bear was taken aback by the fierceness in her voice. "Sometimes I wonder."

"You're a good man." Kelly's voice was quieter now. Distant. "I'm obviously not the best judge of character, but I have a good feeling about you. What you're doing to help me means a lot."

Bear slowed as the path got wider. He walked beside Kelly so he could watch the emotions on her face as he asked his next question. "Speaking of, I gotta ask."

Kelly sighed. "About Chip?"

"He's such a dick." Bear threw his arms up, making Kelly laugh. "I imagine he was charming once."

"Oh, he was." This time when she sounded wistful, it was tinged with sadness. "Not many people want to date a single mom, you know? Especially with a kid so young. He hit on me at the bar, and I didn't think anything of it. Lot of guys flirt when you're pouring their drinks."

"Comes with the territory."

"But he kept coming back, every day. I was at a low point, laid it all out for him. Told him I had a kid at home. This was a couple years ago, so I was really struggling. He said he didn't care. For that first year, he'd come over, cook me dinner, help me take care of Flora. He was good with her. She loves him. Doesn't know any better."

Bear knew how delicate the topic was, but he needed to know what he was getting himself into. "When did it change?"

"I'm not sure." Kelly watched the ground as she navigated the path, avoiding roots and Bear's eyes. The rain had turned the path into a muddy mess, squishing underneath their feet. "It was little things at first. I couldn't even tell you what they are now. At first, I thought it was just normal couple stuff. Honeymoon phase was over, you know? But then it started feeling wrong. I started feeling vulnerable, and like I was in danger around him."

Bear let her words hang between them for a moment, not wanting to press the subject but needing to know. When it seemed like she wouldn't go on without prompting, Bear asked, "Is that why you wrote the note? The one on the dollar bill."

"I did that a few months ago when it looked like things could get even worse. Didn't know what else to do. Never ended up handing that note to anyone. But I kept it because it made me feel like I still had the option."

"Did he ever hit you?"

Kelly looked up at him, a sad smile on her face. "You're not so subtle, are you?"

"Not one of my strong suits."

"He doesn't have a lot of patience. I found that surprising after all he did to win me over. He's hit me a few times. When we were really fighting. Always apologized after. Said he'd never do it again." Kelly stared straight ahead, her lips pressed together so tightly they turned pale. "I'm not stupid, you know."

"Never thought you were."

"You'd be the only one. I fell out of love with Chip a long time ago. I wonder if he's even noticed." Kelly shook herself from whatever memory had floated to the surface. "But having a kid makes you think about your priorities. Makes you realize what you can endure. Whatever kind of man Chip is, he takes care of us. Flora always has everything she needs. I won't deny her that stability for the sake of my own comfort."

"You deserve stability, too," Bear said.

"I know." Kelly looked at him, like she wanted to make sure he understood her completely. "I've thought about this from every angle a thousand times. I have a plan. Right now, that plan means staying on Chip's good side."

Bear filed the information away for later. She was right about what having a kid did to you. As soon as Mandy came into Bear's life, everything shifted. What he found important the day before no longer mattered. He'd done a lot of things to keep her safe, and he didn't regret a single one of them. Understanding Kelly's reasoning, he just wished it didn't have to be that way.

"Where does Ethan come into it?"

A smile crossed Kelly's face. "I've known Ethan for a long time. Since we were in high school. We went out for a while, nothing serious. Lost track of each other when we graduated. Then I started working at the bar. At first, it was like a high school reunion, sharing good memories. He could make me laugh like no one else. Then it escalated. Got away from us. Before I knew it, we—" Kelly broke off to clear her throat, but whether it was from embarrassment or emotion, Bear couldn't tell. "Look, I'm not proud of it."

"You deserve happiness."

"I wish I'd found Ethan first, you know? Things would be a lot simpler."

"Does he know about Chip?"

Kelly laughed, but it was tinged with something dark. "They're friends. Chip didn't grow up here, but he's lived in town for a while. Ethan knows I'm involved with him. Knows Chip isn't the gentlest. But I can't tell him what it's really like. Ethan would kill him. I wouldn't be able to live with myself."

"And if Chip ever found out the two of you were together?"

"You already know."

He did, and now Chip Greyson was his prime suspect. But first, they had to find evidence that something had happened to Ethan. He wasn't convinced that the torn shirt belonged to the bar owner's son. Yet.

The muddy path was difficult enough to navigate, and the footprints he and Mandy had followed the first time would be wiped away. The blood on the tree would be hard to spot, too. This already felt like looking for a needle in a haystack, and it had just gotten ten times worse.

Luckily, Bear remembered how to get back to the spot with the tattered shirt. They'd already made good time, and he kept the rest of the hike light by asking Kelly about easier topics. Most of her answers involved Flora in one way or another, and Bear was happy to trade stories with her about raising a daughter on your own. It wasn't easy, but there was no doubt they both believed it was worth it.

"Do you think they're okay? Back at the cabin?"

Bear had wondered how long it would take her to ask, surprised that it hadn't been sooner. "I'm sure they are." His chest warmed at the realization that he believed that. "Mandy's a good kid. Smart. Too smart for me sometimes. And she's got the energy to match Flora's."

Kelly laughed, and he noticed her shoulders had relaxed. "We'll see about that."

He was glad he'd made her laugh one last time—the next part of this journey would be difficult.

Holding out his arm to stop her from walking forward any farther, he pointed to the tree next to them. Sure enough, the rain had washed away the blood that had been there only the day before. "This is where I saw the handprint." He pointed off the path, down to where he knew the shirt would be. "And that's where we found the bit of clothing." He waited until she met his eyes before he asked her the most important question of the day. "You sure about this?"

Kelly didn't pretend like she was sure. Bear saw every emotion warring across her face. Pain, fear, hope, regret, longing, all of it. Whatever they found out here, it would lead them down a path they couldn't come back from. Whether it was Ethan's body or someone else's, they'd both decided to make themselves a part of the story. And time would tell if they would end up regretting it.

"As ready as I'll ever be." She looked deeper into the woods and tucked all those emotions away. He'd seen that tactic before, had used it himself. Going numb didn't mean it wouldn't hurt later, but it at least helped you get shit done. "Lead the way."

Bear took a second to make sure she was certain. The hardened look on her face was all he got in return. It wasn't a glowing endorsement, but he hadn't expected one. This would be traumatizing if they found something and agonizing if they didn't. He wondered if she'd figured out whether she wanted to find Ethan or not. Sometimes it was better to know, even if the answer shattered your entire world.

Bear led the way toward the shirt, careful to make sure neither of them slipped on the wet grass and leaves underfoot. When they made it to the shirt, Kelly sucked in a sharp breath before crouching down next to it. She picked up a little stick and flattened out the wet piece of clothing, trying to get a better look at it.

"I can't tell," she said, and Bear was glad she sounded logical, almost procedural about it. "He definitely owns a shirt like this, but it could be anyone's."

"My thoughts exactly."

Kelly noticed the slip of paper in the pocket, now soggy and torn. "What's this?"

"Don't know." Bear hadn't told her about the phone number, ConnectCom, or what he'd found in the warehouse. He'd save that line of questioning for when he had more answers. "Didn't notice it before."

"Whatever was written on it, it's illegible now."

"Let's fan out," Bear suggested. "Step carefully. Try to disturb as little as possible. Look closely for anything that could be evidence that a person was out here."

"Like footprints?"

"Doubt you'll be able to see those after the rain."

"Then we're looking for more of the shirt." She swallowed. "And blood?"

"Blood'll be washed away." Bear didn't want to point out the other things they might find, like body parts. He'd deal with that if it came to pass. "Shout if you see anything."

Kelly stood and walked farther down the hill, picking her way over roots and around trees. Bear took off in the opposite direction, doing the same. Right now, he didn't have enough evidence to put together any sort of sequence of events.

Did the bloody handprint belong to the victim or the murderer? Had the victim even been killed? Was the shirt evidence that the person had gotten away, or was it an indicator that animals had found the body and run off with parts of it? If it was the latter, then they'd find what they were looking for sooner rather than later. But if it was the former, they could be out here all day without coming across another scrap of evidence.

Bear hadn't realized how much distance he'd put between him and Kelly until he heard her calling his name from farther down the hill. Bear made his way to Kelly, slipping and sliding and leaving behind a trail. If it rained again, he wouldn't have to worry about it, but that would also make their job more difficult in case they didn't find what they were looking for today.

But the look on Kelly's face as he approached told him that she had found something. Her body was vibrating, whether from fear or anguish, he couldn't tell. He followed her outstretched hand. His gaze fell upon a shovel leaning up against an ancient tree.

"Strange," Bear said, "but could be from anything. We have no idea how long that's been here."

"That's not all." Kelly's voice cracked on the last word.

Bear followed her lead as she walked around the tree and pointed into an animal's burrow on the other side. The yellow laces on the boots made them easier to spot. Whoever had shoved them inside had been in a rush. That confirmed Bear's worst suspicions about what they were looking for.

Bear grabbed a short, thick stick from nearby. He stuck the end into the opening of one of the boots and dragged it out from the hole. It was a well-worn hiking shoe, covered in mud and a few drops of blood. A length of duct tape patched together the heel.

When he looked up at Kelly, he already saw the truth in her eyes.

"Those are his," she choked out. "Those are Ethan's boots."

21

Iris returned to New York soon enough not to be missed. She'd used personal days for her off-the-books investigation, and she'd been careful about not leaving a trace for anyone to follow. They still could have had eyes on her.

Iris had always been a by-the-book kind of agent, aside from her recent stint in Indiana. It was the first and only time she'd ever gone rogue, and her punishment had been worse than the crime. Peake and all his superiors probably thought she'd had enough of desk duty and needed to hit the beach for a few days to recover. He'd even mentioned trying to get her back out in the field when she returned. Once they found out what she'd really been up to, they'd either fire her or promote her. After all the secrets and lies of the last few months from both herself and her colleagues, Iris wasn't sure which she preferred.

Shaking off the thoughts of despair, Iris looked up at the house down the street from where she'd parked. The last time she'd been here, Mrs. Moore had made sure Iris knew she wasn't welcome. That woman would give her no answers about Bear and Mandy, even if she had them —and Iris wasn't convinced she did.

But her son, Marcus? No doubt he had them. Rosie had made it clear that he and Mandy were still close when she and Bear were living in

North Carolina. At one point, Mandy had been friendly with Jenny, but they were no longer friends. Rosie hadn't told her what the incident had been to end their friendship, and Iris hadn't asked. As interested as she was in everything Bear had done prior to their meeting, she had to pick and choose. Jenny was out. Marcus was in.

It was a risk coming back here. Showing up again would set off more alarms than the first time. Maybe she'd call Sheriff McKinnon to deal with Iris. That wouldn't be so terrible. McKinnon had been distant but helpful. But if Mrs. Moore called the Feds, Iris would have a storm to deal with.

Perhaps luck would be on her side today. The driveway was empty. Summer Break hadn't ended yet. But he might be involved in extracurricular activities. Maybe he was out with friends or at a summer camp.

Before Iris could think of more worst-case scenarios, she popped open her door and hurried down the sidewalk toward the house. She'd traded in her suit for a pair of jeans and a t-shirt. She couldn't carry her gun out in the open, but she wasn't expecting trouble from a fifteen-year-old, one Mandy trusted no less. Then again, maybe that would be Iris' first mistake.

Iris didn't need to walk up to the door to know someone was home. The television blared in the living room. Guns and shouting and explosions could be heard from the sidewalk. When she approached the door, she had to bang on it in the hopes that whoever was inside would be able to hear her.

It took a few rounds of knocking, if the ensuing silence was any indication. She waited for someone to open the door. She caught movement out of the corner of her eye. The curtains swayed as though someone had just parted them. Seconds passed. She decided to take matters into her own hands.

"Marcus? Is that you?" She waited for an answer, but none came. "My name is Iris Duvall. I was here yesterday. Talked to your mom. I'm not sure if she told you or not." More silence, and Iris had to decide how truthful she could be. "Listen, I know you don't know me, and you have no reason to trust me. I work for the FBI, and I'm looking for Bear and your friend Mandy. I met them when I was in Indiana a while ago. I lost track of them afterwards. I think they might be in trouble, and I want to do everything I can to help them."

"Why?"

The answer came so suddenly, it took Iris a minute to comprehend what he had said. "Because I care about them. My cousin was killed. Bear helped me find out who was responsible. Saved a lot of people's livelihoods while we were there. I couldn't have done it without him."

"You could've just made that up."

Iris couldn't help the smile that spread across her face. "Sounds like they're rubbing off on you." She waited a beat before continuing. "Mandy didn't want to tell me much of anything, either. But we did get to spend some time together. I helped her pick out *A Wrinkle in Time*. I think she really liked reading it."

The silence from the other side of the door stretched on for so long, Iris began to wonder if Marcus was still on the other side. But then —"She really liked that book. Talks about it all the time. Made me read it."

"Did you like it?"

A pause. "Yeah, I did."

"Good." Iris laughed, feeling lighter, realizing that she'd made an impact on the girl, if only a small one. "It's one of my favorites."

"Why are you looking for them?"

The smile slid from Iris' face as reality came crashing back down. "I'm worried about them. When I made it back to the office, the FBI moved me off the case I was working on. They had information on Bear, but they wouldn't let me see it. I've got a lot of evidence telling me Bear is dangerous. And a lot of witnesses telling me he saved their lives. I just want to talk to Bear and get his side of the story. I want to make sure Mandy is okay."

The hinges of the door squeaked as Marcus pulled it open. He wore a t-shirt with a picture of some sci-fi movie on the front and basketball shorts. His eyes were wide behind thick glasses. But his gaze was sharp and knowing. Iris could see why Mandy had been drawn to him.

"She hasn't been answering my messages," Marcus said, keeping a watchful eye on Iris. "I'm starting to get worried."

"Do you know where they are?"

Marcus shook his head, but it was too fast, too jerky.

"Look, I understand what a big deal it is that Mandy trusts you. I'm not looking to risk that for you. But if you have any idea where they are, I need to know. It'll be better if I'm the one who finds them versus some of my colleagues."

Marcus looked torn. The crease between his eyebrows deepened at the same time he bit his lip. There was a war waging in his mind, and Iris could tell he was weighing the repercussions of divulging any information to her.

When Marcus opened his mouth to answer, she wasn't sure what would come out of it. A phone number? An address? A general location? Or maybe nothing at all. Perhaps he was about to apologize to her and say he couldn't help. That it wasn't worth the risk.

But she never found out what his answer would've been because, in that moment, she heard a car pulling into the driveway behind her. Marcus' eyes went wide, and Iris spun around to see Mrs. Moore stepping out of her vehicle, a finger already pointed in her direction.

"You get away from my son."

Iris held her hands up in surrender. "Ma'am, I just needed to ask him—"

"I don't care." There was a cell phone in her other hand, and she was dialing a number. "Leave now, or I'm calling the cops."

Iris hesitated. If she called McKinnon, it might be worth it. Maybe Marcus would open up to the both of them. Or maybe he'd clam up even further. And she'd run the risk of landing on someone else's radar. Then this investigation would be over before it even began.

"I'm going," Iris said, stepping away from the house. She tossed a look over her shoulder at the kid. "If you've got anything to say, now's the time."

Marcus' mouth clamped shut, and two seconds later, his mother was through the door and slamming it in Iris' face. Dejected, Iris lowered her arms and stared at the house, but the only face in the window was Mrs. Moore's, glaring at her from behind the glass. There was nothing

Iris could do now except turn around and figure out where to go from here.

But when she climbed back into her car, Iris still didn't have a plan. Both Rosie and the Murrays down in North Carolina had no way of getting a hold of Bear. No one else from Cape Hatteras had been as close to him as those three.

Sheriff McKinnon made it clear she couldn't help, and that she probably wouldn't even if she wanted to. No one else in this town knew who Bear really was. That left Indiana. Iris had witnessed firsthand Bear's interactions with the townspeople. Bear had been closest to Amos, and she'd witnessed their goodbye. The old farmer would have no idea where Bear and Mandy were now.

The entire time they'd been stuck in Indiana, Bear had been trying to get to St. Louis. But that was months ago, and the probability of tracking them to their next destination was low. The flash drive had nothing in it about the city or anywhere beyond.

Mandy had mentioned California a couple times, but it could've been a red herring. Besides, California was huge. It'd be harder to find them there than in St. Louis.

Iris banged her hands on the steering wheel a few times, reveling in the sting against her palms. She had been so close with Marcus. If she'd only had ten more minutes, she could've gotten him to reveal something. Maybe if she came back tomorrow, she could try again. It'd be a risk, but she could wait for Mrs. Moore to leave for work and then knock on the door again. Marcus would give her another chance.

Before Iris could plot out the details of her plan, her cell phone vibrated from the cup holder. It was a text message from a number she didn't have in her contacts. She'd given out her card to thousands of people over the years, and without any guess as to who it could be, she pressed a finger to the message to open it.

This is Marcus. I got your number from the card you gave my mom. She threw it away after you left the first time, but I took it just in case.

Heart pounding, Iris tapped out a reply. *I'm glad you did. I only want to help Bear and Mandy.*

The seconds stretched on as Iris waited for Marcus' reply. She could almost feel the debate raging in his mind, pushing away from Iris and pulling closer again. Closing her eyes, she sent up a silent prayer to whoever was listening that he'd throw her a lifeline. All she needed was one solid lead, and she could do the rest on her own.

A vibrating in her hand made Iris' eyes fly open.

They were looking into this phone number when I stopped hearing from her. That's all I can tell you. I'm sorry.

Iris ignored the disappointment of knowing Marcus wouldn't help her again after that, because he'd included the number in his next message. Switching over to the browser in her phone, Iris typed the area code into the search engine with shaky fingers. The results were immediate. She finally had her heading.

Bear and Mandy were in Oregon.

22

BEAR HELD KELLY AS SHE CRIED OVER ETHAN'S BOOTS. OUT IN THE forest, it didn't matter how loud her sobs were. The birds kept singing, the wind kept rustling the leaves, and the animals kept working their way through the underbrush.

After a few minutes, Kelly pushed Bear away. The touch was gentle, and when she looked up at him, her eyes were red-rimmed. "Thank you," she said, her throat raw. "I'm sorry I dragged you into this."

"Wasn't you," Bear said. He knew the feelings warring inside Kelly right now. Grief fought anger while sadness battled denial. He wanted to reassure her that there was still a chance that Ethan could be okay, but they'd both know that was a lie. The only thing left to do was move forward. "What do you want to do now?"

Kelly was silent for so long, Bear wasn't sure she'd actually heard him. Then she looked up, and this time, the pain in her eyes had been replaced by determination. "Find out who did this."

Bear helped her to her feet, then headed back up the trail. Their hike back was grueling now that the day was getting warmer, but neither one of them complained. In fact, neither one of them said much. Bear heard Kelly crying behind him, but a few minutes later, she was silent. There was nothing he could do to make her feel better other than help her find out what had happened, so that's what he would do. He hadn't been lying when he said it wasn't her fault he'd been dragged into this. Fate had done that to him—the chance meeting with Greyson, the tattered shirt out in the woods, the strange phone number and utility van.

When they arrived back at the cabin, Mandy and Flora were playing a game of hide and seek. The little girl was doing a poor job of hiding under the couch, and she gave herself away when she spotted her mom's boots walking through the door. When Flora wiggled out from her hiding spot, Kelly scooped her up and held her close, tears still fresh on her face.

"Everything okay?" Mandy whispered, coming to stand next to Bear. "You find something?"

"Pair of boots and a shovel."

"The boots are his?"

"Yeah."

Mandy sighed, resigned to whatever came next. "What now?"

"You still up for babysitting duty?"

Mandy seemed to know better than to argue her case to go with him. "Yeah, whatever you need." She nodded toward Kelly. "She okay?"

"No." Bear kept his voice low. "But she will be."

They had devised a loose plan on their way back to the cabin, and it was time to put it into action. Greyson had gone out of town the night before; the only reason Kelly had felt comfortable coming to Bear when she did. It also meant they had limited time to do some digging without him knowing. This was the only reason Bear felt it was safe enough for Mandy to watch Flora at Kelly's apartment, where there was actual cell service and more of the kid's toys.

They stayed at Kelly's apartment only long enough to get Mandy settled in. Kelly had trouble leaving Flora behind. But at the end of the day, Kelly needed closure, and that would only come with finding answers.

They drove separately to the bar, pulling in one after the other. The parking lot was empty except for a few of the employee's vehicles. The lack of customers would make what they needed to do next much easier —as long as Bear could get through the door.

Kelly led him around to the side door he'd seen her enter with Greyson the day before. That seemed like ages ago now, after everything that had happened. Everything they'd discovered. Now that he knew her better, he could see the strength inside. The will to endure whatever life threw at her if her kid was safe. Bear knew what that felt like.

Sticking her key in the door, Kelly twisted it to the right and pulled on the handle. On the other side stood the bouncer with red hair and a weapon hidden under his jacket. When he saw Kelly, a smile broke over his face, fading as soon as he locked eyes with Bear.

"You're not supposed to be here."

"Got a personal invitation." Bear pretended to fish it from his pocket, revealing his middle finger to the guy instead.

"He's with me." Kelly stood her ground.

The bouncer wanted nothing to do with it. "Don't matter. Get out before I put you out."

Bear stepped forward, the challenge in the man's words calling to something primal inside of him. He had been willing to smooth-talk his way into the bar. Now he was itching for a fight. And for the first time in a long time, Bear wondered if he'd be able to win this one. Something about not knowing had him clenching his fists at his side in anticipation.

A hand on his chest stopped him, and he looked down to see it was Kelly's. Her arms were stretched out between them, her other hand on the bouncer's chest. "You're a pair of meatheads, you know that?" For some reason, she was glaring up at Bear when she said it. "Play nice."

Robbie didn't move. Didn't take his eyes off Bear. "He's gotta go. You heard Chip. He's not supposed to be here."

"He's with me," she repeated.

"One of two ways we can handle this. I call the cops, or I deal with this guy right here."

Bear didn't miss the way his hand inched closer to the holster under his jacket. Thinking he'd have no trouble getting through the door with Kelly at his side, Bear had left his weapon in the Tahoe. He didn't really think the guy would pull his gun with Kelly between them, but those were the kinds of assumptions that got you killed.

"You're not calling the cops," Kelly said.

Finally, Robbie looked away from Bear and down at Kelly. "Why are you sticking your neck out for him? Who is this guy?"

"He wants to talk to Edison about the business. He might invest. He's got money."

"Chip wouldn't want his money."

"You ever think for yourself, big man?" Bear said. "Or you just do what Greyson tells you?"

"Shut up, Bear." Kelly slapped him on his chest.

"Thought your name was Carl?"

"Only my friends call me Bear." He'd seen the way Robbie had looked at Kelly, and he couldn't help himself. "My good friends."

Robbie's eyes narrowed, and he took a step forward, forcing Kelly back.

"It's not like that," Kelly ground out. This time, she shoved at Bear's chest. There wasn't enough strength behind it to move him, but he got the hint and stepped back. Kelly glared at him for a moment, then turned back to Robbie. When she spoke, her voice was sugary sweet. "How long you known me, Robbie?"

"Long time. Longer than Chip."

"That's right." The smile in her voice was enticing, encouraging. "And in all those years, have you ever known me to do anything that wasn't in the bar's best interest?"

Robbie sounded chastised when he answered. "No."

"Exactly."

"Chip said—"

Kelly's voice turned hard. "Chip doesn't own the bar, Rob. Edison does. It's Edison's decision whether Bear—Carl—is allowed inside."

The change of tone had Robbie looking down at his shoes, brow furrowed like he wasn't sure what he'd done to make her angry. "Fine. He's in the back. But you know I gotta tell Chip." He pulled out his phone. "If he finds out I kept this from him—"

"You don't owe Chip shit." Her ire was now directed at Robbie. "He treats you like a lap dog, and for what? You deserve better."

When Robbie looked up, there was anger in his eyes. "You're one to talk."

"I have my reasons," Kelly whispered.

"So do I."

Bear didn't know how to name the look that passed between them, but it felt intimate and vulnerable. How much had these two been through, and how much pain had they endured because of Chip Greyson? There was no chance in hell Bear and the bouncer would ever be friends, but this brought a new perspective for him. Robbie wasn't the real enemy. Greyson was.

"Robbie," Kelly pleaded.

"I'm sorry, Kells." The bouncer sounded like he meant it. "But I have to."

As Robbie raised his phone to his ear, Kelly put a firm hand on his arm. She'd straightened up, her shoulders rigid. "I know you've been skimming from the register. Known it for a while now. Never said anything. If Chip finds out, he'll be pissed. If Edison finds out, he'll fire you."

Robbie's eyes went wide. He stuttered for a moment before any real words came out. "You know I have nowhere else to go."

"You keep my secret," Kelly said, "and I'll keep yours."

Robbie hesitated, glancing up at Bear, who shrugged as if to say he wasn't gonna tell Greyson. The bouncer shoved his phone back in his pocket and stepped to the side. Kelly gave him an apologetic look, but Robbie's face remained hard. She walked away, and Bear followed in her wake.

When they were out of earshot, Bear leaned close to her. "That's going to backfire."

"I can handle it," Kelly said.

Bear wondered if she felt as confident as she sounded.

23

KELLY LET HERSELF INTO THE BACK OFFICE. BEAR STOOD IN THE DOORWAY and took in the room. Piles of papers littered every surface, more peeked out from the open drawers of several filing cabinets. Bear got the sense of organized chaos, that the Tapps were always trying to catch up but never quite crossed the finish line.

In the center of the room was a metal army-green desk. It was dented on one side and seemed like a relic from the sixties. It looked solid even though it was rusted along some of the edges.

A man sat behind the desk, searching through his papers with his pen clenched between his teeth. He had a beard full of silver that needed a trim, and thick grey hair that fell to his shoulders. If he hadn't been a hippie in a past life, he was certainly playing the part now.

The man didn't look up when they entered the room. Bear wondered if he was used to the constant interruptions, or if he was so lost in his work he hadn't realized they were standing there.

Kelly must've been used to it. She walked up to his desk and rapped her knuckles on it. A hollow echo bounced around the room. The man finally looked at them. His eyes were a piercing blue, curious and kind.

"Morning, Ed." Kelly's voice was softer than it had been with Robbie. "How's it going?"

"Good, good. Just looking for those pay slips from last week. Can't seem to—"

Kelly pulled a stack of papers from the pile he'd already gone through and handed it to him. "You mean these?"

Edison groaned theatrically. "How'd I miss them?"

"You're not wearing your glasses." She leaned forward and pulled them down from the top of his head to place them on his nose. "Better?"

Edison looked down at the papers in his hand. "Oh, will you look at that? I found the pay slips."

With a smirk on her face, Kelly stepped to the side and gestured to Bear. "Ed, I want you to meet a friend of mine. His name's Carl—"

"You can call me Bear." He stepped forward and offered his hand.

"Bear's interested in making an investment in the business. Says he really likes the beer."

"Oh?" Edison grasped Bear's hand in a firm grip. His hands were rough, like he'd spent his whole life working with them. "That so?"

"Best beer I've had in a long time."

Kelly didn't give the man a chance to argue. Shuffling around to the other side of the desk, she ushered Edison toward the door. "I'll finish this up before my shift starts. You two go talk it over."

"You don't have to do that, honey. I can—"

"I don't mind."

This was all part of the plan to get Bear alone with Edison while she got the opportunity to rifle through his desk and look for clues about Ethan's disappearance. "You know I can type faster than you, anyway."

"That's true," Edison said. But he dug his heels in at the doorway and turned to her. "You doing okay? You look sad."

"Didn't get much sleep last night. Flora had too much sugar and kept me up till three in the morning." The lie was smooth. Convincing. How many times had she lied like this to make sure no one knew how difficult her home life had become? "Besides, you know better than to tell a woman she looks tired."

"I said *sad*," Edison answered, but he allowed her to push him from the room. "There's a difference."

Bear chuckled when Kelly shot Edison a look and shut the door in his face. Even though he'd been removed from his own office, Edison appeared to be in good spirits. He gestured for Bear to follow him. They ascended a narrow staircase to the second floor, and Ed opened the door at the top. Sunlight greeted them from open windows, momentarily blinding Bear to what lay on the other side.

He wasn't sure what he'd been expecting, but it wasn't the private bar and lounge area that met him, full of leather couches and recliners. A pool table sat in the middle, with a stained-glass lamp hanging over its center. If the area downstairs gave off an air of comfort and camaraderie, the room upstairs oozed luxury and grandeur.

Bear whistled.

"You like it?" Edison asked.

"Very nice."

Edison turned to him with an eyebrow raised. "I hate it, too." He walked over to the bar and slipped behind it. "Feels like a gentleman's club. Not my style."

"Then why—"

"My son, Ethan." Edison pulled out half a dozen bottles and set them on the counter between them. "Said I needed a space like this for taking meetings and entertaining business partners. It has the intended effect, but I feel like it's promising something I'm not sure I can deliver." He gestured to the beer in front of him. "Take your pick."

Bear took in the line of beer. "Already tried the Magic Brew," he said, remembering the smoothness of the honey flavor. "And the Citrus Cascade. Not sure I'm brave enough for the Good vs. Evil."

"One of my favorites. The balance of chocolate and chili is fantastic."

"Think I'll go for the Dark Roast." Bear picked up the coffee-flavored beer. "Didn't get a chance to have more than a single cup this morning."

Edison smiled and picked up another with notes of ginger and watermelon, according to the label. "Sit wherever you'd like."

Bear chose a pair of recliners near the window and settled into one before taking a sip of his beer. The flavor came a few seconds later, washing over his tongue and leaving no doubt in his mind that this man was a genius. "Wow." It was the only word he could think of to express his surprise. "That's good."

"Give it a few minutes, and you'll feel like you're on top of the world. Really has a caffeine kick. I can't drink it past two in the afternoon or I'll be up all night."

"Good to know." Bear took another swig.

"How'd you hear about us?" Edison asked.

"Came in the other day for a drink, and Monica gave me my first taste. Gotta say, I was hooked." Bear knew that to get real answers out of Edison, he had to play the part. "Couldn't stop thinking about it since."

"Appreciate that." Edison tilted his beer in salute. "Been playing around with flavors for decades, just for fun. Have my own farm and everything. Started off small, making batches for myself. Testing them on my friends. Then they started requesting flavors. Before I knew it, I was selling them at the bar. Never thought I'd have my own brand, but my son wouldn't stop going on and on about it. Wanted to start selling them outside the bar. Eventually, he wore me down."

"I haven't met Ethan yet." Bear threw his hypothetical line into the water and let it sit. "But I've heard a lot about him."

"You'd know it if you did." Edison laughed. "He's the life of the party. Much different from me. Takes after his mother. Should be back in a few days. You're welcome to swing by whenever you want."

"Might need to tell the security that. Don't think he likes me too much."

Edison waved away the comment. "Robbie's a good kid, but he doesn't make friends easily. Very protective of me and the kids. Especially Kelly."

"I got that sense, yeah." Bear forced himself to take another sip of beer, so he didn't seem too eager to get through his questions. "Don't think his feelings were returned, though."

"Nah, Kelly's only got eyes for Chip."

Bear tucked that piece of information away. All of Edison's answers had been natural and easy so far, but if he thought Kelly was head over heels for Chip, then he either didn't know any better or he was maintaining the lie in front of a stranger. Bear's gut told him it was the former. If Ethan and Kelly were having an affair, Ethan likely hadn't divulged that information to his father.

"Think he and I got off on the wrong foot. I seem to be making an impression around here."

"Chip's a tough nut to crack. Doesn't have Ethan's charisma, if you know what I mean."

Bear just came right out and said it. "He's a dick."

Edison's whole face crinkled as he barked out a laugh. "He can be, yeah. But he's been good for the business over the years. And Kelly seems to like him. That goes a long way in my book."

"Good for business?" Bear asked.

"Oh yeah, the kid's got a ton of ideas. Chip knows how to haggle for a good price. Made startup costs a lot lower. I'm in debt to him for that. Look, I know what he can be like. He and Ethan are quite the pair. Surprised I've survived them this long. You'd think a couple guys in their thirties would be more mature." He chuckled at some distant memory. "You got any kids?"

Bear nodded. "A daughter. Fifteen."

"What's her name?"

"Mandy."

Edison nodded, sadness spreading over his face like a shadow. "I had a daughter once. Never got to see her grow up. She and her mother, my wife, were killed in a car accident. Not long after, Ethan and I moved here. He was old enough to understand they were never coming back. Wasn't my fault, but I think he blamed me anyway." Edison shifted in his seat, piercing Bear with his blue eyes. "Not trying to be a sap here. Just want you to know this business means a lot to me. Ethan and I haven't always gotten along, but the brewery helped us mend our relationship. Making our own beer has been an important part of that. Something we can work on together."

"Most dads toss a baseball or teach their sons how to change the oil in their car."

Edison laughed. "Never was good at either one of those."

"Like I said, I haven't met your son, but I've heard plenty about him. I don't think he'd push you so hard to get your beer in stores if it didn't mean just as much to him, too."

Edison's smile was soft around the edges. "Appreciate you saying that."

Bear was almost done with his beer. It was time to reel in his line. "I think I'm more interested in investing than I was before."

Edison had a sparkle in his eye. "It's the room, isn't it? I'll have to tell Ethan it's working."

Bear gave him the laugh he was looking for. "I won't tell him if you won't."

"Good man," Edison said. "But I would like you to meet him. He's got all the numbers. I just make the beer."

"Have you heard from him lately?" Bear asked. "Any idea when he's gonna be back?"

"He's usually only gone for a couple days. His anniversary is this week. Don't think he'd miss that."

"Anniversary?" Bear asked. If Edison thought Kelly and Chip were together, then who did he think Ethan was with?

"Been with his girlfriend Trish for a year. We're all supposed to go out together for dinner. I haven't met her yet, so I'm taking this as a good sign."

"Sounds like everything is moving in the right direction."

Now that he knew Ethan wasn't the only one having an affair, Bear had a new target and a new prime suspect.

24

MANDY BACKED OUT OF THE BEDROOM WITH MEASURED STEPS. THE floorboard creaked beneath her. She froze midstride and held herself as still as possible. She didn't even dare to breathe. When she saw no movement from the other side of the room, she continued to tiptoe backwards and pulled the door behind her, leaving it open a crack. She turned around and went back to the living room where she let out the air she'd trapped in her lungs.

Babysitting was a lot harder than she'd ever imagined.

After Bear and Kelly had dropped her off at the bartender's apartment, Mandy and Flora had played a dozen games, not even bothering to finish one before moving onto the next. Mandy had loved spending time with a kid who could keep up with her and not get bored. Playing pretend was fun, and it made the morning zip by in a blur of colors and activities.

But by the time lunch had hit, she was exhausted, and Flora had started to get grumpy. Mandy's limbs ached from chasing Flora through the apartment and swinging her around the room. A headache had formed between her eyes, and she didn't need a doctor to tell her it was from clenching her teeth together every time Flora fell over and came close to getting hurt. That kid wasn't afraid of anything, and while

Mandy would've applauded that kind of behavior, knowing she was responsible for Flora's safety added a thousand pounds of stress to her shoulders.

Mandy could understand Bear's overprotective nature better now although she'd never admit it to him. More than once, she'd had to tell Flora not to do something or else she might get hurt, and though it broke her heart when Flora cried in protest, Mandy knew she was doing the right thing. Was that how Bear felt all the time?

She was relieved when Flora began yawning after lunch. Mandy ignored the girl's protests and led her to Kelly's bedroom and plopped her down on her little bed. It took Flora a while to decide which book she wanted Mandy to read to her, going through at least seven or eight options, and then she had the nerve to fall asleep before Mandy even got to page five.

That's when Mandy had slipped out of the room. She prayed that Flora wouldn't wake up and demand she keep reading. Mandy wanted to take a nap herself. The apartment was strewn with Flora's toys. Not only was it messy, but it was also a tripping hazard. The least she could do was make sure everything went back where it belonged.

Mandy let her mind wander as she tidied up. Bear had told her what they'd found in the woods, and it didn't take a genius to assume that Ethan Tapp was dead, even if they hadn't found his corpse. Bear suspected animals had dragged his body off. The problem was, they had a crime, but no crime scene. And forget about any real suspects. That's what Bear was doing now—gathering evidence. But he wasn't the only one.

This was a prime opportunity to snoop through Kelly's apartment. Bear hadn't instructed her to do so, but she figured he wouldn't complain about her taking advantage of the situation. Especially if she found something.

As soon as Bear and Kelly had shut the door behind them, Mandy had wandered around the apartment to familiarize herself with the layout and to look for baby cams, hidden or otherwise. Finding none, Mandy relaxed. She could take her time inspecting the apartment once she got Flora down for a nap.

And that's where she found herself now. With the living room clean, Mandy turned in a circle, searching for anything that looked out of place or like it would be a good hiding spot. The problem was that Kelly's apartment was basic. It was lived in, though still neat. You could tell a kid lived there from all the toys, but for the most part, the bartender kept a tight ship, as Bear would say.

That was a problem for Mandy. She wanted to find something.

It's not that she didn't trust Kelly, because she did. Everything the bartender had told them so far had appeared to be the truth. It was what she hadn't said that was starting to bother Mandy—and she could tell it bothered Bear, too. There was some other piece of information, some other angle that Kelly hadn't revealed to them yet. So Mandy would find it for herself.

The living room was clear of any clues or hard evidence, but Mandy hadn't expected to find anything there. Hiding something out in the open like that would be too obvious. If nothing else, Mandy didn't think Kelly was stupid. She'd find a better spot for something she wanted to keep away from prying eyes.

Mandy remained diligent, moving into the small dining room and then the kitchen. Here, she noted a brand new set of pots and pans, and a new coffee maker. Maybe Kelly had needed to replace them, or maybe Chip had bought them for her. Mandy couldn't blame Kelly for taking advantage of Chip's financial support. She was concerned it might be a good reason for Kelly to double cross them somewhere down the line.

The bathroom proved just as boring as the living room. Some people hid medication or drugs in the cabinet or the back of the toilet, but not Kelly. It was spotless except for the area under the sink, which was cluttered with at least a dozen different kinds of shampoos, conditioners, body soaps, lotions, face masks, and hair products. Mandy resisted the urge to check them all out to see if they were really necessary. There'd be time for that later.

A couple of hall closets provided nothing more than an array of jackets and winter coats, plus some empty luggage. Mandy went through every pocket and zipper, then replaced it all right where she'd found it. One positive about arranging things in a particular way was that Mandy had memorized the placement of her items. In this context, it was easier to resist the urge to straighten up when she knew it might lead to her getting caught.

Closing the door to the closet, Mandy turned to the last room in the apartment. It was the only bedroom, and the place Kelly would be most likely to hide something. Mandy had saved it for last to ensure Flora was sound asleep. Exploring the room as silently as possible would put Mandy's skills to the test, and she had to admit that got her a little excited.

Grateful she hadn't shut the door all the way, Mandy pushed it open and slipped inside. She avoided the floorboard that had creaked underfoot earlier. Kelly's bedroom was a little messier than the rest of the house. For some reason, it brought joy to Mandy to see that Kelly hadn't made her bed. A couple of shirts had been tossed on the floor, considered for today's outfit, and then discarded. The nightstand next to the bed held a few books, a bottle of lotion, a lamp, two empty water glasses, and a box of tissues. Mandy felt something deep in her gut as she observed the room. She was close to something.

Time to get to work.

Mandy started with the nightstand, opening the two drawers and rifling through the contents. Nothing seemed out of the ordinary. She had to fight off a blush when she came across a few items that she definitely wouldn't mention to Bear.

She pressed her stomach flat against the floor and slid halfway under the bed to see what Kelly had stored under there. A few extra blankets and a bin full of shoes didn't catch her attention, but a box of paperwork did. After sliding it out from its hiding spot, she opened the flaps and dug in.

In lieu of a desk or filing cabinet, Kelly had shoved all her important paperwork into this little cardboard box. They were separated into folders, which made it easier for Mandy to search. She was careful to keep them in the order in which she'd found them.

Most of the papers were utility bills or bank statements. Everything was in Kelly's name, and her bank account was pitiful. No wonder she put up with Chip. As disappointing as it was to realize Kelly wasn't a secret millionaire or something, this did cross off a few ideas of what she could be hiding. If Chip was the terrible person Mandy knew he was, then he probably kept Kelly in line by threatening to not pay her bills anymore. She only made enough at the bar to cover her basic expenses, let alone any emergencies that might come up. And that wasn't even touching her debt. The credit card statements made it clear how dire the situation was.

The contents of the box left Mandy disappointed. Kelly wouldn't be back until she finished her shift. Mandy felt a ticking clock hanging over her head. If she found nothing else, she'd come back and look through the paperwork more closely. But for now, it seemed like a dead end.

After closing the box and shoving it back under the bed, Mandy got to her feet and padded over to the other side of the room. Flora was still asleep. Mandy turned to the dresser, purple with floral stickers all over it. Despite the serious nature of Mandy's objective, she smiled at the thought of Kelly covering them in something that represented Flora so perfectly. Mandy wondered what she was doing and whether her doubts about Kelly were founded. She shook herself and leaned down to go through the drawers. There was only one way to find out.

Most of the contents belonged to Kelly, and the only suspicious thing about her clothes was that she only owned about four different types of shirts but had each in about a dozen different colors. What was that phrase Bear sometimes said? *Variety was the spice of life.* Apparently, Kelly didn't think so.

Moving on from the dresser, Mandy searched the two drawers built into the base of Flora's bed. She inched them open, careful not to jostle the bed or else she'd have to answer to Flora. Not that the little girl knew what was going on, but she was talkative enough that it could get back to Kelly.

Inside the first drawer were some outfits and accessories, like bows and headbands. A few of them looked too small for Flora, but Kelly probably hadn't had a chance to throw them out or give them away. In the other drawer, there was an old diaper bag, some towels, and a couple of blankets. Nothing special.

Mandy was about to close the drawer when she kicked herself for not being more thorough. This might be her one and only shot to explore Kelly's apartment without interruption. With that thought in mind, Mandy unzipped the diaper bag.

And struck gold.

Inside, there were no diapers to be found. In fact, the contents were so foreign to their environment, that it took a moment for Mandy to realize what she was looking at. A Ziploc bag with an ID, a passport, and a couple of different credit cards. A wad of cash that had to total at least five thousand dollars. Folded papers that revealed three plane tickets had been bought for a trip to Florida.

Mandy's head spun. She knew what this was—a *go-bag*. Bear had one for them, and considering Kelly wasn't in a good situation with Chip, it wasn't surprising that she had prepared for the day when she might have to leave him at the drop of a hat.

No, it wasn't the go-bag that interested her. It was that the three tickets were for Kelly, Flora, and Ethan. This was why she'd known from the start that Ethan hadn't gone on that work trip. Because she was supposed to go with him. The question now was, had she known he was dead all along? And if so, had she been the one to murder him? That wad of cash would stretch a lot farther if she only had to worry about herself and Flora.

Unsure what to make of the bag, Mandy zipped it up and closed the drawer, making sure it looked exactly as it had before. In a daze, she walked over to the closet and pulled open the doors, barely hearing the squeak they made above the sound of her own thoughts. This was the last place she had to look for clues, but after what she'd just found, she wondered if it was even worth her time. She saw a pile of unmarked boxes and bags on the top shelf. No way she'd risk walking away now. She had to finish what she'd started.

The shelf was far too high for her to reach any of the contents. She retreated to the kitchen to grab a chair to stand on. This would more than make up for the height difference.

As soon as Mandy wrapped her hands around the back of the chair to drag it into the other room, the sound of a key being inserted into a lock drew her attention. She dropped the chair and walked into the living room, watching as the knob to the front door turned under someone's hand. The door creaked open as someone stepped inside.

Mandy had just enough time to duck out of his line of sight and sprint toward Kelly's bedroom. Heart hammering and breaths coming in gasps, she swore as loudly as she dared. Out of all the scenarios she had run through her head, this one had seemed like the least likely to come true.

After all, Chip Greyson was supposed to be out of town.

But if that were the case, then what was he doing in Kelly's living room?

25

Edison Tapp led Bear downstairs to the main bar. Several people with drinks in front of them chatted away or watched whatever was on the flat screen. Bear's offer to become an investor was mostly a ruse, but he couldn't help thinking it would be a wise venture, regardless.

Edison invited Bear to stay and keep drinking. Even offered drinks on the house. Bear had other plans. Kelly gave him a subtle shake of her head when he looked over at her. He took it to mean that she hadn't found anything useful in the back office. Bear didn't feel like they'd come up short, given the information he'd gotten out of Edison.

Besides, he'd shaken Edison's hand right in front of Robbie, who had witnessed the old man telling Bear he was welcome to come back anytime. The bouncer had frowned in response, but kept his mouth shut. Bear felt more certain than ever that even if Robbie was in Chip Greyson's pocket, it was Edison who signed the checks.

Bear returned to the Tahoe without incident but stayed in the parking lot. He pulled out his phone and commenced one of his least favorite hobbies—scrolling through social media. Normally, he'd have Mandy do this kind of work; however, she was busy taking care of Flora, and he didn't want to waste any more time.

Ethan Tapp's social media pages were basic. It was obvious he liked to paint a picture of himself as someone who went to far-off places, drank beer, and always had a good time. But there was nothing personal on there. Nothing about the brewery or his father. Nothing about having a girlfriend. Nothing that indicated he had anything other than a picturesque life. His last post had been a single shot from a beach in Florida, staring out at the ocean. It wasn't even that good, and Bear couldn't help but agree with Kelly that it seemed different from the other photos he'd posted previously. The guy liked to be the center of attention. He wanted everyone to know where he was and that he was having a good time.

According to Edison, Ethan's girlfriend was named Trish. Bear didn't have her last name, but it hadn't been hard to find her.

Trisha Oakley tagged Ethan in all of her pictures, and she wasn't afraid of posting photos of them outside her home either. It wasn't hard to pinpoint the street she lived on. After that, it was just about matching the pictures of her house to the real thing.

That's how Bear found himself standing on her front porch, knocking on her door, wondering what excuses he'd come up with to get her to talk to him. Was she worried about Ethan? Did she know Chip? If Bear talked to her, would it get back to Greyson? It wasn't enough to stop him, but it could prove to be another thorn in his side.

When she finally answered the door, Bear had to keep the surprise off his face. Trisha looked nothing like her photos. Heavy makeup and a scowl made her look less approachable than the smiling country girl he'd found on Instagram. As she looked up at Bear, she popped her gum and asked, "Who are you?"

"Name's Carl." Bear adopted that same southern accent he'd tried on before. "I'm looking for Ethan Tapp."

Trisha rolled her eyes. "What's he gotten himself into now?"

Bear didn't know how to respond. This was the first person who hadn't talked about Ethan like he walked on water. And she was supposed to be his girlfriend. Then again, she'd probably know better than most.

"I'm not sure." Bear hesitated. He didn't want to give too much away. "Was hoping to meet with him to talk about his father's business, but—"

"He's in Florida."

"Any idea when he might be back?"

"Nope."

Bear paused a beat. "You're his girlfriend, right?"

"Maybe." Trisha leaned against the door. She popped her gum again. "Look, you want me to be honest with you?"

"Sure."

"You're an investor, right? Looking to make some money?"

"Yeah."

"Don't trust Ethan Tapp. That's the best advice I can give you."

Bear felt more curious than taken aback, but it was the latter emotion that he let crawl across his face. "What makes you say that?"

"It's the truth."

"I guess I'm just wondering why you'd say that about someone you're dating."

"We won't be dating for long." Trish got a cross look on her face, and Bear decided that she'd be more than capable of killing Ethan if she put her mind to it. "As soon as he gets back, I'm dumping his ass."

"Money trouble?"

Trisha shrugged, and the movement drew Bear's attention to her arm, where there was a pale green and yellow bruise.

"Among other things. He's a cheatin' bastard, for one."

That caught Bear's attention. He smoothed out his voice, deepened it a little. "Never understood why men did that. Just be honest, you know?"

"Exactly." Trisha popped her gum again. "But I've got a plan to get back at him." Trisha noticed the way Bear's eyes flickered back down to her bruise, and she laughed. "A little extracurricular activity. Hey, if he can do it, I can too."

"You're not wrong." Bear kept any judgment out of his voice. "Do you know who Chip Greyson is?"

"Course I do. Everyone around here does."

"What do you make of him?"

Trisha eyed Bear, as though trying to read his intentions on his face. There was something smart and scrutinizing in her gaze. She'd been the only one to talk about Ethan like this. Bear got the feeling she was the only one who wasn't wearing rose-colored glasses when it came to the guy. Or maybe it wasn't that simple. Perhaps Trisha was the only one who got to see that side of Ethan.

"You lookin' to go into business with Chip, too?"

"Not exactly," Bear said. "Kind of the opposite, actually."

"Well, they're two for the price of one. You want to invest with Edison, you gotta deal with Ethan. And if you gotta deal with Ethan, Chip ain't gonna be far behind."

"I'm getting the sense you don't like him much."

"Ethan's an idiot, but Chip? He's dangerous. I don't trust him as far as I could throw him." She lifted up a skinny arm with no muscle in sight. "And that ain't very far." Trisha looked Bear up and down, and the look in her eyes was more honest than blustery. "You want to know who Ethan cheated on me with?" She didn't give him time to answer. "Chip's girlfriend, Kelly. They deserve each other. The only reason I haven't called her out publicly is Chip will kill her if he finds out."

Bear couldn't stop thinking about Flora and what would happen to her if Kelly disappeared like Ethan had.

Bear shook his head. That wasn't his problem to solve. Right now, he had several suspects, and Chip Greyson was still at the head of the pack. He had motivation and opportunity, not to mention the ability to carry out the task. Didn't matter if Ethan was his friend. All that mattered was Ethan had disrespected him. That was a death sentence for a guy like Greyson.

"This has been informative. Appreciate your time."

"You're welcome." Trisha's mouth pulled down into a frown. "And look, Edison's okay. He's a good man who raised a brat of a son. Did the best he could. I'm really proud of the business and everything he's been able to do with it. It's not like I want to punish him for Ethan's crimes, but Ethan needs to learn there are consequences to his actions. The bar is worth investing in. But Ethan's not."

"They kind of go hand in hand," Bear said.

"For now." Trisha took a step back, but hesitated before closing the door. "What are you gonna do now?"

Bear thought for a moment. He was the number one enemy of his number one suspect. Now that he knew there was something more going on with Ethan Tapp, he felt the urge to keep digging.

"I'd like to drop off a note to contact me when he returns," Bear said. "You have his address?"

"Sure," Trisha replied. "Only if you promise to egg his house."

Bear gave her a convincing smile. "I'll consider it."

26

Iris had barely made it to her flight out of JFK. She'd been hoping to catch a few hours of sleep on the plane, but she was too wired. Her mind raced with what lay ahead of her. It was like her body knew she was closing in on Reagan, and it wouldn't let her relax until she completed her mission.

It had been a risk, but she'd used her Agency resources to look into the number Marcus had given her. She was surprised when she'd discovered it was one of theirs. Someone had set up an operation in The Dalles, Oregon, but she hadn't wanted to poke any deeper for fear of being discovered. But at least it gave her a heading.

Not that it had done her much good. Iris had driven past the ConnectCom offices a few times in the blue Honda Civic Coupe she'd rented from the airport, but it wasn't worth going inside. She'd show her hand, even if someone was willing to work with her—and she was certain they weren't. Word would get back to Peake and the others, and at this point, that was the worst-case scenario.

But that didn't mean she couldn't stake them out. With a decent lunch and plenty of coffee, she could set herself up down the road and know whenever someone came and went.

Sure enough, a white panel van with a ConnectCom Services logo across the side pulled into the parking lot. The driver stepped out of his vehicle and went inside. Picking up or dropping off? Iris couldn't be sure. About ten minutes later, he returned to his van and pulled back out onto the street.

Knowing what she did about who ran the show behind the scenes of ConnectCom, Iris had a good idea of their protocol. Their headquarters would be somewhere close-by, but outside of their main target area. Their agents would make frequent stops to the places they kept an eye on. It was just a matter of tailing the van and seeing where it ended up.

Without getting caught.

The job was easier than she'd thought it would be. Whether the agent driving the van wasn't concerned or flat out wasn't good at his job, she didn't know.

After a quick stop at a drive-through, the man headed straight into Arlington, then pulled into an empty parking lot in front of a run-down mall and enjoyed his food. This was a stakeout more than a lunch break. Having scarfed down his food, he stayed put, waiting.

As much as it pained her to leave the van behind, Iris had a different target in mind. Luckily for her, Bear would need food and gas, and he stood out in a crowd. With a little luck and more than her fair share of determination, she'd find him sooner or later. She just hoped it was sooner.

She'd already been to a couple of gas stations before she landed on the one that would tell her what she needed to know. Parking around the side of the building, she strolled through the doors. She kept an easy air about her. Stalking the aisles one by one, she got a lay of the store in case anything went down. It's not that she expected trouble—she just preferred being prepared.

"Excuse me," Iris said, walking up to the cash register, where a guy in his twenties with a bored look on his face was reading a magazine. The tag on his shirt read Silas. "Can I ask you a quick question?"

The kid didn't even look up at her. "You just did."

Oh, so it was gonna be like that. Loosening her jaw so her voice didn't come out strained, she smiled at the cashier even though he refused to meet her eye. She slid a picture of Bear across the counter. "Ever seen this man before?"

His eyes never left his magazine. "Not sure."

This time, Iris gritted her teeth in annoyance. "Look at the photograph. It's important."

He glanced up at her. "How much is it worth to you?"

She slid her badge across the counter and waited for Silas to take it in before she spoke. "The satisfaction of putting you in handcuffs would be payment enough."

The gears turned in the kid's head. Silas had a retort on the tip of his tongue—probably a dirty one, too—but he bit it back. Something told her he didn't have much respect for the police, which also led her to believe maybe he was trying to be on his best behavior. Did he have a record? Was he on probation? The question itched at the back of her mind, but he wasn't her problem. All she cared about was tracking down Bear.

"He comes in sometimes. Don't know his name." He looked up at her again. "Or where he lives."

Iris's heart was pounding. She kept any emotion off her face. This was it. After all her hard work, she was finally closing in on him. "What does he buy?"

Silas looked at her like she was nuts. "I don't know, lady. This job pays me minimum wage. I don't pay attention to that shit."

"I want to see the security tapes."

Silas's eyes glinted. Weighing his options. She could tell the second he decided to go for the jugular.

"You need a warrant for that."

She didn't want to give in, but this wasn't worth the trouble. "How much do you want?"

"A hundred bucks." He hadn't even hesitated.

Iris pulled fifty out of her back pocket and slapped it on the counter. "You get the other half if I find what I'm looking for."

Silas hesitated, but fifty bucks must've been better than nothing. He slid it off the counter and into his pocket. He jutted his chin to the back of the store. "Security's back here."

She grabbed the picture and her badge from the counter and followed him into a back room. The room was small and smelled like stale chips. Her eyes lit up at the tiny computer screen in the middle of a desk covered in papers and empty food containers. *Bingo.*

"I can take it from here." Iris shoved the kid out of the room and shut the door in his face. She heard his protests from the other side, but he didn't bother coming back in. Probably because they both knew who would win that fight. He might've been taller, but she had more experience. And more muscle if she were honest.

She swiped some of the garbage from the desk. She wrinkled her nose at the mold growing inside the containers before steeling herself to sit down in the chair. It was old, and the fake leather was peeling in spots, but it was comfortable enough. She wouldn't be here for long anyway.

The system was easy enough to navigate, especially now that it was digital. The days of VHS tapes were a bygone era she remembered and was glad to be rid of. Clicking on a file and choosing a timestamp was much easier. The problem was, she wasn't sure the last time he'd been in there, so she decided to work backwards from that morning, rewinding at a steady pace until she saw him walk through the door.

There he was, the big hulking figure of Riley Logan. Seeing him again brought back memories. Of Boonesville. Her cousin. Mandy. Their goodbye, and her hope that someday they'd see each other again. Maybe fight side by side again. And now here she was, tracking him down like he was a common criminal.

Maybe he was a criminal, but there was nothing common about him. Logan was dangerous. She'd known that before, but after seeing everything he'd accomplished in his life—and knowing there was plenty left off the record—it made her rethink the image of the man she'd created in her head. But every time she tried to think of him in a new light, she came back to the way he cared for Mandy. Dangerous people had feelings about their kids. But Bear was different. His entire life was dedicated to keeping her safe. Why would he risk pissing off Reagan and endangering his daughter's life? Was he that arrogant?

Turning her attention back to the tape, Iris saw that Mandy wasn't with Bear as he strolled into the gas station. Was she in the car outside, or back at wherever they were staying? Not for the first time, Iris wondered what sort of place Bear would pick to stay off someone's radar. A seedy motel might be too dangerous for Mandy, but somewhere nicer might remember his face if the police came knocking.

Bear walked up and down the aisle at a leisurely pace. He looked familiar with the store, which supported what Silas had told her about him making regular purchases. It disappointed her that Silas hadn't lied. She would've liked the excuse to intimidate him a little more and put him in his place. Something told her he wasn't used to that—especially from a woman.

Leaning toward the screen, Iris switched between camera angles to get a better look at what Bear had in his hands. Batteries and lighter fluid. A tingle went down her spine. Was he planning something? Then he grabbed a case of beer. He wouldn't have bought alcohol if he was on a mission. She'd seen him in action before—he was singled-minded in his determination.

The kid behind the cash register was all smiles for Bear. He looked younger and thinner than Silas. Bear pointed to something nearby, and the kid nodded in understanding. There was no sound on the videos, and Iris had to switch angles again to see what he'd been pointing toward.

Bundles of wood.

A lightbulb went off in her head. What if he wasn't staying at a motel? Perhaps he was camping out. Now that she thought of it, that made a lot more sense, and she kicked herself for not thinking of it before. It was the perfect way to stay off the radar. Plus, Bear was more capable of surviving in the woods than most people, and he'd probably taught Mandy the basics, too.

The thrill of the chase made Iris' entire body tingle. It would be a little harder to track Bear down in the woods, but not impossible. The excitement almost had her backing out of the room and getting on her way, but she noticed both Bear and the kid turn to look at something on the other side of the store. Switching the angles and rewinding the video, Iris watched as a man and a woman entered the store.

The guy looked menacing, with bulging muscles and a cocky attitude. The woman looked meeker. When the guy looked at the woman on his arm, she seemed to shrink in on herself. Words were exchanged, and the woman tried to plead with him. Annoyed, he shook her off, and she stumbled, falling into a shelf, and sending its contents sprawling in different directions.

Bear turned around and said something, then the man tried to shove him. But Bear didn't move an inch. Iris couldn't help but smile. She knew this kind of guy, and that would've pissed him off more than if Bear had swung on him.

The interaction was short-lived. The man knocked a magazine rack over and left after the woman. Bear helped the kid behind the counter pick up the store, then he gathered his things and left. A moment later, he came back in to grab a couple bundles of wood and a few bags of ice, then he left again. She forwarded the tape another half hour, but he didn't come back.

Before Iris left the room, she switched over to the interaction with Silas in which she'd slipped him money. No point in giving the guy leverage to blackmail her, or indicating to the authorities why she was in the store. Better to let them wonder in case someone did end up tracking her down. With the click of a button, she deleted it all.

Iris walked up to Silas, knowing the cameras were rolling but that they couldn't hear what she was saying. She kept her face out of view so no one would be able to read her lips.

"Is there a place where people go camping around here?"

Silas looked at her like she was stupid. "You mean a campground?"

"Where is it?"

"Down the road. You can't miss it. Big sign. Bull Pine Campground."

Iris leveled the biggest, fakest smile at him, infusing her voice with so much cheer, it made her sick to her stomach. "Thank you!"

As she turned to leave, Silas called after her. "Hey, where's my other fifty bucks?"

"Didn't find what I was looking for," Iris lied, keeping the same sickly-sweet tone of voice. "Better luck next time, I guess."

Iris ignored his cursing and pushed through the door, hearing the satisfying *ding* of a bell behind her and stepping back out into the dying sun. She had a couple hours of daylight left, and she planned on burning the rest of it tracking down Bear.

It was only a matter of time now.

27

ETHAN HAD A SMALL HOUSE ABOUT TEN MINUTES FROM HIS FATHER'S business, set back behind some trees and down a gravel driveway. It was gray and plain and humbler than Bear had expected. Maybe that made sense. Given the amount Ethan traveled, maybe he didn't care about keeping a nice house. This could just be a means to an end. Somewhere to rest his head between flights.

Bear hopped out of the Tahoe and walked up to the front door. One of the best parts about living out in the middle of nowhere was that there were no prying neighbors to ask why he was hanging around Ethan's house. The kid didn't have any cameras, either, which bode well for what Bear had to do next.

He pulled out his lock-picking tools and got to work on the front door. With a twist and a pop, he was inside in under thirty seconds. He'd taken his chances that there was no security alarm, and the gamble had paid off. Not that Ethan had much to steal. His flatscreen was a pretty good size, but most of his furniture looked used. Not worn down, just broken in.

The house was clean, for the most part. There were a few dishes in the sink, a hoodie thrown over the back of the recliner, and a couple of empty beer cans on one of the side tables. Most people would clean up before they left for a trip.

Then again, Bear knew Ethan Tapp wasn't down in Florida.

Keeping his footsteps light and making sure not to touch or move anything more than necessary, Bear made his way around the house. He wasn't looking for another indication that Ethan had been killed. He was looking for a reason why. But the place wasn't ransacked or disturbed in any way that wasn't natural. There was no crime scene here.

No, Bear wasn't looking for a crime scene, but for evidence. Whoever had killed Ethan had a damn good reason to drag him off to the woods.

There was only one closet in the hallway. Bear opened it and found Ethan's luggage. The zipped compartments didn't lead to any hidden pieces of evidence, but it did confirm what Bear already knew. Ethan hadn't left for Florida. Was that picture from the beach an old one, or had someone flown down there to take it themselves?

Finding nothing of interest in the spare bedroom, Bear made for the master. He dug through the man's belongings. It distracted him from jumping to conclusions he wasn't ready to make yet.

Ethan's room was messier than the rest of the house, with clothes strewn across the floor and the garbage piling up in a trash can in the corner. It smelled a little, and Bear wondered how long it had been like that. He knew Ethan had only been missing for a couple of days, which meant he'd let the trash pile up well before that.

A desk, dresser, pair of nightstands, and a closet might provide Bear exactly what he was looking for. He tackled the closet first. It was filled with clothes and shoes and not the evidence he hoped to find. The man had suits on one side and casual shirts on the other, though the nicer clothes had a little layer of dust on them.

The dresser didn't hold anything of interest, so Bear went for the desk next, hoping he'd find something to lead him to some solid answers instead of all this speculation.

There were disconnected wires and a lone monitor where the computer had likely been. Had the killer taken it? Did that mean they were just as proficient at picking locks as Bear? Or was it someone who knew Ethan well and possibly had a key? Maybe the computer was just at The Magic Tap, and Ethan had been working out of the back office before he went missing.

Bills were piled up around the desk, all paid in full and on time. No overdue notices or threats of small claims courts. Bear had no idea how much money Ethan made, but he couldn't imagine the man struggled to pay for this house. Plus, there were all those trips he went on. The question was whether Ethan had any money left over after his various vacations. If not, that could rule money out as motivation for the murderer.

Bear checked the nightstand to the left of the bed. There were two drawers and most of the items inside looked like they belonged to a woman. Lotion, flavored lip balm, a couple of face masks, even a pair of self-help books aimed at females. This nightstand must've been Trisha's for when she stayed over. He wondered if Kelly ever used it, too.

The other nightstand was Ethan's, and it was much emptier. Some lotion, a pack of condoms, and a pen and paper were the only things in the top drawer. Bear held the paper to the light, but he couldn't see any indentations of whatever Ethan had written down previously. Another dead end.

Bear moved to the bottom drawer and felt his gut turn. The dimensions were smaller, barely enough to hold the couple sci-fi books within. Not only was it not as deep as its mate on the other side, it was also narrower by about an inch. The average person might not have noticed, but it was a glaring discretion to Bear. A jolt passed through his body. Was this what he'd been looking for the whole time?

Kneeling next to the drawer, Bear emptied the contents and ran his fingers along the interior's bottom and sides, then moved to the outside. There were no keys or visible mechanisms, but he'd seen hidden compartments like this before. He pulled the drawer all the way out and lifted from the front. The drawer pulled away from the bottom. A thin drawer revealed itself underneath. And there was only one item inside.

It wasn't much bigger than a flash drive, but Bear knew what it was before he picked it up. He tested its weight in his hands. There was no doubt in his mind that it was a hardware wallet for cryptocurrency.

Bear pushed the top of the drawer back into place and slid it shut, leaving everything else as he'd found it. Now he reconsidered money as the motivation. He just had to get inside Ethan's account and figure out all the details.

It also confirmed everything Trisha had said about Ethan. The man was into more than he let on. And while Trisha knew, it didn't seem Edison or Kelly did. Unless they were covering for him and were involved too.

Kelly seemed like a stretch, since she'd made it clear she was staying with Greyson because he took care of her. Was Greyson getting all his money from Ethan? Were they in on this together? And though he liked the man, Bear couldn't rule out Edison. He and his son didn't have the best relationship. If Ethan had a decent amount of money saved up, Edison might see that as an opportunity to ensure his brewing company continued to grow and profit.

Before Bear could follow those thoughts any further, his phone buzzed in his pocket. Mandy's name flash across the screen. It wasn't time to pick her up yet. Bear's first instinct was that something had happened to Flora. He trusted his daughter, but accidents were unavoidable. He just hoped no one was seriously injured.

"Hey, kiddo." Bear wanted to keep his voice even in case she was panicking. "Everything okay over there?"

Silence on the other end. Bear pulled the phone away from his face to make sure they were still connected. He saw the timer ticking away. Pressed the phone back to his ear.

"Mandy? Are you okay?"

She didn't answer. Bear could hear one other sound. Heavy, panicked breathing.

Mandy was in trouble.

28

MANDY WASN'T SURE WHAT GREYSON WOULD DO IF HE DISCOVERED HER IN Kelly's apartment with Flora. He was volatile and knew she was with Bear from when they'd seen each other at the gas station. Would he hurt her? Maybe not. But he could use her presence in the apartment to get back at Bear. Or maybe even hurt Kelly.

Mandy snuck up to Flora's bed. The little girl was fast asleep, her breaths coming in slow and measured. The last thing Mandy wanted to do was wake her up. If Flora made any kind of noise, then Greyson would discover them. The consequences would be tenfold if she'd tried to hide, and he still found her.

Slipping her hands under Flora's head and back, she did her best not to jostle the girl. Some kids were heavy sleepers, and Flora had been running around all morning. Maybe she'd stay passed out, and Mandy could hide them both with Greyson being none the wiser.

Lifting Flora up and out of bed was harder than she expected. She was probably thirty pounds. Mandy was strong, but the angle was awkward. Every second counted, and she had no idea if Greyson's first stop would be somewhere like the kitchen or the bathroom, or if he'd come straight back here.

What was he doing here, anyway? He was supposed to be out of town for a couple days, so what would've brought him back early? Had he even left? Bear had seen him yesterday at the bar, so maybe he'd pushed his trip back because of them. Or maybe Kelly had lied. Mandy shook the thought from her head. Kelly's panic and concern seemed genuine. It was still possible she'd sell them out if she thought it would protect her kid. But right now, her best interest was to keep working with Bear to find Ethan. Getting Mandy hurt would be the fastest way to ensure Bear never spoke to her again.

Cradling Flora to her chest, Mandy sucked in a breath when the little girl's eyes flickered open, though it lasted no more than a second. Flora was back to sleep, her body limp in Mandy's arms. They had a chance as long as Flora stayed unconscious.

A door banged shut in the other room. Mandy thought it sounded like the refrigerator. If Greyson was grabbing something to eat, that gave her a few more minutes. Then another thought occurred to her. What if he was staying here?

Her biggest priority was finding a hiding spot. There were only two options—under the bed or in the closet. Under the bed would offer a little more coverage, but it'd be harder to slide into a spot without jostling Flora so much that she woke up. And if she did wake up, she'd be pretty confused about being packed in tightly with all the other junk under there.

Mandy turned to the closet. It was her only option. She steeled herself for what might come next. She could be in there for a while, and she'd have to keep Flora quiet the entire time. A stuffed animal would do the trick. She grabbed Mr. Elephant and tucked him under her arm. Now if only she had a weapon.

Heart pounding, Mandy surveyed the closet she had been ready to explore only moments earlier. It wasn't that deep, but it was wider than the width of the doors. If she tucked herself into either corner, she could stay out of view if Greyson came snooping. She wasn't sure why he would. The closet was stuffed with clothes on hangers, and the bottom was littered with luggage, bags, boxes, shoes, purses, and other odds and ends. The top shelf held some other boxes and bags, the ones that had interested her a couple of minutes ago. Now she wondered if she'd ever find out what was inside them.

She was no longer able to hear Greyson in the kitchen. Mandy had a limited amount of time to hide herself, so she scrambled into the closet and stuck to the side where a handful of long dresses flirted with the floor. She was small and flexible, so climbing inside wouldn't be an issue. It was staying there that concerned her.

Heavy footsteps sounded from the hall. She pulled the doors shut behind her, casting the closet in darkness. She had memorized the contents when she had light, so navigating to the corner wasn't an issue. Could she hide herself quickly enough? How long would it take for her eyes to adjust?

Flora shifted in her arms and groaned. Mandy's heart felt like it would leap from her chest and push right through the closet doors where Greyson would be able to follow it back to her. But she had to deal with one problem at a time. Shoving aside the dresses, she crouched in the corner, and pulled the dresses around her, hoping they hid her toes from any prying eyes. She had no idea how long it had been since Kelly had worn these, but it'd been long enough that they were covered in dust. It tickled her nose with each minuscule movement she made.

"Mandy?" Flora asked, looking up at her and wriggling. "Down now."

"Stop Flora." Mandy said, putting just enough authority in her voice, that the little girl listened to her, but not too much that she'd start crying. "You have to be quiet."

"Why?"

Mandy put a finger to her lips and lowered her voice. "Whisper."

"Why?" Flora was quieter.

"We're playing a game."

"With who?"

Greyson answered that question for her. He pushed through the bedroom door loudly enough that both Mandy and Flora jumped. All she wanted to do was shrink deeper into the closet, but instead, she pushed aside one of the dresses so she could stare through the door slats. It was difficult to see anything in detail, but she could make out

Greyson standing in the middle of the room. He was looking around. Did he know she was there? Was he wondering why Flora's bag had been in the living room?

It was only a matter of time before he discovered her and Flora in the closet. He would have a lot of questions for her. Questions she wouldn't be able to answer. The fact that she was watching Flora would make the situation a lot worse. If Chip knew Kelly and Bear were getting close enough for his kid to watch her kid, Greyson would fly into a rage. Mandy would rather Bear be between them when that happened. There was no reality in which she could protect Flora and fend off Greyson at the same time.

Slipping her phone from her pocket, she dialed Bear's number. Every press of the button felt like a gunshot in the silence. Even the ringing was too loud. She held the phone to her face; terrified Greyson would be able to hear her.

Then Bear answered. His voice was cool salve. Her breaths came in quick spurts. She was relieved he'd answered, but what could she do now? If she said anything, Greyson would hear her. She had to last until Bear showed up.

Greyson had other plans. He turned toward the closet and flung the doors open. Mandy didn't even have time to move the dresses back into place beforehand, and she suddenly found herself staring up at Greyson's large frame. Terror snaked through to her soul. The phone slipped from her hands. She heard Bear on the other end of the line, calling her name. Mandy couldn't say anything. Couldn't move. Couldn't breathe.

It took her a moment to realize Chip hadn't tried to grab her.

He wasn't even looking at her.

His eyes were glued to the top shelf.

Flora opened her mouth and drew in a breath to say something. Mandy couldn't give her a chance. Placing her hand over Flora's mouth, she drew as far back into the corner as possible. She hoped Flora would think this was just part of the game.

The little girl froze in her arms. But Mandy didn't dare remove her hand. One loud breath, one stray movement, and Chip would be able to see them. It was a wonder he hadn't noticed her looking up at him yet.

Chip didn't seem to suspect someone else in the apartment. He pulled down a floral box from the top shelf and stared at it for a few seconds as though he was debating whether he wanted to open it. Mandy couldn't get a good look at the box from her angle. It didn't seem very large. She supposed it didn't have to be to hold something important. Was it filled with cash? A weapon?

Chip lifted the top and looked inside. Mandy wanted so badly to lean forward and look at what it was, but she wouldn't risk being discovered, even if it could break their case wide open. They'd have to find another way to uncover what he took.

After a few seconds, Chip closed the lid and tucked the box under his arm. Then he walked out the door and down the hall. Mandy breathed a sigh of relief. She dropped her hand from Flora's face. The little girl looked scared and uncertain, and Mandy was trying to figure out how to apologize for frightening her without making things worse. Flora loved Chip because she didn't know any better, but Mandy sensed the little girl could tell this was more than just a game.

Before she could decide her next move, Chip walked back into the room. She couldn't help the breath she sucked in, and her hand twitched back to Flora's mouth. Chip didn't hesitate. He reached forward and grasped the closet doors, sliding them shut and casting the space back into darkness.

Mandy felt Flora's body tense, reaching toward the doors, wanting to be out of the closet. Mandy had prepared for this. She brought Mr. Elephant up and placed it in Flora's arms. Flora squeezed the stuffed animal to her chest and buried her face in the soft fur. It would tide her over for a couple of minutes, at least.

Mandy waited until she heard Chip leave the room again before daring to speak.

"It's okay," Mandy whispered, consoling the little girl. "We're winning!"

But it didn't seem to be a comfort to Flora. Mandy couldn't blame her.

29

THE TAHOE ROCKED AS BEAR THREW IT INTO PARK BEFORE COMING TO A full stop. He launched himself out of his vehicle and up the front steps to Kelly's apartment building. She lived on the fourth floor. He took the stairs three at a time. He'd feel it later in his sprained ankle, but for now, his adrenaline kept him moving. He only had one objective.

Find Mandy.

Bear made it to the fourth floor. Through the door. Down the hall. Found Kelly's apartment. Hesitated. What would he be walking into? He didn't hear anything on the other side. No cussing or screaming. From Mandy or anyone else.

He forced himself to take a deep breath. Pulled out his gun and switched the safety off. Mandy had called for help. She hadn't had to say anything for Bear to know.

Bear tested the doorknob. It twisted beneath his fingers. Unlocked. He pushed it open and took in the scene before him. He blinked a few times before he realized it was just Kelly's apartment. A few toys here and there, but no disaster. No dead bodies.

No Mandy, either.

Bear stepped inside; panic affected his decision making. His instincts kicked in a second too late. He didn't have time to react when he saw movement from the corner of his eye, behind the door. Something heavy hit him from behind. One minute he was standing, the next he was on the floor. Someone jumped over him. Bear lifted his gaze just enough to see Greyson fleeing the apartment.

The adrenaline pumping through his veins got him to his feet. He wanted nothing more than to go after the man. No, that was a lie. He did want one thing more. To make sure Mandy was okay. But the apartment was silent. Was he too late?

Bear forced himself to breathe. To stay calm. He shut the door behind him and locked it. He'd hear if someone else tried to get in. It was time to move forward. Find his kid. Once she was safe, he'd deal with the rest. Deal with Greyson.

Sweeping through the apartment, Bear looked behind all the doors and curtains. It was a small place, but there were plenty of hiding spots.

The back bedroom was all that was left. Bear didn't hesitate. No point in worrying about the inevitable. Whatever he found, he'd deal with it. If Mandy was okay, he'd comfort her in whatever way she needed. If she wasn't, he'd burn down the whole fucking town.

The bedroom was a little messy. Lived in. Bed, crib, dresser, the usual stuff. Another option presented itself. If Mandy wasn't here, where was she? Had she escaped? Had someone else taken her?

Before Bear could go down that path any further, he heard muffled sobbing from the closet. Without thinking, he crossed the room and wrenched the doors open. Right there, in front of him, Mandy and Flora were cowering in the corner. It took a moment for the three of them to realize who they were looking at. Then Mandy dropped her hand from Flora's mouth, a breath of relief making her whole face relax.

Bear bent down and gently tugged the little girl from Mandy's grasp. Flora wrapped her arms around Bear's neck and squeezed, still shaking from her sobs. When Mandy extricated herself from the closet, Bear pulled her into a hug too. She squeezed back before gently pushing away.

"You okay?" he asked. "Hurt?"

"No, he never found us." Mandy looked up at him, and he could see her pulse jumping in her throat. She was safe, but terrified. "It was Greyson."

"Yeah, he made his introductions." Bear rubbed the back of his head. It would be tender for a few days, at least. "You sure you're okay?"

"I'm fine," Mandy insisted. Then her face pinched in concern. "Flora's freaked out. I didn't mean to scare her. I just didn't want him to know we were here."

"I know." Bear winced, and this time it wasn't from the pain. "And now he saw me walk right into her apartment."

Mandy's eyes grew wide. It was time to leave. Bear kept Flora close while he headed out of the apartment and back down to the Tahoe. Mandy stayed close behind, her head swiveling back and forth as much as Bear's.

Greyson was already gone. Now that Bear was thinking about it, he hadn't even seen his car. Maybe he'd parked out back. Or maybe he hadn't been alone. Who else could've been with him? What was he doing in Kelly's apartment by himself, anyway?

There was no other choice than to go back to the bar, so Bear put the Tahoe into drive and peeled out of the parking lot. He could hear Mandy talking to Flora in a soothing voice in the backseat, but his mind was too chaotic to make out any of the words. Kids were resilient anyway. And it already seemed like she'd forgiven Mandy for scaring her.

The parking lot of The Magic Tap was busier than he'd seen it so far. It was late afternoon and the usual patrons had arrived for their liquid dinners. The extra witnesses could be a hindrance if he and Greyson got into it. According to the woman at the Meadowlark Diner, Greyson had a reputation, and Bear doubted any regulars of the bar would take anyone else's side.

What other choice did he have?

Bear twisted in his seat to look back at Mandy. "Stay here. Keep an eye on her. I'm leaving the engine running. Lock the doors when I get out."

Mandy looked like she wanted to argue, but something on Bear's face or in his tone must've told her it was a losing battle. She was as worried about Kelly as he was, and every second counted. She and Flora would just be a liability. As much as Mandy wanted to be part of the action, she needed to stay with the little girl.

Grateful that it hadn't turned into an argument, Bear kicked his door open and stepped outside, shutting it behind him. He resisted the urge to look back over his shoulder. Mandy was safe now, but the adrenaline pumping through his body told them they were still in danger, even if the logical part of his brain knew they weren't.

Bear took a step forward. Then another. One foot in front of the next until his shoe hit the front steps of the brewery. All of a sudden, the bouncer was in front of him. One hand on his chest. Pushing him back. Shaking his head.

"You can't be here right now, man."

Bear swatted the guy's hand away. The sound was like a crack of lightning. Robbie looked down at the red mark on his skin, then back up at Bear. There was a challenge in his eyes. One Bear desperately wanted to meet.

"I need to talk to Kelly."

"Don't care. Already told you that you can't be here. Those are the rules."

"You heard Edison. He said I could come back here any time."

"Don't matter. Chip don't want you here. As soon as he explains to Ed that you're putting the moves on his woman, Ed ain't gonna be on your side no more." Robbie let the threat sink in. "Leave. Before I make you."

"What are you, his lap dog? You seem to be pretty low on the totem pole, buddy."

"Higher than you." Robbie stepped forward. "We gonna have a problem?"

"We already have a problem. I need to talk to Kelly. And you're in my way."

Robbie shoved Bear in the chest again. "You've got no business talking to her."

Bear debated whether he should tell Robbie that he had Flora in the car. It could either make the man step aside, or make everything a helluva lot worse. Had Robbie called Greyson after their last encounter? That could explain why he'd come back early. Bear craned his neck, trying to see inside the dimly lit bar. Kelly had to know he was outside. Why wasn't she coming out? Was Chip in there with her? Was he hurting her?

Robbie shoved at his chest again, and something snapped inside Bear. He didn't let most men lay a finger on him like that, let alone three times. He was trying his best to hold back for Flora and Mandy's sakes. He sure as hell didn't need to make any more trouble for himself in this town, but Robbie was pressing all his buttons. And after missing his chance with Greyson, Bear really, really wanted to punch someone.

So he raised his fist and connected with Robbie's jaw.

The man took the jab well, barely stumbling back a step.

Then he reached inside his windbreaker for his weapon.

Before Bear could react, a siren sounded behind him. One loud, quick burst.

Game over.

30

EVERYTHING HAPPENED AT ONCE.

A cop car screeched into the parking lot. Two officers threw their doors open, yelling over each other for Bear to put his hands up. He didn't need to turn around to know they'd drawn their weapons.

Robbie backed up a step. Out of range, in case they decided to shoot Bear. He had a smug look on his face. His eyes screamed *I told you so.* Bear wanted to punch him again. Harder this time.

Kelly flew out of the front door of the brewery in a rage. She shoved Robbie out of the way, and even though he barely budged, the pride on his face turned to shame. Kelly ignored him, making her way toward the cops and planting herself between them and Bear.

"Kelly," Bear hissed, turning to face her and the officers. "It's fine. Get out of here."

"The hell it is." Kelly pointed at one of the cops, and it took a second for Bear to remember his name. Officer Padulano. "What do you think you're doing, Jeff?"

"Got a complaint." Padulano looked taken aback but holding his ground. Nodded at Bear. "This one's not supposed to be here."

"You got a complaint, huh?" Kelly shook her head like she couldn't believe how stupid they were. Hooked a thumb over her shoulder.

"Robbie called you before Bear even got out of his car. He didn't even do anything."

"He's not supposed to be here," Padulano repeated, his voice deflated.

"According to who?" Kelly didn't even wait for an answer. "Chip Greyson? He doesn't own this bar. Edison told Bear he could come back any time. Does Chip have a restraining order?"

Padulano said something, but his voice was so low, the wind carried it away.

"What was that?" Kelly asked. Bear had never seen her like this. Angry. Fierce.

"No," Padulano repeated. "No restraining order."

"Then he didn't break one by coming here."

"He hit me," Robbie said, stepping forward.

Kelly rounded on him. "You started it, you big idiot." She wagged a finger in his face. "I saw everything. Bear should be pressing charges against you."

"Go inside, Robert," Padulano called out. "Let us deal with this."

Robbie turned on his heel and went back inside. Bear stepped closer to Kelly. "Is Greyson here? Have you seen him?"

Kelly's eyes were wide. "What happened?"

"Have you seen him?" Bear repeated with more force.

"No, he's not here. Is everything okay? The kids—"

"They're fine. But Greyson saw me at your apartment."

"Shit. That's not good."

"You got anywhere to lie low for a while?"

"I can go to my mom's. He won't be able to get in." For the first time, she sounded a little afraid. "At least not before I can call the cops on him."

"Try to find somewhere else. If you can't, go there. Lock up. Don't talk to him."

Padulano stepped out from behind his car door for the first time. He had tucked his weapon away, but his hand still rested on it, just like the first time they'd met. "You should get out of here, son."

Bear growled in response. "There's someone I would like to press charges against." Bear stepped closer. He wanted to see Padulano's reaction in his eyes. "Chip Greyson. Assault."

The officer's eyes narrowed. Bear heard the other one scoff. "What evidence do you have?" Padulano asked. "Any witnesses?"

Bear pointed to the back of his head. "Got a goose egg here to prove it. My daughter is my witness."

"Neither of those will hold up. Need something better than that."

Bear took another step forward. Now he was toe to toe with the man. He stopped short of jabbing him in the chest. But only just. "How deep does he have you in his pocket, huh? What's he paying you? Is it worth it?" Padulano opened his mouth to retort, but Bear used his large hand to wave away the statement. "You've got your head so far up his ass, you don't know what's really going on around here."

"What's that supposed to mean?" the other officer asked.

Bear didn't take his eyes off Padulano. "It means Ethan Tapp has been missing for four days and no one seems the least bit suspicious."

Padulano's eyes narrowed. "The only one who strikes me as suspicious is you."

Before Bear could answer, Mandy was there, her hand on his arm, the other holding onto Flora. When he looked down at his daughter, his anger receded. Not gone. Still simmering. But manageable. He could think again. When she spoke, her voice was steady. Calm.

"We should go. Now."

Flora pulled from Mandy's grasp and flew into Kelly's arms, squeezing tight. Bear met Kelly's eyes. "Don't finish your shift. Go to your mother's. Lock the door. I'll be in touch."

Mandy took Bear's hand, and they walked toward the Tahoe, its engine still running. Padulano stepped out into their path. Raised a hand, like that was going to stop them. It did, but only out of necessity. He couldn't give the cops any reason to arrest him.

Padulano waited until Bear looked him in the eye. "Don't leave town."

"Wasn't planning on it." Bear stepped around the man. He wanted nothing more than to shove past him, but Mandy's grip kept his head on straight. He wouldn't risk it. Not with her here.

They were all lucky.

Bear got into the front seat and waited for Mandy to jump in next to him. He put the car in drive and spun around, kicking up dust and pebbles as they peeled out of the parking lot. Bear didn't look back and only realized he was death-gripping the wheel when Mandy placed a soft touch on his arm.

"We have to work on your people skills."

Bear couldn't help the chuckle that escaped his lips. Then it turned into a laugh. A loud one. His kid knew exactly what to say to calm him down. To stop him from acting irrationally. Maybe she'd be able to put that skill to good use some day.

"Would help if people weren't so stupid," he said.

"You're not wrong."

Bear passed the campground and kept going. It was dark now. Traffic was light except for one car behind him. He wasn't sure where to go or what to do. Greyson was in the wind. Kelly would be safe for now. The cops weren't following, but it was only a matter of time. The last thing he wanted to do was sit and stew back at the cabin. He'd done his interviews. Dug around Ethan's apartment. The crypto wallet was burning a hole in his jeans, but it would be encrypted. Usually, he had someone to help with that. But for now, he was on his own.

The headlights behind him flashed. He ignored them. Until they flashed again. And then a third time.

Mandy looked up at him, questioning.

"I'm over this day." He pulled over to the side of the road.

It wasn't the cops. Maybe it was Kelly. Had she left the bar so quickly? Whoever it was, they weren't being subtle. If they wanted to ambush him, they wouldn't have flashed their high beams.

"Stay here," Bear said, then climbed out of the car. The adrenaline hadn't left his system. He was feeling reckless. Wanted to do something. Even if that something was stupid.

The person in the other car kept their engine running. High beams still on. But they opened their door. Stepped out. Bear squinted at the light. It was so bright; he could only make out their silhouette. No defining features. Couldn't even tell if it was a man or a woman. Then they spoke.

"Riley Logan," she said. Her voice was harsh. Determined. "Born in North Carolina to Martha and Chuck Logan. Enlisted into the Marines at age eighteen. Recruited to a CIA-sponsored program. Became an independent contractor. Killed a lot of people. Righted a lot of wrongs. Committed some crimes along the way. Then you got out." A soft chuckle. It held no humor. "Settled down in Upstate New York with your daughter. Solved a cold case and brought HealTek to justice. Went back to your old stomping grounds. The Outer Banks should've been a vacation, but you stumbled into something else there, too. Couldn't stay out of it. Then to Indiana. Where we met for the first time."

"Iris Duvall." How had she found him? "Nice to see you again."

"Wish I could say the same." Her voice shook. Was it from anger or fear? "I've got enough to bring you in, Logan. Lots of people are looking for you. But I want to know the truth."

"What truth is that?"

"Who are you?"

Bear let the question hang in the air. The passenger side door of the Tahoe opened and closed. Footsteps tapped on the asphalt.

"He's my dad." Mandy's voice carried easily. There was no hesitation or fear. "Whoever you think he is, and whatever you think he's done, you're wrong."

31

IRIS RODE BEAR'S BACK BUMPER UNTIL THEY MADE IT TO THE PARKING LOT of a diner one county over. She thought about blocking him in but didn't want to show her desperation. There was no way she could let him out of her sight now.

Bear was already leaning against the side of his Tahoe by the time she approached. The look on his face was impassive and unreadable. In a way, that was comforting. A part of her thought Bear would be nothing like the man she'd met in Indiana, but here he was, as inscrutable as ever. It almost brought a smile to her face—until she caught sight of Mandy's expression.

The girl stood a couple feet away, arms crossed over her chest, glaring at Iris. It wasn't lost on her that while she and Mandy had buried the hatchet back in Indiana, they still had a complicated relationship. Iris thought she'd proven herself in the end, but here she was, having tracked them down from the other side of the country. Both of their hackles would be raised, and as much as Iris wanted to demand answers out of Bear, she knew honey was better than vinegar. She'd have to swallow her pride a little.

"Hey," Iris said, and this time she let the smile crest her lips. "How are you?"

Neither of them answered. Bear stared at her as though he'd be able to read her mind and surmise why she was there and how she'd found him. Or maybe he was still debating the merits of talking with her at all. Iris still had her weapon on her, but she wasn't about to hold him at gunpoint. Confused as she was about Bear, Iris couldn't deny that she cared about Mandy. A lot. There was something about the girl. She stood out. She reminded Iris of herself. Iris didn't want to jeopardize their connection. At least without the full picture.

"Come on." Bear pushed off the car and headed toward the diner. "We haven't eaten yet. Your treat."

Iris' smile spread as she followed them into the diner. It was called The Grape Leaf, and they certainly stuck to their theme. Anything and everything to do with grapes had been tacked to the wall, though the atmosphere was less Old-World Italian and more easy American dining.

They were seated as soon as they walked through the door. Bear requested a booth in the back without any trouble. That put them far enough away from anyone else to have a private discussion. Mandy chose the bench facing the door, forcing Iris to sit with the room at her back. The smile on Mandy's face said she knew exactly what she was doing, and Iris had to resist rolling her eyes. This was going to be an uphill battle.

Silence hung heavily around the table as the waiter approached and took their orders. It continued until the three of them received their meals. Iris got a meatball sandwich that looked about four sizes too big for her, while Mandy got a twelve-inch pizza and Bear dug into a calzone that smelled incredible. While the other two ate, Iris pushed the plate away and crossed her arms over her chest in her best impression of Mandy.

"You can't ignore me all night," she said.

"Can try," Bear answered. His mouth was full of calzone.

"Come on, I'm buying. The least you can do is answer some questions."

"You're the one stalking us," Mandy said. "I think you need to answer our questions first."

"Fine." Iris threw up her hands, and then dug into the sandwich. She couldn't hold out any longer. When was the last time she'd eaten? "You go first."

"How'd you find us?" Mandy asked.

Iris looked between the two of them. Was she leading this interrogation? Bear seemed perfectly at ease, enjoying his calzone in silence. "It wasn't easy, if that's what you're worried about. Took a lot of time and money. And luck." Iris gestured to Mandy with her fork. "Marcus is worried about you."

Mandy groaned and fished her phone out of her pocket. "He texted me, like, eighty times."

Finally, Bear spoke. "He told you where we are?"

"No." Iris had no interest in being the reason Marcus ended up on Bear's shit list. "He gave me the number you've been looking into. It wasn't much, but I found ConnectCom's offices. Followed their van to Arlington. Asked around at some gas stations. Saw some security footage." She was barely holding back a laugh. "Then I just followed the sirens."

Bear shrugged. "Wasn't my fault."

Iris sobered. "What are you—"

Before Iris could get the rest of her question out, Mandy almost jumped out of her seat. "Oh shit! Oh shit!"

Bear froze, eyes roaming the restaurant. "What is it? What's wrong?"

"I forgot to tell you!" Mandy was oblivious to the reaction she'd caused in Bear. "Greyson pulled something out of the closet when he was at the apartment."

"Greyson?" Iris asked. "Who's Greyson?"

Bear ignored her. "What was it?"

"Dunno." Mandy shoved a piece of pizza in her mouth and didn't bother swallowing it before continuing. "It was a floral box. Not that big. Couldn't see what was inside. Big enough to hold a weapon, maybe. Or money? Anything, really." She held out her hands and approximated the shape. "About this big."

"What'd he do with it?"

"Left the room. Made sure to close the closet doors after, so maybe

Kelly didn't know it was there? Or he didn't want her to know he took it."

Iris leaned forward over her meal, careful not to let her hair fall into it. "Who's Kelly?"

"Got any other secrets you haven't told me?" Bear said.

"Tons." Mandy grinned. It dropped a second later. "But actually, yeah." When she spoke this time, she sounded somber, almost sad. "Found a go-bag hidden, too."

"Was it Greyson's?" Bear almost sounded hopeful.

Mandy shook her head. "It was in one of Flora's old diaper bags. Cash. Plane tickets. Guess where she was going?"

"Florida." The two of them exchanged a look that Iris couldn't begin to read.

"It was for all three of them—"

"Okay, that's it." Her voice came out louder than intended, and from the corner of her eye, she saw the waiter veer away from their table, where he'd been heading to check on them. Probably for the best. "Can someone please tell me what the hell is going on?" She stared Bear down. "What are you mixed up in? Who *are* you?"

Bear took another bite of his calzone, and for a moment, Iris thought he was going to ignore her again.

"I've never pretended to be anyone other than who I am."

"That doesn't answer my question."

"Let's not pretend like you didn't show up in Indiana under false pretenses with a cover story of your own."

"I'm a federal agent. It's my job."

"How do you know it's not mine?"

"I don't, and that's my point." Iris leaned back in her seat, massaging the bridge of her nose to relieve some of the pressure building there. After a few seconds, she felt calmer, but no less determined. "Look, you have no reason to trust me. But I'm just trying to figure out the truth here."

"Why do you care so much?" Bear said. "You have to give a little to get a little."

Iris chewed the inside of her cheek. "When I got back to the office after the last time we met, my boss had your file. Wouldn't tell me anything about you other than you were dangerous. It's not like I hadn't figured that out on my own, watching you that night outside Amos' house. But that's not what he meant. He thanked me for finding you. Said he'd take it from there. And then I was sidelined for weeks."

Bear went stiff. He dropped his fork onto his plate, finally giving Iris his undivided attention. "He say anything else?"

"No," Iris bit out, her frustration flaring again. "That's the problem. It took a helluva lot of digging to find you, Bear. Your official records are wiped. No paper trail or anything. I had to talk to a lot of shady people to dig up any kind of information on you. And I swear, half the information is wrong. Or, at least, it's not the whole picture."

"What makes you say that?"

The question felt like a peace offering. Iris didn't want to miss the opportunity. "I don't know everything, okay? But I know enough. Enough to bring you in as a person of interest. You keep getting mixed up in all these things—HealTek, the shit in North Carolina. Indiana. It raises eyebrows."

"But?"

"But *I* know who *I* met in Indiana. Saw what you did for that town. And everyone else I talked to since then? McKinnon. Marcus. Rosie. The Murrays. They say hi, by the way." Iris caught a smile flicker over Mandy's face. "All of them say you're a hero. That you saved them in one way or another. None of them knew where you'd gone, but even if they had, they wouldn't have told me. Not because they were afraid of you, but because they're loyal to you."

Bear was silent for a moment, searching Iris' face for something she couldn't begin to imagine. "Yet the first thing you did was threaten to haul me in."

"Can you blame me? After everything I've read, everything I've heard? I have no idea who you really are."

"Yes, you do." Bear picked up his fork again. He seemed much more relaxed now. "We wouldn't be here right now if you didn't." When he looked up at her, there was a lightness in his eyes that hadn't been there before. "So, who do *you* think I am?"

Iris' gaze traveled to Mandy. It'd only been a couple months since she'd seen the girl, but Mandy seemed older, somehow. Still the same chaotic girl she'd met in Indiana, but she'd grown. Iris couldn't help but think about everything that happened when they were together. What Mandy had done attempting to save Lily's life. There's no telling how that affected her.

When Iris looked back at Bear, she had her answer. "I think you're a dad. A good one, at that. And you're a great man. But even great men get mixed up in terrible situations. I know you don't owe me anything, Riley. But I'm asking you, please. Give me the whole picture. Let me help you if I can. If you can't trust me, trust that I don't want you separated from your daughter. If my boss finds you, that's what will happen."

Everyone at the table knew it wasn't a promise to keep Bear out of handcuffs, but it was as honest an answer as Iris could give.

"I'll tell you what you need to know," Bear said, wiping his mouth and throwing the napkin down on his plate. "But I have to take care of some business first. You can either wait it out, or you can help. Up to you."

Iris looked first at Mandy and then back to Bear. Both of them waited for her answer. If she helped, she could be an accomplice to whatever they were involved in. If she didn't, it'd give them a chance to slip away again. She thought Bear was serious about telling her what she wanted to know, but he'd likely take an opportunity to dodge that bullet if given the chance.

"Okay." She pushed away the now-cold sub. There was a finality about it that they all felt. "I'm in."

32

WHEN BEAR HAD REALIZED IT WAS IRIS WHO HAD BEEN FOLLOWING THEM, his first instinct was to get the hell out of town. He didn't like the idea of anyone being able to find them, no matter how difficult it had been for her. That ever-present paranoia wrapped its hand around Bear's lungs and squeezed. Several measured breaths saved him from acting irrationally.

Out of those who could've tracked them down, Iris wasn't the one he would've hoped for. She wasn't their worst option, though. Back in Indiana, they'd gotten to know each other, fought side by side. He liked to think they had a mutual respect, even if that didn't translate into mutual trust. She would have to work a lot harder for that, and even then, it'd be a coin-toss to determine whether he went through with his promise to tell her everything.

It's not that he didn't like Iris, because he did. Mandy did, too. But her profession put her at odds with Bear's ultimate objectives, which were to stay off anyone's radar and avoid getting involved in anything that jeopardized Mandy's well-being.

Not that he'd done a good job with either of those things.

But Iris was here now, and she wouldn't go away anytime soon. It wouldn't be too difficult to give her the slip, but then he'd be looking over his shoulder until she found them again. And despite the information Mandy had revealed at dinner, Bear still felt responsible for Kelly and Flora. Plus, Ethan's murder was driving him nuts. He wanted answers, if only to put his own mind at ease.

After giving Iris the bullet points, she'd suggested they follow the money. The crypto wallet he'd found at Ethan's hinted to the heart of what was going on here, but the thing was about as useful as a brick until he could find some way to crack it.

And he still had a debt to settle.

Greyson had gotten in a lucky hit at Kelly's apartment, and Bear wasn't planning on waving that off. From the moment they'd met, Greyson pushed all of Bear's buttons, and he'd been surprisingly good about keeping his temper in check up until this point. But Greyson had been inches from Mandy without realizing it.

With that thought in mind, the three of them headed over to Kelly's mother's place. Iris was still riding his bumper, but for now, it felt like they were on the same side. When all of this was over, he'd make the call. Give her a version of the truth she could live with, or ditch her the first chance he got. Any other option seemed unrealistic.

Having someone like her to work alongside hadn't given him any sense of relief. He just hoped he wouldn't regret opening the door to her, even this much. The decision had been made. No turning back now.

Bear knocked on the door. He saw someone's shadow pass by the gap at the bottom. After a brief pause, Kelly pulled it open. The look of intense relief turned to confusion when she spotted Iris. Her gaze flicked to Bear.

"Who's this?"

"A friend," Bear said, even though it was only a half truth. No point in burdening Kelly with all the details. "I trust her."

Kelly didn't hesitate. She nodded her head in greeting Iris and opened the door wider. Mandy slipped inside first, heading straight for Flora, who giggled and ran into the other girl's arms. Apparently, all had been forgiven. Mandy looked relieved as she wrapped the little girl in a hug.

Bear didn't follow her inside. As much as he wanted to grill Kelly on everything Mandy had found inside her apartment, Bear needed more evidence first. And he wanted a face-to-face with Greyson before the man could make any more moves. Bear wanted the contents of that box sooner rather than later.

"We can't stay." Bear watched as Kelly's face fell. "But we'll be back soon."

"Where are you going?"

"Greyson's. I need his address."

Kelly's eyebrows pinched together. "Are you sure that's a good idea? If you make him angry—"

"He's made me angry," Bear said. "Trust me, that's worse. For him."

"What if he comes after me? After Flora?"

"You're safe here. Mandy will keep an eye out. I'll be back soon. I just want to talk to him."

Kelly lifted an eyebrow. "Something tells me you're hoping he doesn't want to *just* talk to you."

Bear gave her a lazy shrug. "If he wants to cross that line, I'll be ready. But we need answers. I've got too many questions and not enough patience. It's time we figure out what happened to Ethan, and I have a feeling Greyson knows more than he's letting on."

A mix of fear and anticipation crossed Kelly's face, finally settling into a look of determination. She'd asked Bear for help, and here he was, offering it. She'd be smart to take advantage. All she had to do was hold down the fort. No skin off her back.

Once Kelly gave him Greyson's address, he and Iris piled into the Tahoe and made their way over. The ride was silent except for a few questions from Iris about the problem at hand, like what they could expect from Greyson when they showed up at his house unannounced. Bear didn't have a solid answer the way he'd thought he would, and it drove them both back into a tense silence, wrapped up in their own thoughts.

Wanting the car close-by, Bear pulled into Greyson's driveway without bothering to hide himself or his vehicle. A direct approach wasn't always the best, but considering Greyson's reaction to Bear showing up unannounced last time, he wanted to make sure the guy wouldn't act impulsively. Between Bear and Iris, he was sure Greyson wouldn't do much, but better safe than sorry.

Iris leaned forward to look out the windshield and up at Greyson's home. "Nice house." Her gaze moved over to his vehicle. "Nice car."

"He's not subtle," Bear said. "Makes me wonder where he gets his money from."

"Works at the brewery, right? With Kelly and the Tapps?"

Bear nodded. "All Edison said was he was good at getting resources at a discount."

Iris raised an eyebrow. "That's not suspicious at all. Maybe he and Ethan were mixed up in something else. Could've been the reason he was killed. Explains the crypto wallet."

"Ethan's place wasn't as nice as this."

"Doesn't mean he wasn't making money. Just means he was smarter about hiding it than Greyson."

"There's a good chance that's true. Come on. He's probably noticed us by now."

BEAR KICKED open his door and slammed it shut behind him. Iris did the same, and they both waited for someone to come to a door or window to see who it was. When no one did, Bear started forward with measured steps. He and Iris were both armed, but he didn't want Greyson to think this was an ambush, so he kept his hands visible.

When they arrived at the door without a welcome party waiting, Bear didn't hesitate to knock. He'd given Greyson long enough. Was he sleeping, or doing something else? Maybe he had a second car and wasn't home.

Iris must've read his thoughts. "Got any other ideas?"

"One." Bear reached over and tested the handle. The door swung open with ease.

"Not what I had in mind, and you know it," Iris said. "This is still breaking and entering."

Bear pulled out his gun, and Iris followed suit. "Only if we're caught."

Iris mumbled something under her breath, but Bear was no longer paying attention. Straining his ears, he tried to pick up on any sounds indicating someone was waiting for them around the corner. Greyson had pulled that trick once before, and Bear wouldn't fall for it again.

But there was nothing. Other than the slight breeze at his back and Iris' soft breathing at his side, he heard silence. No TV or creaking floorboards. No whispers or the cocking of a weapon. For now, they were in the clear.

Bear waited about thirty seconds until his eyes adjusted to the room. Given the way the house was situated, with an upper and lower driveway, Bear figured they'd approached the door that led to the basement. He stepped inside and waited for Iris to do the same before closing the door behind them without a sound.

The basement had been turned into a man cave with a couch and a pair of recliners in the middle, plus a bar along the far wall. Though it lacked any real decoration aside from a couple of neon beer signs, it was clean and looked new.

Iris didn't need instruction to peel off and check the closet on the other side of the room. Once she cleared it, she gave him a curt nod. If they needed to, they could come back down here and look around, but their priority was ensuring no one was home.

Bear led the way up the stairs to the main level, noting no pictures on the walls. Greyson didn't strike him as someone who was into interior design, but if he and Kelly had been together for any length of time, she'd probably have helped him make the house cozier. Her apartment had been covered in framed pictures, after all. Was the lack of décor a testament to their rocky relationship, or was this a newer purchase and Greyson hadn't finished setting up house?

Bear ascended the stairs with his weapon at the ready and Iris covering his back. The main floor contained a living room as big as the den downstairs, plus a kitchen, bathroom, and master bedroom. Instead of lingering, Bear led them to the second floor.

The floorplan up here was tighter, with a hallway that led to a handful of smaller rooms. Iris and Bear split up, taking them one at a time, listening for movement before flinging the doors open and searching inside.

It wasn't until they reached the end of the hall that Iris called for him. Turning his back on the spare bedroom he'd just cleared, Bear crossed the hall into what looked like an office. This was messier than the rest of the house, and it wasn't hard to guess that Greyson had probably spent the majority of his time here.

But that's not what drew Bear's attention.

In the center of the room was a wide wooden desk. Sitting behind it was the man of the hour. But there was no smug grin on his face or vengeful mirth in his eyes. Instead, they stared forward without seeing, blood dripping down from a wound at his temple.

Chip Greyson was dead.

33

"WELL, SHIT."

Iris said it, but Bear thought it. His head spun, and he wondered what this meant.

"Talk to me," Iris said, looking at Bear. "What are you thinking?"

"Not sure yet." Bear ground his teeth together. "This complicates things. And puts us back a few steps."

Iris walked over to Greyson's body and used the back of her hand to touch his arm. When she met Bear's eyes, hers were hard. "He's still warm. He hasn't been dead for long."

"Killer's gone." Bear felt the hairs on the back of his neck rising. "We cleared the house. Must've left right before we got here."

"If they saw us arrive, our time could be limited. We should search for what we can now and get the hell out of dodge before the cops show up."

Bear had no interest in arguing. For the first time, he let his eyes roam the office. It was the only room in the house with any sort of decoration other than the bar down below. More attention had been paid to this room, and Bear wondered if it was because Greyson had planned to take meetings here. Suppliers? Investors?

A single bookshelf next to the door drew Bear's attention, but the titles seemed random. Some old classics, like *Moby Dick* and *Frankenstein*, sat next to at least a dozen books on various cars. On the next shelf down, there were some books on chemistry and brewing beer. Was Greyson just trying to look intelligent, or had he read these? Was he helping Edison with his business, or looking to start a rival one?

"Handgun in the desk drawer," Iris said, drawing Bear's attention. "It was right here. Why didn't he go for it?"

"He knew the person who pulled the trigger." Bear walked around the desk to stand on the other side of the body. "No forced entry to the house. Greyson let them in. Maybe led them up here to talk business."

"What kind of business?"

"Don't know. Could've been about the brewery, maybe something else." Bear studied the wound at the man's temple. "They were talking, maybe just shooting the shit or brokering a deal. Greyson's dressed how he's normally dressed, so he wasn't looking to impress whoever it was."

"A friend?" Iris suggested. "Business partner?"

"Ethan was his closest friend, and he's dead. Edison could be considered a business partner."

Iris studied him for a moment, long enough that Bear knew she was staring. "And then there's Kelly."

He met her eyes. "Trust me, I'm thinking it too."

"Greyson never treated her right. She could've done it while we were at the diner."

"And then led us here?"

Iris shrugged. "It would make her look more innocent."

"I just don't think she'd do this. Plus, she's got Flora. She wouldn't risk losing her."

"Are you telling me you wouldn't commit murder to keep Mandy safe?"

Bear *had* committed murder to keep Mandy safe, but he wasn't going to tell Iris that. "Like I said, she's still a suspect. She's just farther down on my list."

"No sign of struggle," Iris continued, gesturing to the area around the desk. "No stray bullets. Greyson doesn't even look like he was trying to get away. Whoever did this was quick and efficient. I don't think there was any hesitation."

"Then it was planned," Bear said. "As soon as the killer walked through the door, they knew how this meeting would end."

"But how long had they been planning it? And why?"

"That's the million-dollar question, isn't it?" Bear stepped toward the back wall to peer out the window. The area was deserted. "The sense I've gotten is that not a lot of people like him. Ethan was a lot more charismatic, so if they were working together, he would've been the face of it. Greyson would've been the money or the muscle."

"Or both."

"Right. He had plenty of enemies."

"Being disliked is one thing," Iris said. "Being hated enough that someone shoots you at pointblank range is another."

Bear turned to face the room again, spotting a flash of color under the desk. He bent down and pulled it closer. It was a little smaller than he'd expected, but it was exactly as Mandy had described it.

"The floral box." Iris leaned over to peer inside. "Empty."

"There's our motivation," Bear said, straightening up. "Greyson came back early from his trip, maybe because the bouncer called him and told him I'd shown up at the bar with Kelly. But instead of confronting her, he went to Kelly's to get this. Then he came home for a meeting with someone he knew. Someone he trusted."

"Maybe they were making a deal for the contents of the box," Iris suggested. "And the other person decided it'd be easier to take what they wanted."

"Or it was blackmail. Greyson didn't strike me as a guy who was content with what he had. Maybe he overstepped his bounds."

"Could've been the killer. Greyson might've known who killed Ethan and tried to strike a deal."

"And failed," Bear finished.

Iris nodded. "Any idea what was in the box?"

Bear had plenty of guesses, but no evidence to support his ideas. "No, but whatever it was, it resulted in two men dying."

Iris checked her watch. "We should go. Where do you want to head next?"

"There's only one place, really." Bear looked at Iris, knowing he wasn't doing a good job of keeping the frustration off his face. "It's time we get some straight answers from Kelly."

34

Kelly looked relieved to see Bear and Iris return to her mom's place. Then she stilled, likely noticing the seriousness on their faces. Before she could ask anything, Mandy popped into the room with Flora on her hip. It made Bear smile and calmed him down. Above all else, Mandy was okay.

"Any problems?" he asked her.

"No. Been pretty quiet. What about you?"

Bear gave her a look that he hoped she could read before turning to Kelly. "Can we talk with you? In private?"

Kelly looked between Iris and Bear a few times before nodding her head and gestured for them to follow her.

"I'll be back in a minute," Bear told Mandy.

Mandy hesitated before leaving the room. "Did you find him?"

"Yeah."

She must've caught the meaning in his tone before, then nodded her head once and turned on her heel. As Bear moved further into the apartment, he heard Mandy asking Flora if she wanted to play another game and Flora responding with excited giggles.

Kelly took them to the back bedroom, which must've been the master. It was simple, with a bed and a dresser and not much else, but tidier than all the other random bedrooms Bear had been in over the last twenty-four hours. He had an urge to search the place, wondering if it held any secrets to the mystery they were trying to solve, but he resisted. As far as he could tell, Kelly's mother didn't know anything about what was going on. Kelly hadn't even told her mom how Greyson treated her.

"What's wrong?" Kelly asked, stopping in the middle of the room and turning to face them. "Did you find Chip?"

Bear waited until Iris closed the door behind him before he answered. "Yes, we did."

"And?"

"He's dead."

Kelly's eyebrows knit together, and she cocked her head to the side like a dog trying to assess something it didn't understand. "What?"

"We found him in his home office."

Kelly backed away from him, as though trying to walk back in time and unhear the truth. When the backs of her knees hit the bed, she sank down onto it. The look in her eyes was distant. Searching. When she looked up again, there were no tears.

"When? Why?"

Bear searched her face, trying to get a better read on her emotions. Shock was all he could see. The better question was whether it was real.

"Shortly before we arrived. The body was still warm."

"Was he shot?" Kelly asked.

"Bullet to the temple." Bear didn't mean to be crass, but the more straightforward he was, the better read he could get on her. "No forced entry. No struggle."

Iris stepped up to the plate. They hadn't discussed an interrogation tactic. Not like they'd needed to. Neither of them was an amateur. "We were hoping you could tell us why?"

"Me?" Kelly looked worried. Maybe it was because she still didn't know Iris, still didn't trust her. Or maybe she had something to hide. "Why me?"

"You were Greyson's girlfriend," Iris said. "You told us to go there."

"You asked me where he lived. All I did was tell you the truth." Kelly looked over at Bear. "Do you think I did this?"

"No," Bear said. "But it doesn't change the fact that he's dead. Or that you haven't been telling us the whole truth."

The dam finally broke, and tears erupted from Kelly's eyes, sliding down her face and off her chin. She didn't bother wiping them away or denying what Bear had accused her of. All she did was stare up at him, pleading. "I'm sorry."

The apology tugged at Bear's heart. They weren't friends. Weren't even that close. But her story had touched him. Their lives were worlds apart, yet he knew some of her struggles. Knew what she woke up to face each day. It wasn't easy. That earned her some sympathy, if nothing else.

"First Ethan," Iris said, volunteering as the bad cop. "Then Greyson. You gotta know how this looks."

"I do." Kelly sniffled, standing up to grab a tissue and then settling back down on the bed. "Trust me, I do." Then burst into tears again.

"Which one are you crying for?" Iris asked. "Not like you had a good relationship with Greyson."

"This changes everything," Kelly said, between sobs. When she looked up again, she was torn between frustration and something else that Bear couldn't put his finger on. "My first thought was relief. Chip's gone. He can't hurt me anymore." Even Iris looked sympathetic to that statement. "But now what? He always made sure we were okay financially."

"He did that to control you," Iris said.

"Don't you think I know that?" The question came out less venomously than if Kelly hadn't been crying. "It was just easier to take care of Flora. Oh, God." Kelly looked to the door, like she could see through it to her daughter on the other side. "What am I going to tell her? Both of them are gone now."

"Kids are stronger than you think," Iris said, softer than she had before. "She'll be okay."

None of this was going to be easy, but Bear needed answers sooner rather than later. "Did you know about Trisha Oakley?"

Kelly jumped a little at the name, then looked down at her hands, which she was wringing in her lap. "Yes."

"Well, she knew about you, too."

"Figured it was only a matter of time." Kelly swiped at some tears. "I never wanted to hurt anyone. Just wanted a better life for Flora. Ethan and I—we didn't plan that. Didn't mean to fall in love."

"Is he the one who gave you the money and bought you the tickets to Florida?"

Kelly looked up sharply, pinning Bear with her gaze. "You know about that?" When Bear didn't answer, only stared her down, she took a deep, shaky breath. "Yes, he gave me the money. Bought me the tickets."

"Why didn't you tell me?" Bear asked. "Money is a big motivation. You checked the office computer at the brewery. Said there was nothing there. You lied. We could've caught the person who killed him by now."

"I was scared," Kelly said. "And ashamed of ... everything."

"If there was ever a time to be honest," Iris said, "it would be now."

Taking another deep breath, this one steadier than the last, Kelly kept her gaze on Bear. "Like I said, Ethan and Chip had been friends for a while. Always coming up with new schemes, new ways to make money. Wasn't always legal, either. But Chip's been paying off Padulano and a few other guys on the force, so he never had to do time. I didn't like it, but the money was nice. Not worrying about bills was nice."

"You have a kid to take care of," Bear said. "If I was backed into a corner, I'd do the same thing."

Kelly nodded her thanks. Bolstered, she continued. "Ethan didn't like the way Chip treated me. They argued about it a few times, but they stayed friends. Or I thought they had. Ethan and I started hooking up, and he made promises. Lots of them. Of a better life, away from here. Said he was going to take Greyson for everything he had. Teach him a lesson."

"And you liked the sound of that," Iris said.

"Of course I did," Kelly said. "I'd fallen out of love with Greyson a long time ago."

"You never questioned how he could do that to his best friend?" Bear asked.

"At that point, I think Chip was just a means to an end. He was good at what he did. Shaking people down, getting them to do what he wanted. It let Ethan be the good guy, to keep his reputation as the fun one. The charismatic one. Ethan needed Chip as much as Chip needed Ethan."

"What were they planning?" Bear asked. "Before Ethan disappeared?"

"I don't know." Kelly turned desperate when Bear and Iris exchanged a disbelieving look. "I swear, I don't know. Ethan wouldn't tell me anything, even when I asked. It felt like it was bigger than their usual schemes, but I was afraid to push. I didn't want him to change his mind about taking me with him."

"What usual schemes?" Bear asked.

"Usually something small. Chip would get a shipment of electronics, like stereos or something, and Ethan would sell them. I was pretty sure they were stolen, but people trusted Ethan and it didn't seem to hurt anyone. They'd make a couple thousand bucks, something like that."

"You didn't want to ask questions," Iris said. "In case it was something bigger. Ignorance is bliss."

Kelly threw up her hands. She sounded angry, but tears were spilling down her face again. "Fine. Yes. Are you happy? I didn't want to ask. It was easier not to. All I care about is Flora. All I knew was that I was getting out of here, one way or another."

"Did you know about the box in your closet?" Bear asked.

"Box?" Kelly's eyebrows pinched together. "What box?"

"Yellow and red," Bear said. "Floral. Mandy saw Greyson pull it down from the top shelf of your closet. It was empty when we found him."

"I have no idea. I didn't know he was hiding anything at my place."

Bear studied the woman's face and found only truth there. "Any idea what could've been in it?"

She shook her head. "Money, maybe?"

"You think they already pulled off the job?"

Kelly shook her head. "I don't think so. I think I would've known."

"What makes you say that?"

Kelly took a deep breath before she answered. "Because I think it had something to do with The Magic Tap. Ethan and his father had been fighting a lot lately. I'm not sure what it was about, but I know there were a lot of hard feelings. At least on Ethan's side. Edison was trying, but they could never see eye to eye. The business was doing well thanks to Ethan, but he was always talking about how his dad didn't know what was going on right under his nose."

"You think Edison could've done this to either one of them?"

Tears welled in Kelly's eyes again. She kept her focus on Bear. "I don't know anything anymore. About a week ago, I was closing up the bar late. I don't think they knew I was there. I heard them arguing upstairs. I was so used to it at that point, I just ignored them. But then Ethan came stomping down the stairs. He had a piece of paper in his hand. He was shaking it at Edison. I couldn't read what was on it, and I was too scared to say anything. I've never seen Ethan that mad before. Neither of them noticed me." Kelly swallowed before continuing. "All I heard was Ethan saying, 'You're gonna regret this, old man,' before slamming the door behind him. He left, and Edison went back upstairs. I left a few minutes later. I never brought it up to him. I didn't want him to know I heard."

"Is there anything else?" Iris asked.

"No," she said, staring up at Bear. "I swear. That's all I know."

"All right," Bear said, and Kelly's face was flooded with relief. "That gives us somewhere to start." He turned to Iris. "I could use a beer. What about you?"

A smile spread across her face. "Thought you'd never ask."

35

BEAR STILL WASN'T SURE HOW HE FELT ABOUT IRIS TAGGING ALONG, BUT she'd been useful in getting answers out of Kelly, and even more so when they rolled up to Edison's brewery. Robbie tried to stop them at the door, the bruise Bear had given him shining in the outside lights, but all Iris had to do was flash her badge. Without acknowledging Bear, Robbie led them upstairs, where Edison was having a drink with a couple of his buddies.

"Mr. Larson," Edison said, getting up to greet them. "It's good to see you again. I'm sorry to say, my son hasn't returned yet. But you're welcome to join us. Your friend, too!" He held his hand out to her. "My name's Ed."

"Iris Duvall." She offered her badge instead of her hand. "FBI."

Edison's face fell, and he looked over his shoulder at the others in the room before turning back to Bear. "What's this about?"

"Can we talk?" Bear asked, not waiting for an answer before grabbing a couple of bottles of beer from behind the bar. "Privately."

Edison searched Bear's face for a moment before turning to the room and asking his friends to grab a couple of drinks downstairs. None of them seemed put out, and the room cleared in under a minute.

Bear handed a Citrus Cascade to Iris while he kept the Magic Brew for himself, saying, "You're gonna like that one." Then he settled into one of the leather chairs, waiting for the other two to join him.

Edison hesitated before sitting across from them. When he did, he stayed on the edge of his seat.

Bear weighed his options. He could be subtle about this, but he wasn't sure how much good it would do. Better to drop the bomb and see how Edison reacted, like they'd done with Kelly. "Chip Greyson is dead."

Edison stared at him for a moment, taking in the words. "You're sure?"

"Yes." No point in telling him they'd found his body.

Edison could only choke out a single word. "How?"

"Shot in the head, pointblank. Not quite execution style, but close enough."

"Jesus." Edison let the information sink in before letting out a few choice curse words. "I've known that man for twelve, maybe fifteen years. Felt like I half raised him myself." He took a long swig of his beer, then let his gaze rest in the distance. "He had a penchant for finding trouble. Worse than Ethan. But he tried. Helped me out with the business when he could."

"What'd he do here to help?" Iris asked.

"This and that." Edison's stare was distant, as though trapped in memory. "Mostly helped Ethan with the books. Shipments. Supplies. Deliveries. He's the one who took cases of beer up to Portland and dropped them off."

"You ever suspect him of anything? Stealing from you?"

Edison opened his mouth as if to argue, but seemed to think twice about it. "Not at first. In the beginning, everything was going great. Had a ton of money coming in. We could barely keep up."

"Until it wasn't so great?" Iris asked.

Edison looked over at her like he'd forgotten she was there. "Yeah. Then things got weird."

"Weird how?" Bear asked.

"Kept finding out they'd ordered double batches of supplies. I was worried about spending the money all at once, so I wanted to call and asked if we could return some of it. Ethan told me not to worry about it. That he'd take care of everything."

"Did he?"

"Yeah. They were gone in a couple days."

"Did you check to make sure the money was back in your account?"

Edison shook his head. "Ethan did all that. He's better at the numbers than I am. Got me all organized. I had trouble figuring out that program he used. What the hell was it called?"

"QuickBooks?" Iris said.

Edison snapped a finger. "That's it. He was trying to teach me, but he'd get frustrated."

"So, you don't know if you ever got your money back," Bear said.

"I assumed we did." Edison thought for a moment. "But then it happened again. Bunch of boxes in the storeroom. Could hardly walk in there. Ethan told me not to worry about it."

"You ever look inside the boxes?" Iris asked. "Make sure it was what you'd ordered?"

"Yeah, it was stuff for the farm." Edison frowned, his whole face falling as a result. "Nothing out of the ordinary. But they kept ordering more and more. I got mad about it."

"You say something to them?" she asked.

"When I asked, Ethan blew up at me. Told me now wasn't the time to be his father. That opportunity had passed a long time ago."

"You weren't totally honest with me, were you?" Bear asked. "About your relationship with your son."

"Thought you were an investor," Edison said with a shrug. "Wasn't gonna get into my rocky relationship with him."

"All the rest of it was true? Your wife and daughter?"

Edison's eyes snapped up. "Yes. I wouldn't use that for sympathy, if that's what you're implying."

Bear held up a hand in surrender, then took a sip of his beer. "Just making sure. We heard your relationship was a bit worse than just rocky."

"From who?" Edison scrunched his face in confusion, then realization seemed to dawn on him when he clicked his tongue. "Kelly."

"She said she heard you fighting one night. Ethan seemed upset, had a piece of paper in his hand. Told you that you'd pay for something. What was he talking about?"

Edison looked away. Took a sip of his own beer. "We fought a lot. Could've been anything."

Bear rattled off the numbers from the slip of paper he'd found with the tattered shirt. It was a shot in the dark, but worth a try. "Ring a bell?"

Edison's head snapped back in their direction, casting glances at Iris. "I have no idea what you're talking about."

"Don't bullshit us, Ed." Bear leaned forward, elbows on his knees. "Kelly saw you and Ethan fighting. He had that piece of paper with him. We want to know how you got it."

Edison's brow furrowed. He stared at Iris. "One of you gave it to me."

"One of you?" Bear asked. Then it dawned on him. Federal Agent. That's who was behind ConnectCom. The FBI. He'd seen it himself. He looked at Iris. "You know about this?"

"Had a hunch. Not the full picture." She never took her eyes off Edison. "Tell me everything. From the beginning."

"Not much to tell." Edison settled back into his chair. He looked defeated. "Some guy came up to me. Told me he was FBI. Didn't believe him until he showed me his badge. Said he was offering me a deal. Either I turn in my kid, or I lose my business."

"Why?" Bear asked.

"Said Ethan was into some illegal stuff. Using the business to hide what he was doing. I told him he was lying, and he laughed in my face. Said I was either dumb or lying to myself. Then he handed me that number. Said if I didn't want to lose everything, I'd call it. Talk to them about it."

"Did you?"

"No."

"But Ethan found it, didn't he?" Iris said. "That's what the fight was about."

"He saw it on my desk. Figured out what it was for. I told him I didn't call it, but he didn't believe me. Stormed out of here. That was right before he left for his trip. That's why he's not speaking to me right now."

Bear and Iris exchanged a look. He hated to be the bearer of bad news, but Edison would find out sooner or later. And maybe he'd have a better idea of who might've wanted Ethan dead. Besides, it would be better if Edison contacted the authorities about his missing son than if Bear did it. Maybe they'd be able to get some dogs together and finally find a body.

But before Bear could open his mouth to deliver the news, the door burst open. Three cops entered. Two of them had their guns drawn. The third stepped forward. Padulano.

Bear's heart plummeted. He'd be tied up for days if they arrested him. And they were so close to the truth.

Bear looked at Iris, eyes wide in concern. There weren't many exit points to the room, just the door and a couple of windows. He was sure they'd catch up to him before he could get out. Even if he managed to escape, what would be the fallout? Either Edison or Iris could be injured —or killed.

Iris must've read Bear's mind. She reached for her pocket, probably to draw her badge and slow them down. If she said she'd take Bear into custody, maybe they'd lay off. Small town cops never liked when the FBI stepped on their toes, but Bear could deal with the repercussions of that later.

But when Padulano opened his mouth to speak, he wasn't looking at Bear.

"Edison Tapp," he said. "You're under arrest."

Edison stood. "For what?"

"The murder of Chip Greyson."

36

It was utter chaos in the bar when the police dragged Edison Tapp downstairs in handcuffs. Iris hadn't been in Arlington for as long as Bear, and even she knew what a big deal this was. Apparently, the cops had gotten a tip about Greyson's death and found a gun registered in Edison's name hidden in one of the bushes out front. They hadn't said anything about motivation, but a judge had already signed a search warrant for the brewery, so it wouldn't be long before they found discrepancies in the money coming in and out of the business. The cops would use that for motivation and say Edison found out and killed Greyson for betraying him.

"It's bullshit," Bear spat, sitting behind the wheel of the Tahoe. The police had been too busy trying to control the crowd to notice them slipping out the side door. "He didn't do it."

"You're sure?" Iris asked. She didn't want to doubt Bear's instincts, but the evidence lined up.

"Positive." Bear shook his head, threw the car into drive, and slipped out of the parking lot before anyone could stop them.

"Any other theories?"

Bear gripped the wheel so tight, his knuckles turned white. She could hear him grinding his teeth together. "I've got bits and pieces.

They were using the brewery as a front. Kelly mentioned stealing money, wanting to run away together. And what Edison said about excess product showing up one day, then disappearing the next."

"If the FBI is involved, this isn't a small operation. It's big enough that it caught their attention, but it sounds like this had been going on for a while. Why didn't they take them down? What are they waiting for?"

"Maybe we should ask them," Bear said.

"See, that sounded serious, but you'd have to be crazy. And you don't strike me as—" She broke off. "Never mind, I take that back."

One side of Bear's mouth lifted up into a half-smile. "I'm joking," he reassured her. "Mostly."

"That's comforting."

Bear drummed his fingers on the steering wheel. "But you're right. There's something bigger going on here. Something we haven't found yet."

"Is there any place we haven't looked? Anyone we haven't talked to?"

Bear turned the wheel so sharply, Iris hit the door with a grunt. "There is one spot I haven't been to yet."

It was only a fifteen-minute drive from the bar, but it felt like a whole new world. The trees gave way to cultivated fields, pastures with cows, rows of ready-to-harvest wheat, barley, and corn. When they pulled into a long driveway with a white farmhouse and a red barn at the end of it, Iris had finally caught up with Bear's line of thinking.

"Is this Edison's house?"

"And his barn."

"Instead of buying supplies to make his own beer," Iris said, "he was growing his own."

"Cheaper and easier to control the product."

"And the barn—" Iris started.

"—is where they kept their supplies." Bear hopped out of the car and began walking through the mud. "Something tells me Ethan wasn't just buying in bulk at a discount and turning it around at a profit."

Lightning traveled up Iris' spine as they approached the barn. "We better be quick. Once they discover the discrepancies in the money, they'll want to search here. If they don't already have someone on the way to do just that."

Bear made quick work of the padlock on the door with his lock-picking tools. Iris made a mental note to lock up after they were done here. Slipping inside after Bear, she stopped short at the sight before her.

The barn wasn't particularly large, just big enough to fit a packing truck. Though it looked out of place in the space in front of her, Iris' eyes were drawn to hundreds of green and white bags stacked along one wall. On the other sat a couple dozen army-green metal gas cans. Next to it sat a large, nondescript, white tank. Iris was starting to paint a picture of exactly what was inside.

Bear walked over to the bags and took a closer look. "Fertilizer. A lot more than they would need for the size of their farm. *A lot* more."

Iris approached the little army of gas cans and picked one up. Even before she took the lid off, she could smell the gas inside. Unscrewing the cap, she angled it so she could see the contents—or, more specifically, their viscosity. "This is diesel." She looked over at the tank. "And I bet that's full of it."

"Both are needed for farming," Bear said.

"And for making bombs."

Bear stood, inspecting his surroundings more. "My guess is Ethan could get these supplies without raising suspicion. I've heard a lot of stories about Greyson's exploits. He must have contacts willing to take the extra product off their hands."

"It would explain why the FBI is involved. Domestic terrorism?"

"Ethan and Greyson were both looking to make money here," Bear said. "Greyson because it fit his lifestyle, and Ethan because he wanted to get out of town and provide for Kelly and Flora. The business was a perfect cover to order the supplies and launder the money. But it still doesn't tell us who killed either of them."

"Could've been the buyers. Maybe they were unhappy about how their last exchange went down?"

"Or a rival group. Or a third business partner we don't know about yet." Bear shook his head, and Iris read the frustration on his face.

"None of this is gonna get Edison out of jail or give us the answers we're looking for."

"But you know who might?"

Bear turned his head and met Iris' eyes. "Who?"

"The FBI."

37

OUT OF ALL THE PLANS BEAR HAD EVER HATCHED, WALKING STRAIGHT into the secret headquarters of a team of FBI agents was not at the top of his list. Having Iris by his side relieved some of the tension in his shoulders, but not enough to make him relax.

As far as he knew, the team had no idea who they were. Even if they'd managed to get his name, they wouldn't be able to find anything other than a meticulously curated backstory. But if they got his image, it would become a whole different ballgame.

Bear kept his camera jammer in his pocket, knowing the agents would be able to tell they were coming as soon as their feeds crashed. Maybe even before. Not that he and Iris were trying to sneak in. They'd pulled up to the front of the abandoned factory building and parked a couple of feet from the door. And by the time they had climbed out and walked up to the entrance, Bear could feel the tension from inside.

"You sure about this?" Iris asked out of the corner of her mouth.

"No," Bear replied. "But we need them."

Iris sighed. "Then let's get this over with."

Bear didn't bother knocking. What was the point? He swung open the front door. A pair of agents greeted them on either side of the door, their weapons raised and aimed at Bear's and Iris' heads.

Raising his hands, Bear stepped forward. Iris mirrored his moves. The agents swung the door shut behind him while a third patted him down. It was the kid he'd taken out the other day. What was his name? Byers.

"Found it." Byers pulled out the camera jammer from Bear's pocket.

"Kill it."

Bear looked up to see the woman with the braids. She stood without a weapon raised, instead her arms were crossed. A sense of knowing her team was capable of handling these two. There was only one other person left in the room, a man with a bald head and a scruff of a beard. He stood by her side with his weapon raised.

"You don't want to do that," Bear said.

"Oh?" the woman replied. "Why not?"

"The cameras will come back on. You'll grab my image. Run it through your system. And it'll come back with my name and a whole lot of interesting information."

The woman shrugged, her stern expression unchanged. "Doesn't sound all that bad to me."

"It'll be bad," Bear said, "when a couple dozen agents show up on your doorstep, demanding to know where I am. They'll ruin your operation."

Her brows furrowed and her eyes squinted. "Who are you?" she asked.

"Someone who just wants to help you."

"Prove it."

"My name is Special Agent Iris Duvall," Iris said from Bear's left. "Check my pocket."

Byers waited for the woman to nod her head, then obliged, pulling out Iris' ID. "Checks out." The kid kept patting her down, pulling out the crypto wallet Bear had taken from Ethan's house. "And there's this."

"You can have that," Iris said. "We brought it for you anyway."

"You gonna tell me what you want in exchange?" the woman asked.

"You gonna lower your weapons?" Bear said.

"They're clean," Byers said.

The woman nodded her head. Every agent who had raised their

weapon tucked it back into their holster. The two who'd greeted them at the door went back to their desks while Byers handed Iris her badge. He kept the crypto wallet, and Bear's jammer. The woman and her bald-headed sidekick surveyed the newcomers as Bear and Iris lowered their arms.

"Thanks," Bear said. "Was starting to get tired."

"Who are you?" the woman asked again.

"Name's Carl."

The woman eyed him. "You're the one who snuck in here and took down one of my agents."

Bear looked over at Byers. "Sorry, kid. Nothing personal."

"What do you want?" the woman asked, drawing Bear's attention back to her.

"You got a name?" Bear asked. "Only seems fair."

After a pause, she said, "Whetstone."

"Like I said, we're here to help you." Bear pointed at the crypto wallet. "That's Ethan Tapp's."

Whetstone raised a single eyebrow, but otherwise gave nothing away. "How'd it come into your possession?"

"I found it."

"Found it?"

"That's what I said." Bear grinned. "Doesn't really matter how."

"Ma'am, we're not here to derail your investigation," Iris said, stepping forward. "Far from it."

"No, but you want something."

"Less suspicious than if we didn't," Bear said.

For the first time, there was a glimmer of emotion behind Whetstone's eyes. Was that approval? "You're not wrong. But I can't divulge private information about our investigation."

"Then let me tell you what we know," Bear said. "Ethan Tapp and Chip Greyson have been friends for years, pulling together small jobs to gain a buck. Then they got the bright idea to use Edison Tapp's farm to stockpile fertilizer and diesel fuel. Sell it to the highest bidder. I assume it was a domestic terrorist group."

"You'd assume correctly," Whetstone said.

"They got a name?"

After a pause, Whetstone said, "The Free Society. Anti-government, mostly. They were low on our list up until the last couple of years. Got a new leader and a new lease on life. It's been hard to track them down."

"I've heard of them," Iris said. "They have a penchant for blowing things up."

"You got wind of this operation," Bear continued. "And you set up shop. Arlington's a small enough town that you couldn't do it there, where someone would notice. But you didn't care about Greyson or Tapp. You wanted their buyers."

"Go on," Whetstone said, as though Bear weren't accusing her personally of anything.

Iris picked up where Bear left off. "The Free Society spooks easy. Their members are the types of people who live in bunkers and wear tinfoil hats. They wouldn't come within a hundred miles of this place if they thought you were onto them, so you had to hang back. It was too dangerous to follow them to the exchange, wasn't it?"

"We couldn't risk it," Whetstone said. "We'd been on them for too long, and this is the closest we've come. Had to make sure it counted. Otherwise, they'd scatter, and we'd lose them again. No telling how many people would die in the meantime."

"Only way to track the buyers back to their headquarters, to the leadership, was to have an inside man. My guess is you approached Ethan first. He's the more reasonable out of the two. But he didn't go for your plan. That's when you approached Edison."

Whetstone sighed, looking defeated. "We told Ethan we didn't care about him or Greyson. We just wanted the buyers. We couldn't let him walk away with the money, but we could give them both immunity. Ethan didn't go for it. Then he skipped town."

"Hate to be the bearer of bad news," Bear said, "but Ethan Tapp is dead."

Whetstone exchanged a look with the bald guy. When she turned back to Bear, the shock was still apparent on her face. "Are you sure?"

"As sure as I can be," Bear said. "Found a bloody shirt and his boots in the woods. No body. Animals probably dragged it off."

"We assumed the trip to Florida was to throw us off his tracks, but we figured he had made it out of town one way or another."

"Did you approach Greyson after that?" Iris asked. "To be your inside man?"

"Didn't have a choice." Whetstone shrugged. "Turns out, we probably should've gone to him first."

"He accepted?" Bear asked. "Just like that."

"Pretty much. We put some pressure on him. He'd gone to prison for a few years at eighteen. Didn't want to go back. Knew he'd be better off working with us. We knew about his crypto wallet, told him he had to turn it over. He agreed to it all."

"Then he wound up dead," Bear said.

"Do you have Greyson's wallet yet?" Iris asked. When Whetstone shook her head, Iris turned to Bear. "That must've been what was inside the box."

"Box?" Whetstone asked.

"My kid saw Greyson pull a floral box down from a shelf in Kelly's closet," Bear said. "It was obvious he was hiding it there. Took it with him back to his house." Bear hesitated. He didn't want to tell them this next part, but it was too relevant to leave out. "He attacked me on his way out of Kelly's apartment earlier. Iris and I went to confront him at his house. But he was already dead."

"You're the ones who called it in?" Whetstone asked.

"No." Bear exchanged a look with Iris. "We went right over to Edison's to ask him about it. Was trying to avoid getting involved with the cops."

"The point is," Iris said, "we found the box there. Empty. Someone killed Greyson and took the money."

"You got any idea who that could be?" Bear asked Whetstone.

"No, I don't." She gestured to Byers. "Give the man his tech back and go see what you can find out about where that money came from."

Byers looked dubious, but did as he was told. Bear took the camera jammer back, sticking it in his pocket and giving Whetstone an appraising look. "After you found out Greyson was dead, you had to come up with a contingency plan."

"Send one of my men in," she said.

"That's not going to work."

"I know." Whetstone surprised Bear by flashing him a wide smile. "That's why you're gonna do it."

Bear laughed. "What makes you think that?"

"Because you want something. You're desperate enough to walk in here, willingly giving up that wallet in exchange. Means you don't want money. You can't be bought. But it's something you can't do on your own. You seem quite resourceful. So if you need help, it's something only I can do. What is it?"

"Pretend like we were never here," Bear said. "When you write up your reports, when you talk to your superiors, don't mention anything about me. Not my name, not what I look like. Nothing."

"Won't be hard," Whetstone said. "I don't know anything about you."

"That goes for me, too," Iris said. "No one can know I was here either."

Whetstone's brows furrowed. "What are you wrapped up in?"

"Nothing good."

"You gotta give me something," Whetstone said. "If you're working outside the law in any capacity—"

"It's not like that," Iris said. She hesitated before she spoke again, and Bear got a sense she was weighing her words carefully. "I'm after someone. Problem is, he works for the government. And I'm pretty sure he's got friends at the FBI. Carl here is helping me out. We're just trying to stay off the radar until we find more information."

Whetstone's gaze bore into Iris. But Iris didn't back down. When Whetstone gave Bear the same treatment, he didn't shrink either. Whatever the woman saw in them, it must've been something she trusted. Or at least recognized. "Fine. You've got your anonymity. But nothing comes back to me on your end either. Deal?"

"Deal," Bear said. "There's one more thing. Edison Tapp."

"You want him out of jail," Whetstone said.

"He didn't kill Greyson. That man was just trying to do right by his kid. Whatever he did wrong, it doesn't justify a prison sentence."

"We'll talk to the local authorities, see what we can do. Would be better if we found out who did kill Greyson."

"One thing at a time," Bear said. "What's the gameplan?"

"The deal's going down tonight. We've got the location. We just need to pick up the truck full of—"

"We already have it," Bear interrupted.

Whetstone leveled him with a look. "You already have it?"

"We gave you the money," Bear said. "We couldn't give you everything. We had our own contingency plan."

"Fair enough." Whetstone looked more resigned than annoyed. "They'll sweep you for a wire, so you're on your own."

"Prefer it that way," Bear said.

"They'll also sweep the supplies for tracking devices."

"If we can't use tracking devices, how are you gonna follow them?" Iris asked.

"You'll have to plant the devices afterwards. Preferably on the fertilizer or the fuel, not the truck, in case they switch vehicles."

"Sounds easy enough," Bear said.

"Don't count on it. These guys are paranoid. They're expecting Greyson. You'll need a cover story. If they suspect you of being anyone other than who you say you are, they'll pull out of the deal. Might try to kill you."

"Lady," he said, "that's the story of my life."

38

MANDY TRIED TO NOT MAKE IT TOO OBVIOUS THAT SHE WAS KEEPING AN eye on Kelly, but it was getting more difficult as the night went on. After Bear left, Kelly filled in her mother, Erin, on everything, including the fact that Chip Greyson was a giant asshole.

Erin was shocked and angry and upset all at once, but she comforted her daughter as Mandy took care of Flora in the other room. Kelly had decided not to tell Flora just yet, not until everything settled down and she had all the answers.

After that, Kelly busied herself by cleaning her mother's entire apartment. Mandy volunteered to help, and they worked side by side in silence, only breaking the tension to ask for the other to pass the cleaner.

Mandy didn't mind the work, mainly because it allowed her to observe Kelly more closely. Not that there was much to observe at this point. The woman was upset, but confused and angry, too. Mandy didn't understand everything Kelly was going through, but she did understand what it felt like to lose someone.

Now that the apartment was spotless, Mandy wasn't sure what to do next. She tried not to be too obvious when she followed Kelly from room to room. Part of her wanted to give the woman some space, but at the same time, she needed to know if Kelly was up to anything. Bear was pretty sure she didn't have anything to do with Greyson's death, but he wasn't one to leave anything to chance.

It was only because Mandy had been watching Kelly so closely that she noticed the way the woman went rigid as she was scrolling through her phone. It was on silent, so Mandy had no idea if a phone call or a text message had come through. Maybe it was some other notification, or maybe just something on social media.

Kelly stared at her screen without moving for a good sixty seconds, then slipped her phone into her pocket and stood abruptly.

"I need to get some air. Watch Flora?" She didn't meet anyone's eyes. And Flora was asleep in Erin's arms. There wasn't much to watch. "I'm just going to take a lap around the building."

"Are you sure?" Erin asked. "What if someone is out there waiting for you?"

"No one's out there," Kelly said, though her voice shook a little. "I'll be right back."

Kelly kissed the top of Flora's head, and the girl barely stirred. It was close to midnight now, and she was exhausted from the day's activities.

Mandy waited until the front door closed before she stood and walked out of the room.

"Where are you going?" Erin asked, more curious than suspicious.

"Stomach hurts," Mandy said. "Might be a while."

Erin made a face, and Mandy had to grin. She wouldn't be checking on her any time soon, which was exactly what she'd been hoping. But instead of going to the bathroom, Mandy snuck to the front door and pulled it open an inch at a time. Before she stuck her head through, she waited for the elevator to ding, and for the doors to close behind Kelly as she stepped on board. Mandy slipped through the door and headed in the opposite direction, toward the staircase.

They were on the seventh floor, so Mandy had to haul ass to get down to the first. There was no guarantee Kelly wouldn't stop off on another floor instead, but the best lies held versions of the truth. Kelly was going outside, but not to get some air.

On the bottom floor, Mandy peered out the little window set in the door to the lobby when she saw Kelly rush by. On instinct, she ducked, but it wouldn't have mattered. Kelly wasn't looking around, only ahead. Wherever she was going, she wanted to get there fast.

Once Kelly was through the front doors, Mandy counted to ten before following her. After everything she'd been through in the last couple of days, Kelly would probably be more paranoid than ever. And Mandy didn't want to get caught and sent back to the apartment, or worse—make Kelly miss out on whatever she was after. If Mandy could get some serious answers for Bear, he'd trust her even more than he already did. And maybe she'd be relegated to babysitting duty less often.

Not that she minded Flora. The kid was great.

Mandy pressed her face to the glass doors at the entrance of the building, spotting Kelly in less than two seconds. The woman strode down the sidewalk and veered to the left, moving in a walk-jog. When she disappeared behind a line of trees, Mandy pushed through the doors and stalked after her, doing an uncanny impression of her walk. It was the best way to get where she needed to go without drawing too much attention to herself. Kelly was probably thinking the same thing.

When Mandy reached the line of trees, she ducked behind one and peered around it, just barely catching Kelly as she made her way toward the parking lot. Erin's building was one of the bigger ones outside of Arlington. There were over a hundred cars in there. Maybe closer to two hundred.

As Mandy continued to follow in Kelly's wake, a thought made her stumble in her tracks. If Kelly was heading toward the parking lot, there was a chance she'd get into her car to drive somewhere. There'd be no way Mandy could follow her if that happened.

Speeding up a little, Mandy sprinted forward from tree to tree. There was no one around, so she was less self-conscious about looking suspicious. Once she made it to the parking lot, Mandy swung wide and crouched low, running from car to car, only popping her head up occasionally to make sure she didn't lose Kelly.

With her mind still racing with ideas to try if Kelly did get into her car—none of which would've feasibly worked without getting caught—Mandy didn't realize that Kelly had stopped or how close she'd gotten until she heard the woman speak. The first thing that came out of her mouth was just a jumble of sounds and incoherent words. But one finally broke the surface.

"How?"

"We don't have time. I'll explain everything later. I need your help."

"My help?" Kelly laughed, and she sounded unhinged. "Why? Why would I help you? And after everything you put me through. Everything that's happened?"

"You need to trust me."

"Well, I don't," Kelly said, with an air of finality. "Not anymore."

Mandy was dying of curiosity, and even though she was a little too close, she couldn't stop herself from peering around the backend of the car she was crouching beside. One quick glance was enough to catch a glimpse of Kelly and the person she was talking to, but not enough to take in any detail. How did Bear do that? She'd seen him look for the span of a single heartbeat and take in everything about the room and the people occupying it. Yet another skill she'd have to hone if she wanted to be as good as him one day.

Taking a deep breath, Mandy shifted forward and crawled to the next car, grateful the parking lot was paved and not made of loose gravel. It allowed her to stay silent as she positioned herself a little closer. There were two cars between them now. When Mandy took another quick glance, she could clearly make out Kelly, though the man she was talking to was still partially hidden by the roof of a jeep.

Letting out a string of curse words in her head, Mandy shifted around to the car's back bumper. She was still out of sight, but if Kelly turned too quickly, she'd be able to see her. Staying silent, Mandy pushed up just enough to peek over the top of the car for two seconds. When she ducked back down, her head was spinning.

She'd seen who Kelly was talking to, but it didn't make any sense. She recognized the face but couldn't connect him with the name. That person hadn't even been on their radar. Had Kelly known the whole time?

Thoughts in a panic, Mandy slipped out her phone. Her hands shook as she tried to concentrate on what she was doing while her mind was in a whirl. There was no way she could put together a coherent thought, other than she had to contact Bear *right now*.

Muscle memory had her pulling up her contacts, but instead of hitting Bear's name, her shaking fingers hit Marcus'. This time, Mandy swore out loud as she hit the *End Call* button several times. She'd deal with Marcus later. For now, she needed Bear.

She realized she couldn't call him. Kelly and the man would hear her. Know she was there. Instead, Mandy opened her text messages to Bear and started typing something out. Then a shrill sound emanated from her phone and Marcus' name popped up on her screen.

"Oh shit," she said, and it came out louder than she intended.

She'd left her ringer on in case Bear had called with an update. Marcus had called after she'd hung up, probably making sure she was okay. He'd be so worried about her, but that was the least of her worries now. The conversation two cars over had died. Footsteps pounded on the pavement. Mandy whirled around and found herself looking up into the last face she thought she'd ever see.

Kelly yelled something, but Mandy couldn't think straight. The man whipped out his hand and knocked the phone from her grasp. It hit the pavement. Then he wrapped one large hand around her mouth while his other arm grabbed her and pinned her to his chest.

She couldn't move. Could hardly breathe. Kelly kept yelling. The man dragged her backward toward his car. And the phone was there, just out of sight, a half-formed text to Bear explaining the impossibility of everything she'd seen.

But it didn't feel impossible right now.

In fact, it felt all too real.

Out of the chaos of her mind, only one coherent thought formed.

If I survive this...Bear's gonna kill me.

39

THERE WAS AN OLD, ABANDONED STEEL MILL ABOUT HALF AN HOUR outside of Arlington. They only had a couple of hours until Greyson was meant to meet the buyers there. Bear had to scramble to get back to the truck, come up with a variety of backup plans, and get back on the road to head to the location.

Whetstone hadn't been kidding when she said Bear was on his own. They hadn't allowed Iris to tail him in the truck in case she was spotted, but she was closer than they were in the next town over. With no communications device other than his phone, Bear felt vulnerable. If he were killed, they wouldn't know for at least an hour. Plenty of time for the buyers to get away.

It was nearly two in the morning now, but Bear was wide awake. There was something about being up while the rest of the world slept. He should've been tired after everything he'd been through the last couple days, but he was so close to answers, he could taste them on the air. His mind kept circling back around to Ethan and Greyson's dead bodies, to who could've killed them. But it was like punching a brick wall.

The Feds had provided him with a layout of the steel mill, and when he approached in the truck full of fertilizer and diesel, he was glad the mill had matched their records.

Abandoned some fifty years ago, the building had been gutted and all the equipment had been moved out. The structure was sound, but apparently no one had been able to repurpose it into something else. A couple hipsters tried turning it into a restaurant or boutique, but the location wasn't ideal, and most of the surrounding residents weren't interested in what they were trying to sell.

When Bear turned off the road and into the lot, it wasn't hard to spot the loading dock that had once been used to transport various products out of the factory and across the United States. The box truck was small compared to the opening. He pulled in and put the truck in park.

The issue would be the half-dozen men with assault rifles who had appeared out of the shadows and pointed their weapons at him as soon as he came to a stop. They were dressed in all black, with Kevlar vests and a sidearm in addition to their rifles. Some of them wore balaclavas underneath their helmets and goggles, but a few of them had pulled the material down to reveal their faces.

One man stepped forward, emotionless except for a slightly disapproving look. He had dark eyes and a heavy brow and looked like he meant business. Bear would've bet money this guy was the leader. Whetstone had said he went by the moniker Adder, like the snake. Bear's thought was confirmed when the man started giving orders.

"Roll the window down. Stick your hands out the door, open it from the outside. Hop down, then face the truck with your hands over your head."

Outmanned and outgunned, Bear couldn't refuse. He moved slowly but deliberately as he complied. Once his face was pressed to the side of the truck, another man broke off and patted him down. He heard the scan of some electronic device, and Bear knew they were checking him for a wire.

"All clear."

Adder waited until the other man moved away before he spoke. "Turn around."

Bear did as he was told.

"You're not Greyson."

"What gave it away?"

"Where is he?"

"Not here."

The man didn't hesitate. He shifted his weapon and swung the butt at Bear's temple. With only a split-second to react, Bear was able to turn and reduce the force of the hit, but it still made him stumble.

"You got a big mouth on you for someone who's about to die."

"You're not going to kill me," Bear said, doing his best to remain calm despite the growing tension in the air. "You need us."

The Feds had enough on the buyers to know that they usually held up their end of the bargain. Money wasn't an issue for them. Getting the product was. They couldn't purchase the materials themselves, not in bulk, so they relied on farmers. Most of their suppliers were unwilling participants. Ethan and Greyson had volunteered, and thus had become their most reliable sources.

"Greyson was supposed to be here. He's the only one I deal with."

Bear shrugged, the pounding in his face only a slight distraction. "He got tied up. Couldn't make it. Sends his apologies."

"Are you Tapp?"

Bear had to make a decision. If he said he was Ethan, that would gain him credibility. But if this guy already knew Tapp, then Bear would be knee deep in shit with no way out.

"You know I'm not Tapp." Bear forced his posture to stay relaxed even as his heartrate ratcheted up into his throat.

"Just checking." The guy grinned, but it didn't meet his eyes. "What's your name?"

"Carl."

"Carl what?"

"Just Carl. It's not important." Bear gestured to the men with their weapons aimed at him. "Look, I'd be an idiot to walk up in here and try to double-cross you. I've got the stuff in the back of the truck. I just want to get paid and get home. I've been working doubles, man. I'm exhausted. Can we do this?"

The guy in front of Bear never took his eyes off him. "Check the back."

Two men peeled off and circled the truck. Bear couldn't see them, but he imagined one opening the door while the other kept his weapon trained on the opening. If anyone was inside, they'd be ready for them. Luckily for Bear, the truck contained exactly what he'd promised.

The doors swung open and a moment later the truck shifted as one of them climbed inside. There was another electronic sound, this one checking for trackers. But they wouldn't find any. Sure enough—"All clear."

"Is it all there?"

"Looks like it." The leader stared at Bear, assessing. "I don't like changes in the plan."

"Neither do I," Bear said, and it was the truth. "Wouldn't be here if there were any other options."

"What did you say Greyson was up to again?"

"I didn't." Bear's heart rate increased. Whetstone had told him there was no way they'd know Greyson was dead since it hadn't made the local news yet, but that only held true if they weren't the ones who killed him. "Above my paygrade."

"You know who I am?"

"A guy with a gun."

"You know what's in there?"

"Course I do. I loaded it up."

"You know what we're going to do with it?"

"Blow shit up." Bear's annoyance was real now. "Look, man. I don't care who you are or what you're gonna do with this shit. It's not my business. I keep my head down, do what I'm told, and get paid. Greyson doesn't tell me anything else about what we do, and I'm smart enough not to ask."

The leader studied Bear for a moment. There was something skeptical in his eyes. "Last question." He paused, waiting for Bear's reaction. When none came, he asked, "Passcode?"

Bear's heart hammered in his chest. The Feds hadn't told him about a passcode. Maybe they didn't know. That could've been something new, something this guy had messaged to Greyson right before the exchange. Something Greyson wouldn't have known prior to his death. If that were the case, then he was screwed.

"You've gotta be shittin' me." Bear threw his hands up. A few of the other men shifted forward, anticipation causing their fingers to twitch against their triggers. "There ain't no passcode, man. I've passed all your tests. Give me the money so we can both go home."

The man in front of Bear stared at him long and hard for a good thirty seconds. It felt like ages. Then his face split open into a wide grin and a raucous laugh escaped his throat. "Just messin' with you, man. Relax. Yo," he called over his shoulder. "Start unloading."

"And the money?"

"Yeah, yeah." Adder nodded his head. "You'll get your damn money."

Bear pulled out his phone after Adder did. The Feds had temporarily given him Greyson's crypto wallet in case the buyers had demanded to see it, to prove that Greyson had sent him. They'd also linked his phone to the account so he could ensure the money landed.

"There you go," Adder said, after a moment. "Now you can shut up about it."

Bear waited for the notification. Ten seconds passed. Then fifteen. Finally, a little notice popped up. The numbers on Greyson's account rose. The deal was done. "Pleasure doing business with you," he said, infusing some excitement into his voice. "Let me help you unload."

"We got it." Adder moved away. One man still had his gun trained on Bear. "Thought you wanted to get home."

"Can't go home till the truck is empty." Bear opened the door to the truck and tossed his phone and the wallet on the seat to cover for grabbing the tracking device he'd stashed in the cupholder next to the center console. He slipped it into his pocket before turning back around to face Adder. "One more pair of hands won't hurt. The faster we get out of here, the better."

Adder looked torn between not wanting Bear to help and knowing he was right. The quicker they could clear out, the faster they'd be on the road and headed to their next destination. Bear hoped it was back to their headquarters and not somewhere they planned on blowing up with the materials they'd just bought, but that was Whetstone's problem.

"Fine. Make it quick."

Bear obliged, climbing into the back of the truck and helping another guy hand everything down to the men waiting on the ground. Timing it for when everyone's back was turned, Bear stuck the tiny tracking device into one of the bags of fertilizer, hoping they wouldn't spot it during their next stop.

He watched as the bag traded hands two or three times before someone threw it into the back of another truck. Unloading took twenty minutes, and by the time they were done, Bear was sweaty and tired. The night was catching up with him.

When he jumped down from the back of the truck, Adder was waiting for him with a gun to his face. Bear froze. It wasn't the first time he'd had a gun aimed at his head, and it wouldn't be the last. But this wasn't his fight. All he wanted to do was get home to Mandy. Put this all behind him. He was so close now.

"Tell Greyson no surprises next time," Adder said. "Or someone's going home in a body bag."

"You got it, boss," Bear said. He waited for the other man to drop the gun before turning his back on everyone else in the steel mill and climbing up into the truck. His hands didn't shake as he took the wheel, but his heart was drumming in his chest. Would they let him back out only to shoot him before he could get back on the road?

"Clear the way," the leader yelled.

Bear turned the wheel, pushed the truck back out onto the road. No one followed him. For the first time in the last hour, he could breathe. His part of the deal was done. Now it was time to figure out who had killed Greyson and Tapp, then get out of town before the buyers realized they'd been duped.

Bear had just hit the highway when his phone vibrated from the cupholder. Looking down, he saw it was an unknown number. Whetstone had insisted on getting his number before he left, though she'd promised not to call unless she hadn't heard from him for over an hour. He still had some time left.

Hitting the answer button, Bear held the phone up to his ear. The voice on the other end didn't belong to Whetstone or Iris.

"Well, hello there," the man said. "Boy, it's nice to finally talk to you after all this time."

"Who is this?"

"That doesn't matter," the man said.

Bear paused for a beat, knowing the kind of game this guy was playing. "Why are you calling?"

"Mandy," he said, "say hello to your father."

Bear's throat constricted as he listened to the sound of snuffling on the other line. Then Mandy's voice was bright and loud in his ear.

"I'm sorry." She was holding back sobs, but only just. "I'm so sorry. I didn't mean to—"

"That's enough of that," the man said, returning. "You still there?"

"Yes." Bear ground his teeth together so hard, they could've turned to dust. His grip on the wheel was tight enough that his hand hurt. Without realizing it, he'd pressed down on the gas so hard, he was zipping down the highway at ninety miles an hour. "You're gonna regret this, you mother—"

"I'll make this easy for you," the man said. His voice was as sharp as steel. "No cops. No FBI. You and me on The Dalles Bridge. Bring the money. I'll bring your kid. A clean exchange. Then we go our separate ways. We got a deal?"

"You hurt her, and I'll kill you."

"Bring the money," the man said. "Or she goes over the edge."

40

By the time Bear arrived at the bridge, he had close to twenty missed calls from both Iris and the Feds. It was a risk not telling them what was going on, but he didn't want them interfering in what came next. If the Feds showed up, they'd get Mandy killed. If Iris showed up, well, she might play the hero, but still get Mandy killed.

The problem wasn't that Bear didn't trust Iris to have his back, it was that he was willing to do anything to keep Mandy safe, even if that meant burning the world down around them. Iris cared about Mandy, but Bear knew she wouldn't go that far. And that was a liability for him.

At three in the morning, there was no traffic on the bridge other than a single car sitting off to the side. Bear could see three figures inside, but he couldn't see their faces. The smaller figure was definitely Mandy, and the one behind the wheel had to have been the man who called him. But who was in the back seat?

There were lights along the bridge, but they were old and dull yellow in color. Once the people inside the car stepped out, Bear would be able to distinguish who they were, just barely. The clouds in the sky obscured the moon, making it possible for someone to lurk in the shadows.

The rain from the last couple of days had flooded the river. Even before he opened his door, Bear could hear the water rushing by. The way it was moving, anyone who fell off the bridge would be swept away in its current as soon as they hit the surface. There was a good chance they wouldn't make it out.

As soon as Bear parked, Mandy stepped out of the vehicle. Bear thought she was going to make a run for it, but she stepped around the front of the car and opened the driver's side door. The man behind the wheel was using Mandy as a shield, and she had no choice but to comply. A growl formed in Bear's chest. He'd make this piece of shit pay.

Once the man was out of the car, he gestured for the person in the back to join him. Stepping forward, the three of them entered the light. For the first time, Bear could see the expressions on all their faces.

Mandy looked neutral, but he could tell she was hiding her fear. He couldn't see her eyes from this far away, but he could feel the mixture of anger and terror coming off her. But she didn't look like she'd been harmed.

Bear's eyes found Kelly's face as she stepped into the light. His chest squeezed in a mixture of betrayal and concern. For her part, she looked terrified, and kept shuffling closer to Mandy, trying to put a reassuring hand on her shoulder. Mandy shrugged it off, her jaw clenched.

It took Bear a second to place the third person. Mandy's kidnapper. Blond hair. Blue eyes. A hard expression on an otherwise congenial face. He was supposed to be dead, but there was no denying who was standing there with a gun pointed at Mandy's head.

Ethan Tapp.

Scenarios flooded Bear's mind. The evidence in the woods suggested Ethan had been murdered, but they hadn't found a body. Had Ethan escaped his captor? Pretended to be dead, then crawled his way out of a grave? From what Bear could see, the man looked unharmed.

"Out of the vehicle," Ethan shouted. "Bring the money."

Bear did as he was told. He'd jarred at the men during the exchange because that's who he was. It was part of an act, part of the persona. He couldn't look too afraid, and couldn't be too compliant. They would've gotten suspicious. But here? With Mandy's life on the line? It wasn't worth the risk.

"Stop right there," Ethan said.

Bear came to a halt. He was maybe fifty feet from them. Could read the expression in everyone's eyes. But all he cared about was his kid. "You okay?"

"I'm fine." Mandy's voice shook just a little.

Bear looked to Kelly. He couldn't stop the question that came out of his mouth. "You know about this?"

She shook her head. "Not until tonight. I swear. I didn't know."

Bear wasn't sure he trusted her, and Ethan must've seen that on his face. "She's not lying, you know."

"And I'm supposed to trust the word of a dead man?"

Ethan's face split into a grin, and Bear saw the man's former glory. "Have you ever faked your own death?"

"Once or twice." Bear slid his foot forward. If he could get a little closer, he might be able to get the upper hand. "It's overrated."

"I disagree." There was a mania in Ethan's eyes that worried Bear. "I found it quite freeing. Walking around at night like a ghost. Seeing what people get up to when they think you're dead." His eyes cut to Kelly. "Figuring out who your real friends are."

Bear slid his other foot forward. He had to keep Ethan talking. "You use your own blood, or an animal's?"

"Chicken's blood. Didn't need a lot. The farm next door had some. Figured it'd be okay if one went missing."

"You could've just gone with the Feds. They'd have gotten you out of this mess."

"I didn't want to get out of it," Ethan said. "I wanted the money. They wouldn't give it to me. That wasn't an option."

"And you never told your girlfriend? Either of them?"

"Trisha was fun while it lasted. Used her to keep Greyson off my back. Didn't want him getting suspicious."

"Who cares?" Bear asked. "He was kind of a dick."

"And that's what killed him," Ethan said.

Another piece of the puzzle slid into place as Bear took another small step forward. "You knew Greyson had agreed to work with the Feds. You wanted to get his money before he handed it over. Killing him was just a bonus, wasn't it?"

"The plan was to send him to prison, set him up for my murder. Kill two birds with one stone, you know? But then my money went missing, and I needed his. He didn't want to hand it over, so I didn't give him a choice."

"You could've cut your losses and run. You've got enough money there to live off."

"That's my money." Ethan stepped forward, Mandy still clutched to his chest. "It belongs to me. I saw you snooping around all over town. Figured you were the one who had it when Chip came up emptyhanded."

"Your father's in jail, you know. They think he killed Chip."

"Who do you think called it in?" Ethan laughed. "Who do you think planted the gun?"

"Your father's a good man," Bear said. He hadn't known Edison for long, but the man cared about his kid. Not all sons had that luxury. "What did he do to deserve this?"

"Everyone loves good ol' Ed." Ethan rolled his eyes. "Because they didn't know him back then. When I was just a kid. The drunken nights. The neglect. Took him fifteen years to realize he hadn't lost his *entire* family in that car crash. But it was too late. He can't make up for everything he took from me."

"And Kelly?" Bear asked. "You expected her to go with you, after everything you put her through?"

"After everything *I* put her through?" Ethan laughed, and Kelly winced at the sound. "Chip Greyson treated her like shit for years, and she stuck by him. Look at everything I did for her. For us. I deserve this. She owes it to me."

"I didn't ask for this," Kelly said, her voice quiet but clear. "I didn't want any of this, Ethan."

"Are you sure about that?" Ethan jeered. "All those late nights planning what we'd do if we had a million dollars and the whole world at our fingertips? Every day, you dreamed about a life without Chip

Greyson." Ethan swung his arms out, and Kelly flinched at the movement. "Well, you got your wish, baby. A new life."

Kelly looked crestfallen. Bear shook his head. "All this, just to get money you didn't earn and a woman you don't deserve. No one owes you shit, Tapp. Least of all her."

"Be that as it may, I'll have what's mine, regardless." Ethan looked over at Kelly. "Get the money. Bring it back." He turned back to Bear. "Once I have the money, I'm driving to the end of the bridge. You'll stay there until I let the kid go. After that, you can collect her. And I'll be long gone."

Bear seethed. "The money for my daughter. That's what you said."

"You're not really in a position to negotiate, man." He waved his gun around, then pointed it at Mandy's head again. "She'll be fine as long as you don't do anything stupid."

"Ethan, this isn't you," Kelly said. "We can't just pack up and leave. What about Flora? What about my mom?"

"Flora won't ever have to worry about anything again," Ethan said. "And your mom will get over it. We can come back to visit in a couple years when things die down."

"You sold some stuff to some pretty terrible people," Bear said. "The Feds will find you. You're not walking away from this one, Ethan."

There was a gleam in his eye that Bear didn't want to test. "Watch me." He turned to Kelly again. "Go get my money."

Kelly stumbled forward, tears in her eyes. Bear had only made it about five feet closer. Still too far to do anything. He couldn't pull his weapon without risking Mandy's life. His best bet was to hope Ethan would let Mandy go at the other end of the bridge. But he didn't like his odds.

By the time she stepped in front of Bear, Kelly was sobbing. "I'm so sorry. I don't know. I didn't—"

"I know," Bear said. When he'd first seen her, he thought she'd been in on it the whole time, strung him along like an idiot. But it was clear that as much as she loved Ethan, this wasn't the life she wanted to live. He was the one who had played everyone. "It'll be okay."

"What are we going to do?" Kelly asked, reaching her hand out for the crypto wallet.

"Hurry up," Ethan shouted.

"I'm working on it," Bear said to Kelly, handing the money over. "Let me handle it. You just make sure he keeps his word about letting Mandy go."

Kelly nodded as she took the device, then turned on her heel and shuffled back to Ethan. The man kept his eyes on the money. Bear took the opportunity to take another step forward.

"Get in the car," Ethan said, when she'd finally returned to his side.

"Ethan—"

"Do it," Ethan snapped. "I won't tell you again."

Kelly still hesitated, trying to give Bear enough time to make his move. Ethan opened his mouth again, but his gaze shifted and his eyes narrowed. Bear heard a car engine behind him. Ethan lowered the gun from Mandy's head to her stomach. Harder for the driver of the car to spot but just as deadly for Mandy.

"Don't say a goddamn word," Ethan said.

Bear wasn't planning on it. Whoever had made the unfortunate mistake of driving over this bridge at three in the morning better have enough sense to keep moving. If they slowed to ask what was going on and if everyone was okay, it might be their funeral. Or Mandy's.

As the car approached, Bear took advantage of Ethan's distraction to take a few more steps forward. By the time the car passed, he'd have shaved ten or twelve feet off the original distance.

Luckily for them, the car passing kept a steady pace. He looked over, hoping to gauge the driver's reaction to see if they'd slow down or just keep going. He hadn't expected to be greeted with familiar eyes.

Iris.

Before Bear had fully comprehended the situation, Iris slammed on the gas and twisted the wheel of the rental car to face Ethan's vehicle. Bear knew she wouldn't risk mowing down Tapp if there was any chance she'd hit Mandy. Bear realized she intended to take out his car and close off his means of escape.

Ethan must've had the same thought because he raised his gun, pointed it at Iris, and fired.

41

BEAR WATCHED IN HORROR AND ANTICIPATION AS IRIS DUCKED TO AVOID the bullets and slammed her car into the back of his. Time slowed to an agonizing crawl as he took in the sequence of events.

Kelly screamed and jumped out of the way, tripping backwards and hitting the ground hard enough to lose consciousness for a few seconds. The little device in her hand, so small and yet so important, slid across the road and came to a stop at the edge of the bridge, threatening to be lost to the rushing water.

Ethan had seen the car coming before Kelly. He dove to the side, taking Mandy with him. They landed on the ground a couple feet from the crypto wallet.

Iris had hit the other car with such force that when she clipped the end, it spun around and knocked her off course. Instead of stopping when she hit the vehicle, Iris had left her foot on the gas, launching her car up and over the side of the bridge until the only thing holding her in place were her back tires and a shit ton of luck.

Like something out of a movie, Bear saw how this would play out—if she moved the wrong way, the car would careen forward and be lost in the river below. Iris would die having saved Mandy's life, and Bear would never be able to repay her.

"Bear!" Mandy screamed, drawing Bear's attention.

Ethan was dragging Mandy toward the device, and even though she was clawing and fighting to get away from him, his grip was too strong. But he was also no longer paying attention to Bear. He only had eyes for the money.

Bear drew his weapon and fired, hitting the road right where Ethan's next step would've been. Ethan came up short a foot from the device. He whipped around to face his aggressor. The gun was now trained on Bear. Small mercies.

"Not another—"

Ethan was distracted enough that he couldn't see they'd set him up to fail. He was within inches of everything he'd fought so hard for, but he was also inches from the side of the bridge. And he'd made one crucial mistake.

He'd underestimated Mandy.

Elbowing him in the gut and twisting out of his arm at the same time, Mandy made to run, but Ethan was fast. He grabbed her wrist and almost yanked her off her feet. She grimaced in pain, her arm still tender from the run-in with the Tahoe. Instinct took over. She twisted her hand in his grasp and wrapped her fingers around his wrist and yanked.

Already off-balance from lunging after her, Ethan stumbled forward, and she drove her forearm into the back of his elbow, bending it the wrong way. Now she had leverage. She kept the momentum going and swung him in a circle, grunting with the effort and the weight of her anger. He hit the guardrail at waist-height.

One second he was standing.

The next, his legs were up over his head as he fell over.

Mandy had tried to shake him off, but Ethan had grabbed ahold of her wrist and held on. A moment of elation was dashed by pure fear coursing through Bear's veins. In the blink of an eye, she was screaming as Ethan pulled her down after him.

With a burst of speed, Bear crossed the final few feet and launched himself forward, grabbing hold of Mandy's other hand and pulling so hard he thought he'd yank her wrist out of its socket. If it had been just

Mandy's weight, Bear would've pulled her up no problem. But Ethan was at least two hundred additional pounds. Dead weight.

Mandy stayed silent. Tears poured down her face. Bear lifted her high enough to grip the edge of the bridge on her own. Anchoring her there, he reached down to Ethan.

"Grab my hand."

"No!" Ethan shouted. "You'll let me go."

"I won't." Bear wanted nothing more than to make Ethan disappear after everything he'd put them through, but there's was more at play here.

"Bear," Mandy cried out. "I'm slipping."

"Come on." Bear bent further over the side of the bridge.

Ethan hesitated. His hand slipped from Mandy's wrist. Bear tried to grab hold, but their fingers didn't even touch. Ethan stared up into Bear's face with a mixture of fear and defiance. In a split-second, the churning water had swallowed him whole.

Without wasting another second, Bear hauled Mandy over the edge of the bridge and back onto solid ground. Cupping her face in his hands, he looked her over, making sure she didn't have any serious injuries. A couple scrapes and bruises. Probably some sore muscles.

"You okay?" he asked.

Mandy wrapped her arms around his neck. "Thank you," she whispered. "Thank you for being there."

"Always."

The groan of metal on metal drew their attention, and they both watched in horror as Iris' car teetered on the edge of the bridge. They could see her through the driver's side window. She had twisted around in her seat, determination setting her jaw into a rigid line. Bear and Mandy sprinted forward.

"Check the car," Bear nodded to Ethan's vehicle between breaths. "Look for a rope."

"In the trunk." Kelly rose from the ground and limped forward. "There should be one in there."

Bear ran over to Iris, but when he looked through the back windshield, she had her gun aimed at him.

"Duck," she shouted.

Not a second after Bear complied, Iris emptied her gun through the glass, shattering it enough for Iris to punch her way out. If she could get to the other end of the car before it went over, that is.

"Dad!" Mandy shouted.

Bear turned in time to see her toss him a length of rope. Thick enough to hold Iris' grip. He grasped one end in his fist and swung the rest forward, making it through one of the small openings in the glass. It landed short of Iris' outstretched arm. She'd have to crawl to get to it.

"Slow and steady," Bear said.

Iris didn't answer. The car groaned again as she shifted her weight. The back tires rolled forward a few inches. She'd have one shot at this. As soon as she moved, the rest of the car would go over.

"Screw slow and steady," Iris shot back.

Before Bear could talk her down, Iris launched herself forward, grabbing the rope as high as she could, close to the top of the back seat. The car jerked, then rolled over the guardrail. Iris broke through the shattered back window as it did, sliding across the top of the trunk as it fell out from under her. Blood streaked her arms, a gash appeared on the side of her face. She held onto the rope. Bear had hauled her up and over the guardrail. She peered over the side of the bridge.

"Guess I'm not getting my deposit back."

"Could've been worse."

Iris gave him a nod of approval. "Thank you. You saved my life."

Mandy stepped up to Bear, and he wrapped his arm around her. "And you saved hers." Bear watched as Iris wiped blood from her hands. "How'd you know?"

"Wasn't going to let you out of my sight."

"Could've ruined the whole operation."

"It was worth it." Iris looked down at Mandy. "Had to make sure you came home to your daughter."

Before they could trade any more sentiments, a ConnectCom van and a black sedan screeched to a halt beside them. Several agents poured out of the vehicles and began assessing the damage. Whetstone approached, her jaw clenched.

"This wasn't the plan, Duvall."

"Had to adapt," Bear said, drawing the woman's attention. "Tapp didn't give me any other choice."

Whetstone's eyes narrowed. "Tapp?"

"Ethan Tapp wasn't as dead as we all thought. He killed Chip Greyson for being an FBI informant."

"And where is he now?"

Bear hooked a thumb over his shoulder, toward the white-water rapids below. "There's a chance he's still alive."

Whetstone stepped to the edge of the bridge and looked down at the raging waters. "Not likely."

"Either way, I held up my end of the bargain. The supply's been delivered. Money's exchanged hands. Tracker's in place. The buyers are none the wiser." He bent over and picked up the little device on the ground. Handed it to Whetstone. "And there's this."

Whetstone appraised him. "Not how I would've done it, but I won't complain about the result. Edison Tapp will be released in a few hours."

"And us?" Bear asked.

Whetstone smiled and turned her back on them. "You were never here."

42

BEAR DROVE KELLY BACK TO HER MOTHER'S PLACE IN THE TAHOE, THE only working vehicle left. Erin had noticed that Mandy had snuck out. After Kelly hadn't come back either, she'd called the cops, who were waiting for them when they arrived.

Kelly explained the situation, ensuring Bear was not the suspect. Padulano didn't like it, but he didn't have much choice. Flora had run into her mother's arms, awakened by all the commotion. The young girl didn't understand the reality of the situation, but she knew her mother was upset.

When she and her mother parted, Flora dragged Mandy over to the corner to play one last game together. Kelly watched with a sad smile on her face. She'd stopped crying, but her eyes still gleamed with the fear of an uncertain future.

"Are you gonna be okay?" Bear asked.

"I think so," Kelly said. "Things will be strange for a while, but we'll bounce back. We always do."

"I know it's easy to compromise yourself for your kid. You bend over backwards to make sure they get to lead the type of life you never did. But you deserve to lead that life, too. And they'll be happy if you're happy."

"Thanks, Bear." Kelly leaned forward and gave him a chaste kiss on the cheek. "For everything. I'd say I'm sorry you got dragged into this, but I think it would've ended up a lot worse if it weren't for you."

"For what it's worth, I'm sorry about Ethan."

"I know." Kelly looked down at her hands. "Wish I could say I was surprised, but I knew the darkness that lay behind his charm. I'd picked up on it from being with Chip. But I just didn't think he'd put other people at risk. Not a kid." She looked over at Mandy. "She'll be okay, right?"

"Mandy's tough," Bear said. "She'll be fine." Was it the truth? Time would tell.

They fell into a comfortable silence before Bear and Mandy left to meet Iris at the jailhouse. Mandy was already asleep by the time they arrived, and Bear was sure to close the door quietly behind him. The kid deserved some rest.

Iris was waiting on the steps, Edison Tapp at her side. His tired, dark-rimmed eyes lit up in gratitude as Bear approached.

"Heard what you did for me," he said, offering his hand. "Means a lot."

Bear returned the handshake, even though guilt ate away at him. "About Ethan—"

"Agent Duvall explained everything." Tears welled in Edison's eyes. "I know I wasn't the best father."

"You tried your best."

"Sometimes," Edison said. "I'm not sorry for the man I became, but I am sorry for the time it took me to get to this point. Ethan bore the brunt of my mistakes. And I'll never be able to tell him how sorry I am."

Iris caught Bear's eyes. "The Feds pulled out all the stops. Found his body. He'll get a proper burial."

"Looks like I might be the only one at his funeral," Edison said. "Can't say I'd blame anyone for not showin' up after everything he did. But he's still my son."

Bear didn't know what to say, but Edison saved him from having to answer by shaking both his and Iris' hands again. A car had pulled up— one of the regulars at The Magic Tap—and Edison climbed inside.

"Hey," Bear called. Edison rolled down the window. "You still looking for investors?"

Edison's smile was sad. "Maybe someday."

"Then I'll be in touch," Bear said.

Edison nodded and rolled his window back up, waving his goodbyes as the car pulled away.

Iris waited until the car left the lot before turning to Bear. "I half-expected you to have Oregon in your rearview by now."

"I thought about it," Bear said. "More than once."

Her face lit up as she smiled. "I'm sure you did."

"I can't thank you enough for what you did for Mandy. For us."

"I did it because I care about her," Iris said. "And you. Even though you're a pain in my ass."

Bear chuckled. "I've heard that one before."

Iris sobered. "Bear … I know I'm asking a lot from you. To trust me. To go out on a limb and help me track down Reagan. It could put a target on your back."

"According to you, I've already got a target on my back."

"This will be different. I might not know who he is, but Reagan's important. He controls a lot of people. Has a lot of resources at his fingertips. It'll change everything."

"Sometimes change is good," Bear said. "Besides, I owe you."

Iris nodded, conflict in her eyes. "What about Mandy? She can't come with us."

"I know."

"She needs to be with kids her own age."

"*I know.*"

"She won't be happy."

"You're tellin' me."

"What are you gonna do?"

"I've got a couple ideas."

"How long do you need?" Iris asked.

"Couple days. Week at most. Then I'll be ready."

"You sure?" She looked at the sky. The sun had started to crest the horizon. "There's no turning back after this."

"Yeah, I'm sure," Bear said.

The two didn't bother saying goodbye. They'd see each other again soon.

When Bear pulled open the door, Mandy stirred in the back seat. And when he turned the key in the ignition, the sound of the Tahoe's revving engine had her sitting up. "What's going on? Did Mr. Tapp make it out okay?"

"The Feds held up their end of the bargain."

"Where's Iris?"

Bear's stomach twisted. He wouldn't lie to her. Not after all they'd been through. "She's gone on ahead."

Mandy caught his eyes in the rearview, and hers narrowed in suspicion. "Are you finally gonna tell me where we're going?"

"Yeah." Bear put the car in drive and pulled out of the parking lot.

"Something tells me I'm not going to like it."

Bear forced a chuckle. "You got good instincts, kid."

As much as Mandy wouldn't like being sent away, Bear knew it was for her own good. He'd be able to concentrate better on the task at hand, knowing she was safe. After this, maybe she and Bear would be able to settle down for longer than just a couple of months.

If that were the case, then Bear couldn't help but feel like it'd be worth every second of turmoil knowing that, in the end, there'd be one less target on his back.

BEAR & MANDY'S story continues *Between the Lies*, coming late 2023. Click the link below to preorder now:

https://amazon.com/dp/B0C8ZKV437

JOIN the LT Ryan reader family & receive a free copy of the Jack Noble prequel novel, *The First Deception, with bonus story The Recruit.* Click the link below to get started: https://ltryan.com/jack-noble-newsletter-signup-1

LOVE BEAR? **Mandy? Noble? Hatch?** Get your very own L.T. Ryan merchandise today! Click the link below to find coffee mugs, t-shirts, and even signed copies of your favorite thrillers! https://ltryan.ink/EvG_

ALSO BY L.T. RYAN

Find All of L.T. Ryan's Books on Amazon Today!

The Jack Noble Series

The Recruit (free)

The First Deception (Prequel 1)

Noble Beginnings

A Deadly Distance

Ripple Effect (Bear Logan)

Thin Line

Noble Intentions

When Dead in Greece

Noble Retribution

Noble Betrayal

Never Go Home

Beyond Betrayal (Clarissa Abbot)

Noble Judgment

Never Cry Mercy

Deadline

End Game

Noble Ultimatum

Noble Legend

Noble Revenge

Never Look Back (Coming Soon)

Bear Logan Series

Ripple Effect

Blowback

Take Down

Deep State

Bear & Mandy Logan Series

Close to Home

Under the Surface

The Last Stop

Over the Edge

Between the Lies (Coming Soon)

Rachel Hatch Series

Drift

Downburst

Fever Burn

Smoke Signal

Firewalk

Whitewater

Aftershock

Whirlwind

Tsunami

Fastrope

Sidewinder (Coming Soon)

Mitch Tanner Series

The Depth of Darkness

Into The Darkness

Deliver Us From Darkness

Cassie Quinn Series

Path of Bones

Whisper of Bones

Symphony of Bones

Etched in Shadow

Concealed in Shadow

Betrayed in Shadow

Born from Ashes

Blake Brier Series

Unmasked

Unleashed

Uncharted

Drawpoint

Contrail

Detachment

Clear

Quarry (Coming Soon)

Dalton Savage Series

Savage Grounds

Scorched Earth

Cold Sky

The Frost Killer (Coming Soon)

Maddie Castle Series

The Handler

Tracking Justice

Hunting Grounds

Vanished Trails (Coming Soon)

Affliction Z Series

Affliction Z: Patient Zero

Affliction Z: Abandoned Hope

Affliction Z: Descended in Blood

Affliction Z : Fractured Part 1

Affliction Z: Fractured Part 2 (Fall 2021)

Love Bear? Mandy? Noble? Hatch? Get your very own L.T. Ryan merchandise today! Click the link below to find coffee mugs, t-shirts, and even signed copies of your favorite thrillers! https://ltryan.ink/EvG_

Receive a free copy of The Recruit. Visit:

https://ltryan.com/jack-noble-newsletter-signup-1

ABOUT THE AUTHOR

L.T. Ryan is a *USA Today* and international bestselling author. The new age of publishing offered L.T. the opportunity to blend his passions for creating, marketing, and technology to reach audiences with his popular Jack Noble series.

Living in central Virginia with his wife, the youngest of his three daughters, and their three dogs, L.T. enjoys staring out his window at the trees and mountains while he should be writing, as well as reading, hiking, running, and playing with gadgets. See what he's up to at http://ltryan.com.

Social Medial Links:

- Facebook (L.T. Ryan): https://www.facebook.com/LTRyanAuthor
- Facebook (Jack Noble Page): https://www.facebook.com/JackNobleBooks/
- Twitter: https://twitter.com/LTRyanWrites
- Goodreads: http://www.goodreads.com/author/show/6151659.L_T_Ryan

Made in the USA
Middletown, DE
01 February 2024

48925337R00146